BROOKLYN

THREE

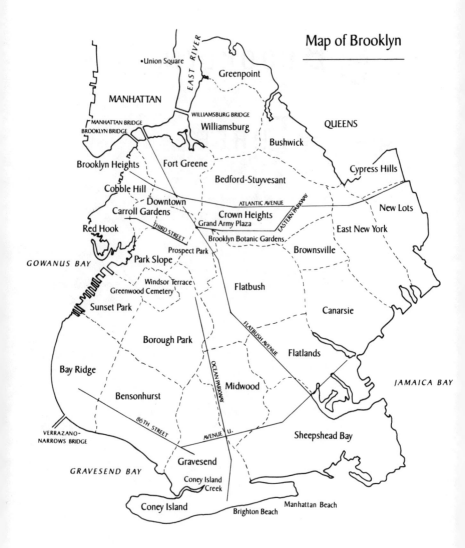

Map of Brooklyn

EAST RIVER

•Union Square

Greenpoint

MANHATTAN

WILLIAMSBURG BRIDGE

Williamsburg

QUEENS

MANHATTAN BRIDGE
BROOKLYN BRIDGE

Bushwick

Brooklyn Heights

Fort Greene

Cypress Hills

Cobble Hill

Bedford-Stuyvesant

Downtown

ATLANTIC AVENUE

New Lots

Carroll Gardens

Crown Heights

EASTERN PARKWAY

Red Hook

THIRD STREET

Grand Army Plaza

East New York

Brooklyn Botanic Gardens

GOWANUS BAY

Prospect Park

Brownsville

Park Slope

Windsor Terrace

Flatbush

Greenwood Cemetery

Canarsie

Sunset Park

FLATBUSH AVENUE

Borough Park

Flatlands

Bay Ridge

OCEAN PARKWAY

JAMAICA BAY

Bensonhurst

Midwood

VERRAZANO-
NARROWS BRIDGE

86TH STREET

AVENUE U.

Sheepshead Bay

Gravesend

GRAVESEND BAY

Coney Island
Creek

Coney Island

Manhattan Beach

Brighton Beach

BROOKLYN

THREE

Thomas Boyle

VIKING

Best Books for Public Libraries

VIKING
Published by the Penguin Group
Viking Penguin, a division of Penguin Books USA Inc.,
375 Hudson Street, New York, New York 10014, U.S.A.
Penguin Books Ltd, 27 Wrights Lane,
London W8 5TZ, England
Penguin Books Australia Ltd, Ringwood,
Victoria, Australia
Penguin Books Canada Ltd, 2801 John Street,
Markham, Ontario, Canada L3R 1B4
Penguin Books (N.Z.) Ltd, 182–190 Wairau Road,
Auckland 10, New Zealand

Penguin Books Ltd, Registered Offices:
Harmondsworth, Middlesex, England

First published in 1991 by Viking Penguin,
a division of Penguin Books USA Inc.

1 3 5 7 9 10 8 6 4 2

Publisher's Note:
This is a work of fiction. Names, characters, places, and incidents either
are the product of the author's imagination or are used fictitiously, and any
resemblance to actual persons, living or dead, events, or locales is entirely
coincidental.

LIBRARY OF CONGRESS CATALOGING-IN-PUBLICATION DATA
Boyle, Thomas.
Brooklyn three / Thomas Boyle.
p.   cm.
ISBN 0-670-83019-4
I. Title.
PS3552.0933B76   1991
813'.54—dc20   90-50745

Printed in the United States of America
Set in Times Roman

To the descendants of James Taylor, a clogmaker
who settled in Brooklyn in 1812

ACKNOWLEDGMENTS

Many native-born Brooklynites have guided me in my fictional explorations of the borough. I am particularly grateful to my old friend Peter deFrancis; and Gina Bellocchio and Christine Ruriani, women of Bensonhurst.

BROOKLYN

THREE

CHAPTER 1

MEGAN MOORE'S ASS was a miracle, plump in the *glutei maximi,* lean in the haunches, and punctuated on each side by a dimple embedded in the otherwise smooth flesh just beneath the widest expanse of pelvic bone.

Detective Inspector Francis DeSales blinked, rubbed the sleep from his eyes, and raised his head from pillow to headboard to better take in the lay of the land. Megan was lying on top of the sheets on her stomach, facing the television set on the table against the opposite wall. Her nightgown was pulled up above her waist. Otherwise, she was wearing nothing but the long earrings fashioned out of miniature .38-caliber Police Specials which DeSales had given her to commemorate the Feast of the Immaculate Conception, the day after Pearl Harbor Day, when he had moved in with her, some ten and one-half months before. She had not yet summoned the courage to wear them on the air—such irreverence about the criminal justice system in a TV police reporter might not be looked upon kindly by the Suits on the fortieth floor—but she wore them to bed each night.

Religiously, one might say.

DeSales, known in tabloid parlance as the Saint, chuckled with pleasure.

"You're awake," she said, not looking back.

The musculature of her back had a way of merging with the nape of her neck—just above where the silky fabric had bunched—that could give a dead man goose bumps. Now, propped up on her elbows, she gathered her dark red hair with one hand in a girlish topknot; with the other she held the remote control to the TV. By way of an answer, DeSales began to massage the elegant arches of her feet.

"I'm glad you're up," she went on. "I wanted you to see this. They're using my piece on the network feed. This kind of national exposure is just what I need to break out of my local rut."

The whirr of the air conditioner, the darkened room with the digital alarm clock reading 7:00 A.M., the sensuous glow of the boob tube bathing Megan's body: all of this conspired to make DeSales conspicuously horny.

Naughty puns seemed to have infiltrated every phrase. *Up, piece, exposure, rut. Boob.*

He straddled Megan's torso, careful to not appear too eager in touching her. When his head hovered over hers, he paused, holding back on the delicious moment when he would press his lips onto the erogenous zone just beneath the point at which she had pulled her hair up off her neck.

Megan raised the volume on the TV, disrupting DeSales's reverie. He looked up. On the screen, a squadron of blacks, led by a fat man with a naughty child's face and a gleaming Little Richard hairdo, was marching down a city street carrying placards calling for justice, chanting. On the pavement white people gesticulated angrily. Some were giving the finger. Most of these whites, seen in close-ups as the panning camera zoomed in and out, were young males with dark hair and underdeveloped mustaches.

"*Paisans,*" DeSales said bitterly. "*My* people. The *cugine* element."

"I wouldn't go *that* far," said Megan. "Just because your mother's side of the family is Italian and you grew up in Bensonhurst doesn't make you the same as those *Saturday Night Fever* characters who shot the black kid. Or the ones waving the watermelons at the Reverend Luke and his minions." She pointed at the screen, where indeed the whites were holding watermelons over their heads with muscular tattooed arms and the marching blacks were shouting threats in return.

"They *look* like my cousins," DeSales chortled. "Except my cousins never shouted 'Nigger go home.' Maybe because they never took a chance on getting close to any persons-of-color."

"Everybody's got skeletons in the closet. At this very minute, my mother's family in Ponte Vedra are expressing their social consciousness by getting ready to tee off at the club, the men all wearing shirts with whales on them and the women in pastel Lilly Pulitzers, killing time before the martinis at lunch. You read Pat Ham in the *Post* yesterday? Guidoville, he's calling your old neighborhood."

"Let's not let it get in bed with us. I got out of there twenty-five years ago with no intention of going back and now it's taking over my professional life. For the moment I'm *off*-duty and *on* you." DeSales lowered himself, making simultaneous contact with Megan's buttocks and shoulder blades. He ran his lips lightly over the bump at the top of her spine.

She slapped at him with the remote control. "Frank! What are you doing? Look! Here I am."

Megan, fully dressed in the regalia of the liberated woman on the job—shirt, long skirt, leather boots bunched at the ankles, hair neatly coiffed, sunglasses propped on top of her head, no revolver earrings—came on screen holding a microphone.

"What does it *feel* like I'm doing?" DeSales breathed into her ear.

"It feels like you're trying to stick that thing of yours where it doesn't belong."

Onscreen, it was last month and she was interviewing Harrison Dillard, the black candidate for mayor. She was asking him whether the Bensonhurst situation had helped his chances in the upcoming primary election.

"Roll over, then," said DeSales.

"This is my *career* you're messing with."

"*My* career is messing with careers."

Harrison Dillard was evasive. Megan asked: "Isn't it true that this could result in all sorts of backlash?"

"No," he said. "We're going to keep campaigning on the issues."

She persisted: "But the issues—by your very presence in this campaign—have been centered on black-white relations, and this ups all the antes, no?"

Dillard fidgeted. Finally he exhaled heavily, as if suppressing anger. "I've said it a thousand times before. The root problems of this city have to do with color, but not black and white or brown or yellow. This city's color problem is spiritual. You hear my opponents speaking of infrastructure: Well, our true infrastructure is our spirit, and our spirit has become corroded and drab, the color of monotony, of rusted incinerators, of children bruised beyond ethnic identity . . ."

The camera closed in on Megan, who looked pleased with herself, as she introduced a tape montage of the events of the long hot summer which had just passed.

In her bedroom, Megan sighed. "Is this a *pressing* need, Frank?"

"You got it."

"So roll me over. No. Not there. I want my head here at the edge. There. I've never watched upside-down before."

She drew in a sharp breath. "Very nice, Frank. Oh. *Penetrating.*"

"Raunchy bitch."

"Macho man. Look, there's the Metropolitan Museum. I thought it would work as a backdrop to the summer of racial violence. You know, a nice counterpoint to the wilders in the park behind it. Touch me there. With your finger. Up and down. Now in. The *long* stroke."

DeSales notched up. He began to bump, more and more quickly. Megan's hair had fallen loose, hanging plumb to the floor, where she had dropped the remote. He felt her fingernails on the backs of his ribs. He saw a bead of sweat emerge on her brow in the eerie green light from the screen, then run back down to disappear in her hairline. On the tube, an unhappy dawn: the lines and shadows where they had discovered the white woman jogger who had been raped and beaten in Central Park. The wilding black boys who had been apprehended covering their faces as they were led into the station house. Mug shots of the boys. Scenes of drug dealing and garbage on the Harlem streets where they had been raised. A videotaped confession. Megan's voice-over reading the prosecutor's prepared statement.

"I'm coming," gasped Megan.

DeSales reached forward and hit the mute on the control with his other middle finger.

The black boy with the puffy eye and scratches on his face gesticulated in an empty room. He seemed to be addressing himself to the wall. The camera, still and relentless, was unfazed by the boy's resistance to eye contact. He was wringing his hands. A close-up of the hands cut sharply to white hands twirling pizza dough. A feast. Eighteenth Avenue in Bensonhurst. Pastries and pasta and tarantellas. The Italian flag and the saint and Christmas lights hanging between telephone poles. A black boy lying shot on a street corner, then the corner empty except for the chalk outline where the body had lain. More watermelons.

"God," said Megan, lifting herself at the waist, "that's *it!*" For a moment she held her torso out from the bed, in midair. "All that work on the Cybex at the gym," she said. Her breath came faster, then the embrace was complete and DeSales's mouth met hers as they ground together in a last convulsive shudder.

Onscreen, Megan, mouthing silent words, standing on the blood-stained street corner, interviewing a very fat white man wearing a sleeveless undershirt, his stupid eyes speaking mayhem. Megan with a priest, also wearing his sunglasses on top of his head, squinting toward the sky as if in search of some divine intervention. The news feature concluded with a stop-action shot of the dead black boy in close-up, lying in the casket at the funeral, the twisted faces of his mourning family behind him. Then the show segued into a commercial for a new fall children's program; slowly Megan began to fall away, from bed to floor; one knuckle grazed the control; the sound came back on. Interactive TV. Kids would be allowed to buy their very own weaponry and shoot their favorite enemies on screen in the relative safety of their own living rooms.

DeSales was back at the headboard, smoking. Megan crawled up to his shoulder: "How was I?" Her voice was eager.

DeSales cradled her to him: "No complaints. Our timing gets better every week. You keep up with that personal trainer, you'll be able to do it standing on your head."

"I don't mean that, dummy. I mean how was my story?"

"Biased."

"Biased? How?"

"Very liberal. Anti-Italian."

"You know I'm not anti-Italian. You must be kidding." She ran her fingers across his nipples, twined them in the hair on his chest. "You're Italian, and you complain about Italians more than I'd dream of. Besides, I satisfy your every lustful whim."

"*Every* whim?"

"Within reason."

"That's the problem. Reason. The law and the media don't know shit from shinola about reason. I watch those Sicilians with their watermelons and their pizza and their big bellies right next to ghetto kids living out of garbage cans and I don't only get a distorted vision of the real worlds these people live in, I catch a terminal case of liberal guilt for the dark-skinned and downtrodden. Send the marines to Eighteenth Avenue and blow the freaking dagos off the face of the earth."

Megan rolled over. The ass again. Then she rolled partly back, propping herself up so she was eye-to-eye with her lover. He exhaled smoke to the side, then stubbed the cigarette out in an ashtray next to the digital clock, which now read 7:30.

"Some speech, Inspector. Would you give that again, on camera?"

"I don't give interviews anymore, remember."

"So how does the media get itself free of its built-in capacity to distort if people like you don't set the record straight?"

DeSales was out of bed. He scratched his groin and stretched his lean hard frame. The scars where the bullets had entered were a striking white against the olive skin. "Your problem," he said. "What's your schedule today?"

"Dillard is going ahead with his plans for a motorcade from Central Park to the Staten Island side of the Verrazano Bridge. I'm going to try to pick up coverage somewhere near downtown Brooklyn. But I have to look in on the RICO prosecution at Borough Hall. The Wall Street front the mob was using is supposed to cop in exchange for a reduced sentence."

"Dillard is a crazy fuck. After this Bensonhurst mess, he could lay up in Harlem until Election Day and still win."

"Harlem indeed! You seem to forget that Dillard lives

among, and on an equal footing with, the gentry of Brooklyn Heights." Megan put her head on DeSales's chest. "I'm scared, Frank. I think someone is going to kill him. Before the election, before he can move closer to Harlem, to Gracie Mansion. I've seen these people. They're not like anyone I've met. In court or out. They're animals. I heard they invited the K.K.K. up from Alabama this weekend. A woman who saw me with my crew the other day spit on me. A guy in a tenement window pulled down his pants and stuck his ass out and spread his cheeks. I'm scared for myself and for Dillard."

DeSales closed his eyes, rearranging his features into a semblance of concern:

"Don't worry. Kavanaugh is running security our end and he's the best."

They moved by rote, as they were talking, into the bathroom. DeSales took out his shaving gear and stood at the sink. Megan turned on the shower. Suddenly, she embraced him from behind. He dropped the razor in the sink. She pressed her breasts into his back. The mirror began to steam up. Her hands moved below his waist. There was a scar she touched when she was nervous.

She asked: "Why are you so interested in my schedule? Trying to plan a nooner?"

"Get outta here. I've got three unsolved homicides on my desk right now and some very weird bomb threats. I guess I gotta work harder to keep the city safe from my own people. I can take a break around eleven, though. When you're at Borough Hall. I wanted to do some house hunting. There's a big place Aunt Sally told me isn't on the market yet, on First Place between Court and Clinton."

"Frank, do you think this is the best time to try to get a Wasp from Manhattan who's experiencing a certain amount of Guidophobia to move to South Brooklyn?"

"They don't call it South Brooklyn anymore, it's Carroll Gardens. And it's mixed. There's yuppies all over the place."

He grinned evilly at his foggy image in the mirror. "All the *bad* goombah boys got driven to Bensonhurst by the yuppie invasion. This leaves only the *good* goombahs, who of course keep the neighborhood safe from criminally inclined crack-crazed outsiders, of whose ethnic background we dare not speak."

"Frank! There you go again. I had a teacher at Vassar who always said irony was the last refuge of the scoundrel."

"Sorry. Gallows humor is an occupational hazard. Anyway, you promised you'd give it a shot. Just look at the apartment. It's a buyers' market, I hear."

"I'll meet you in front of the State Supreme Court at eleven-thirty."

"You got a date." DeSales squirted shaving cream in his hand and began to lather up, resisting the temptation to add that he'd rather be a scoundrel than a Vassar professor.

Any day.

CHAPTER 2

IT WAS AN UNSEASONABLY HOT day in October. The overripe smells of late summer had re-emerged, and there were places in the sun where the heat seemed to rise from the Brooklyn pavements. On Kings Highway, solitary men in strap undershirts straddled tool kits in the backs of darkened vans. In Flatbush, Jamaican girls wearing cowboy boots and mini-skirts hung out with the homeboys in front of abandoned Loew's movie palaces. In Park Slope, fair-haired young entrepreneurs in Bugle Boy shorts sat on brownstone stoops cradling cellular phones and plastic bottles of Evian water. From Cadman Plaza to downtown Fulton, Borough Hall lawyers, all gray suits and hairspray and breath mints, bustled, sweating, to air-conditioned lunches, while on park benches and the concrete stockades which enclosed the plazas of the newer municipal high-rises, armies of overweight office workers indulged themselves in the forbidden pleasures of carryout bags from Burger King and Dunkin' Donuts.

The sky over the harbor was dark with imminent thunder.

Stokely Carmichael Dillard, known as Karma, emerged from the climate-controlled interior of the video store, and the heat surprised him. It had been chilly in New Haven the night before, and coming home for a few days to entertain his long-absent sister seemed to have taken on the dimensions of a major season warp. He blinked, adjusted the plastic bag so it hung from one of his smooth angular cocoa-colored elbows, and proceeded to wipe his round rimless spectacles with the tail of his green Lacoste shirt. He crossed Adams Street against the light and sprinted over Court Street, out of the riffraffery of the legal milieu and into the happily prosperous and genteel environs of Brooklyn Heights, his home turf. He inserted a Tracy Chapman tape into his Walkman and proceeded, head bobbing, silently mouthing the lyrics about welfare lines and Salvation Army shelters, oblivious to the vintage LTD which cruised in his wake.

He was on an errand. He shifted the plastic bag from one arm to the other and pressed on past the Federal mansions and cul-de-sacs and flowering annuals and international boutiques to his own block. Certainly, Garden Place kept up an extraordinary front in a city whose corpus was plagued by drugs and thuggery, filth and ineptitude. It was noontime, a Tuesday. In East New York, a family of ten was being systematically gunned down by a crack-crazed former Eagle Scout and Pentecostal minister; on a walkway over the Cross Bronx Expressway, a group of eleven teen-age boys on their way home from an arraignment for criminal mischief at the county courthouse was dropping heavy chunks of concrete onto the windshields of vehicles heading for the George Washington Bridge; in Kings County Hospital, a team of foreign-educated surgeons was removing some cartilage from the wrong leg of a Guyanese taxi driver, while another operating room was being shut down by the Board of Health because of an over-abundance of flying insects; in Gravesend, two grown men were cutting one another with knives over an insult perpetrated on one man's family by the other's some fifty years before in the city of Palermo, Sicily.

But Karma, in spite of his minority status, had been effectively sheltered from direct contact with such realities—by his family and by his private school, only a few blocks away. And now his Yale experience had given a sense of privilege to his particular sort of blackness, a sense which had only been heightened by his father's current high-profile adventure as the first serious African-American candidate for the office of mayor of the Big Apple. In Garden Place one could hear the pigeons cooing in the eaves of the brownstones on the river side; backpack bookbags, safely untended, were tossed on the stoops; a blond woman wearing a long flower-print skirt, blouse tied in a knot at the waist, walked a sheltie and dangled her keys carelessly; a group of well-scrubbed kindergartners emerged from an ornate cast-iron security gate beneath a stoop crooning "Oh, Susanna!"; overseeing them, but just barely, two West Indian nannies conversed on the corner in high keening voices. Stokely Carmichael Dillard took it all in, paused to contemplate his boat shoes and sockless ankles, and felt justifiably at home.

He did not notice the old Ford pulling up at the fire hydrant at the corner.

He sang aloud with the voice on the headset. He too was talkin' about a revolution.

At that moment, three black youths turned the corner from State Street and blocked Karma's path. The two males had hair shaved in intricate designs on the sides of their heads, baseball caps worn backwards, unlaced hightop sneakers, gold chains and gold teeth, empty eyes. Their female companion had wide nostrils, hair twisted into short rattails, and wore the uniform of a parochial school administered by the Holy Roman Catholic Archdiocese of New York: a dark beret, a white blouse with tie, and a plaid skirt.

Then Karma saw the dog, and the frisson of fear that went through him was accompanied by a terrible sense that the block had emptied out. That he was standing there trying to look very chill without anyone to back him up. The nannies had disappeared, the bookbags abandoned, the singing children taken in to rest before their Suzuki violin lessons and short sessions in preventive psychotherapy. The pigeons in the eaves were sleeping. And Karma Dillard was left alone to defend his turf against three wilders and their dog.

The wilders were laughing now, eyes undead with joyous anticipation: they had, however inadvertently, tracked down and isolated one of those rare black boys, a wannabe, highly desirable as prey, whose very existence was a rebuke to their own. One of them whistled to the dog. The dog was unleashed, a brindle pit bull carrying the severed head of a Barbie doll in his slavering jaws. He dropped the head onto the pavement, rolled it toward the gutter with his snout, then gathered it up again into his mouth and renewed his methodical gnawing. Barbie's once-blond hair was indistinguishable from gutter litter. Barbie's nose was abraded and her left ear chewed off. The pit bull got a clump of dingy hair caught in his teeth and began to shake his head, and the doll's head, violently.

Now the wilding boys advanced toward Karma, menacing. One of them commanded the dog to be ready to attack. The girl was bent over double, shrieking with hilarity at the spectacle of the brindle dog tearing up the severed head. Karma felt dizzy. He needed to escape. Run run run run, screamed the tape in his ear. He put his hand in his pocket, looked puzzled, peered into the plastic bag—all the while evading eye contact with his imagined tormentors—then snapped his fingers like a fellow who has just remembered that he left his car keys at home. It was, he realized as soon as he did it, the lamest of gestures, but in any case he was on the balls of his feet poised for flight. He made an abrupt about-face.

The car that had pulled up at the fire hydrant now accelerated and screeched up onto the curb. A young white male, heavily muscled and wearing a Jets cap, leaped out and went for the black boys. The first of the blacks poised himself for self-defense; the second hit Karma on the side of the head with a glancing blow; the girl started to run; the dog backed away snarling. There was a skirmish, but Karma was unable to follow it. He was seeing stars. It was Alice-in-Wonderland-awesome time: a sense of falling, a rabbit-hole fantasy—instead of dodo birds and giant caterpillars he was surrounded by headless Barbie and Ken dolls, growling and grinding in acts of grim and bestial fornication; he heard the dark unforgiving laughter of ghetto children; he hit bottom and the bottom was hard and dry. His consciousness ebbed and flowed.

The blacks were gone and the white guy was climbing back in his car. The skies opened. Rain was falling. Thunder rumbled over the Statue of Liberty. Karma Dillard was not even sure he had been unconscious, merely inept. Amazingly, he had managed to hold on to the bag with the videotape. He gathered himself up from the pavement and headed for the refuge of his front door.

CHAPTER 3

WHEN KARMA DILLARD WENT into his house the boy wearing the green Jets cap in the car at the corner slapped his hip with pleasure, thinking about the way the Bloods had scattered in the face of serious power. He shifted back into Drive. The mint '69 LTD had oversized foam rubber dice hanging from the rearview mirror and the bumper sticker that said: "Don't Like My Driving? Dial 1-800-EATSHIT." He burned rubber pulling away from the curb on Joralemon Street, at the same time inserting a Creedence cassette into the tape deck. "Fortunate Son" resounded on the boom speakers built in where the back seat should have been.

Fortunate indeed. He had been on the verge of running out of clandestine options, of having to take a chance on being seen simply dropping his delivery through the Dillard mail slot. If it would fit. But then the ghetto kids had hit on the young Dillard and afforded the opportunity for exchanging packages. A window of opportunity.

He turned onto Adams near the Criminal Court on two

wheels and gave the finger to a couple of uniformed court officers crossing the street with the light. The LTD roared down the broad expanse of Adams, then into narrower Boerum Place, left on Dean past the nancy-fancy restored brownstones, then right on Bond, in the direction of the low-income projects, where it pulled up at a hydrant outside a row house that had been overlooked by the gentrifiers. So far.

The landlady's sons, as usual for midday, were sitting on the stoop, all five hundred pounds of them, drinking Colt 45 from brown paper bags. To the driver of the LTD they showed a certain deference. The elder of the two hung his head and spit between his feet; the other crushed his empty can inside the paper bag. Their mother, Bessie Raney, was sitting in the hallway among the stacks of mildewed religious tracts—sepia covers of bleeding Jesuses—and odd lots of impaired furniture. There was an iron gate at the end of the hall opening onto the back yard, and the dogs bellowing there were large and underfed.

After a while, she noticed her visitor. She sighed. "Coughs all night, your friend. Ain't paid no rent. You all tryin' to make a problem. You wanna know what I think? I think he got the AIDS." She sniffed. "You all got some nerve. I raisin' young boys in this house." She nodded toward the front door, outside of which her middle-aged children sat in graduating degrees of stupefaction.

The boy with the Jets hat pulled a roll of bills from his pocket. "What's he owe?"

"Sixty dollar." Her chair squeaked.

The boy turned the peak of his cap to one side with the hand which held the money. He put the other hand to his hip and executed a partial knee bend. "It was fifty last time."

She produced a fan and passed it in front of her eyes. "That was before he use so much water. Toilet flushin' all the time."

"There's other toilets in the house. He ain't usin' all of them."

The landlady had plucked her eyebrows and covered her lower forehead with a series of charcoal smudges. Under the hair net she had bald spots. She intoned: "This his toilet. I know my plumbin'. Been workin' on this place since 1952. Mr. Raney come home that year from Seoul Korea with that there GI Bill? Thass when we bought the house and start makin' the improvements."

She held out the hand without the fan. Her dressing gown had fallen open, revealing a red velvet pants suit underneath. Slowly she looked up and down the grimy hallway. "But it a losin' battle. Where's a person to go? Ain't safe in the streets no more. They got those projects down the block and then these rich liberals come over from the City and the thieves from the project hang around lookin' to rob them." She fanned herself. "Lord's sake, what would Mr. Raney say if he lived to see the state things come to. Used to be plain folks around here. Now there's the Welfare and the yuppies and regular law abiders like us got caught in the squeeze. It's all the boys and I can do keepin' the house together." The popping sound of fresh beer cans opening could be heard from the stoop. "Only neighborhoods we can afford—workin'-people neighborhoods thass safe—they lynch our black asses down there." With the fan she pointed south, in the general direction of Bensonhurst, and with the other hand gathered in the bills. She breathed deeply, profound resignation hanging about her like chains. "So we gotta stay here with the likes of Mr. Social Disease upstairs." She stuffed the money in her pocket. She held up the fan: "What *you* doin' here? White boy. You don't look like no faggot, but I reckon appearances don't mean nothin' these days."

The boy pulled his peak around to the front. His dark hair was cropped close above his ears and trailed out the back of the cap in a kind of fall. He wore acid-washed jeans and a black T-shirt with white Gothic lettering that said "Too Fast to Live Too Young to Die."

"He was in the war with my dad," he said. "Nam. Saved his life." The boy's cheek twitched.

"Him"—she gestured upstairs with her eyes—"don't act like no sojer, let alone no hero."

The boy shrugged his shoulders.

"Listen," she went on, contemplating a page ripped out of a hymnal. "I find out he got that disease, he's out, you hear. They's a line of niggers all the way from here to Brownsville waiting for that upper suite of mine."

"I'd like a receipt."

She reached into the drawer, pulling out a pad. She licked the tip of a pencil with her tongue, poised to write. "To who do I make this out? Mr. Typhoid Mary?"

"To me. I paid you, didn't I?"

"You got a name?"

"Bono." He spelled it out: B-O-N-O. Hendrix. H-E-N-D-R-Y . . . no, I . . . X. Mr. Bono Hendrix."

"You got any title, like from work?"

"I'm a self-employed contractor now, but I used to be an associate producer for Cable Systems of America."

"Sure," said the woman, scrawling large letters across the pad. "And I'm Geraldine Ferrari. With a F. I use to be the next vice-president of the United States. Except I use to be Eye-talian too."

There were four doors on the top-floor hall but only one was accessible. The others were blocked by stained mattresses, upended against the doors, as if the Raneys were warehousing them against a future shortage of SRO furnishings. Bono tapped on the available door and turned the knob, entering a good-sized room, barren except for a toilet, washstand, and tub, two store-window dummies, a moth-eaten overstuffed chair, a standing metal closet the color of a safe, and a narrow bed. On the peeling wall over the bed were some publicity photos of celebrities and some faded newspaper clippings. An emaciated black man with a shaven head lay under mauve linen sheets. He was watching a small-screen TV at his feet. On the TV a woman in a skimpy teddy unbuttoned the shirt of a heavy-breathing dude and stuck a silver letter-opener into his hairy chest.

"How's it going, Remi?" the boy asked.

Remi raised a limp arm and let it rest again on the sheet. "Not bad, Junior," he replied. His voice was starkly resonant in the barren room; he had the timbre and diction of a trained public speaker. He shook his head. "That Lilith is just too much. But"—he turned off the volume—"that's not exactly what you mean by your question, is it dear? You're not even interested in the plot of my soap." Remi's eyes were white-and-brown abstractions. He rolled them in their cavernous sockets at his visitor.

"I meant, like, how are things with you?"

"Bo-ring. Energy the pits. I suppose Aunt Jemima down-stairs had ghastly tales to tell. She suspects I have the Big A."

"And she's no rocket scientist," said Bono. "You should go back to the doctor."

"To Bellevue? To one humiliating indignity after another? The segregated water fountains? The nurses with the gloves? The dementia of my cherished ward mates? Forget it, baby. I got you and . . . what was it Thomas Wolfe said? . . . a room of one's own. Miz Raney"—he raised an eyebrow—"calls it her upper suite."

"I heard her. Here's your papers," said the boy, dropping a stack of tabloids and slick magazines on the bed.

"Yum yum." Remi had a coughing fit. He pulled a blood-stained towel from under the bed, spat in it, and began to riffle through the pages of the periodicals with enthusiasm.

Bono went to the steel cabinet, selected a key off a ring attached to a belt loop, inserted it in the security lock, then inserted another, smaller key in a second lock. The door creaked open. One side of the cabinet was stacked with boxes, the other side had an impressive assortment of weaponry. Bono took out an AK-47 assault rifle and began to remove the cumbersome arching thirty-round magazine from in front of the firing mechanism.

"Crapola!" cried Remi from the bed. "It's *Fragrance* Week and here I am confined in this slum. I'd *kill* to go to the gala at Roseland tonight. They're celebrating the late forties. *Guess* who's going to be there?"

Bono put the long rifle aside and picked up a Tec-9, a short item with a long straight magazine. Thirty-six rounds. "Can't," he said, brows knit as he inspected the threaded barrel and fitted a silencer onto it.

"Gloria De Haven, Claire Trevor, Joan Bennett," exclaimed Remi. "Those three would be something to get into an elevator with."

Bono discarded the silencer and put back the Tec-9. He rummaged around in the cabinet and came up with a smaller cartridge for the AK-47. Opening one of the boxes, he inserted the small five-round cartridge into the AK-47 and tried it out for size against his side, as if he were concealing it under a long coat.

Remi sniffed the air like a hound. "*Cocoa* butter! You wearing cocoa butter, Junior?"

Bono had come up with an orange claylike substance. He brought a quantity of it over to the sickbed. Remi leaned over and smelled.

"Gross," he declared.

Bono laughed heartily. "It's not supposed to smell nice. Semtex, they call it. Arabs use it to blow up charter flights with Jews on them. Stuff like that."

Remi made a moue, then rolled his eyes in mock horror. "Junior! Guns and *plastique?* How absolutely perverse."

"Saving the planet," answered the boy with gravity.

"Saving the planet indeed! Is that all? How?"

Bono put the explosive material back in its box. He picked up the AK-47 with the five-round cartridge, then as an afterthought put a larger cartridge in one of his pockets. He looked knowingly over his shoulder at the emaciated figure in the bed: "I don't know, but I reckon one way to start is to waste some mushrooms."

Remi sank back onto the mattress. His cough was a hack. Bono handed him a clean towel to wipe his face, but he didn't seem able to lift his arms. The boy did it for him.

"I wish you could save *me*."

Bono dropped the dirty towel into a garbage bag and produced a clean one from under the stacked boxes of Semtex. "I wish I could too, but I'm just the gofer. I bring things, I take things away. I do the best I can to make the rest of the world better off. You need a doctor."

Remi was crying into the pillow.

"Don't cry. That's part of the deal. Nobody cries. Hey, Remi, lemme bring you something special. Maybe something you see in one of those columns you read. C'mon, what's your fantasy?"

It took Remi a while to turn over on his back again: "My first choice there's no question. Even *New York Nightlife* says it. John John Kennedy is absolutely the sexiest man alive." He read from one of the papers: "And he can be seen *regularly* at Delia's, 197 East Third Street. Can you believe it! When I was first on the afterhours scene, you couldn't find anything but Hell's Angels and beer-bellied Polish Princes on East Third Street. Rough Trade Boulevard, we called it."

Bono was thoughtful: "John John Kennedy has like heavy security. Somebody could get hurt."

"Well, you could get me them." He pointed at a clipping affixed to the wall at eye level: a grainy news photo of two large muscular people wearing matching mink coats walking down Fifth Avenue. The man had long dark hair. The woman had a crew cut and her hair was platinum blond. The caption under the photo said, "Buzz has a secret message, but only Reno knows for sure."

Remi's voice had regained some of its timbre. "It's Buzz Derma, the Olympic diver, the one with the fizz-eek and the itsy-bitsy swimsuit? And his girlfriend Reno Sheeny. She played the outer-space nympho in *Star Whores?* They're the hottest couple on the club scene now. He's just left his pregnant wife and their permanently disabled five-year-old daughter for Reno. And she's renounced drugs and group sex. Buzz and Reno are going to open a chain of health spas. Dry-out clinic and fat farm combined."

Bono wrinkled his brow at the picture on the wall. Derma looked like a kid he had grown up with by the name of Sonny Grosso who used to pick on all the other kids on the block. Buzz and Sonny both had swollen cheeks and those eyes. Eyes like dogs with hangovers. Eyes that told you that even if they felt cornered and nervous they were still very pleased that they were bigger than you and had sharper teeth. Sticking it to Buzz would be in a way like getting back at Sonny. That would be a pleasure. He looked over one of the mannikins, the black one, pins sticking out all over it and a newspaper pattern covering the head. Remi was into hats at the moment.

"Where do I find these people? Fuckin' Hollywood Boulevard?"

"Hardly, they greet the dawn at Disaster Area every day. I read about it on Page Six just last week."

"Is that the club where you don't know where it is until it opens?"

"Right. A new location every night, to keep ahead of the Liquor authorities—and the bridge-and-tunnel crowd, of course. Once a place is discovered by New Jersey and the O.B.'s, it's dead in the water. Autopsy time. But forget about it. Even if you find where the club is going to be on a given night, they wouldn't let you in."

"Yeh? Why?"

"The look. Acid-washed jeans. Too Outer Boroughs for *words*. You've got to work on your wardrobe, kiddo. Disaster doesn't even let in preppies. Show up in penny loafers and you're on the pavement. Strictly for the people riding the fashion wave."

"Like Buzz and Reno?"

Remi didn't answer. He seemed to be fading into a reverie.

Bono had loaded the semiautomatic assault weapon into a long box, which he was carrying to the door as a delivery boy might carry flowers. "Why do you want them?"

"I never had such famous visitors. Maybe they'd show me their tattoos. They've got messages to each other tattooed in secret places."

He was crying again. Then the coughing started. Bono took him the towel, holding him in his brawny long arms until the sobbing subsided. Remi's eyes were bloodshot. As he spoke, Bono could see the sores in his mouth. You could say that Remi got the sores in the first place from licking the disco floors where the sleaze-stars of New York nightlife struck the pose. This Buzz and Reno business was only the latest break-out of the lingering disease.

"No, Junior," said Remi. "Don't feel sorry for me. I was beautiful once. I had my fifteen minutes of fame. I was the most beautiful piece of ass at the Pines for ten summers and ain't nobody gonna forget it. Now"—he twitched—"my energy is like *down*." Then he was asleep.

"I'm gonna be famous too," Bono muttered. "Save the planet. Waste some mushrooms."

Bessie Raney and her sons did not look up as he carried the long box down the stairs and loaded the artillery into the LTD. The rent was paid.

CHAPTER 4

THE DILLARD HOUSE was unique on Garden Place. Unlike its brownstone neo-Grec and brick Federal neighbors, it was a house wider than it was deep, with mullioned windows and a phony Gothic pointed roof-line above its two terra-cotta stories. Karma was greeted at the door by his older sister Angela, who had just come home from her junior year abroad in China.

Angela was starved for American popular culture. She grabbed the video-store shopping bag and demanded: "Where you been, boy? Rousting out with your rowdy friends from St. Ann's? The *Extreme* skateboarders?"

Karma dropped into the cream sofa in the sunken living room. "I was mugged," he sighed, without much conviction.

"Mugged? Who'd mug you? They run *away* from big black boys 'round here. Beside, you don't *look* mugged."

Karma despaired at the notion of trying to explain with any detailed understanding what had just befallen him. He would tell his father later. For the moment it was better that Angela tranquilize herself with the movie. He had forgotten how hyper she could get.

He sighed again, resigned. "You hear from Dad?"

"No. He must still be in that motorcade."

"Where's Mom?"

"She just called. She's staying over at the conference in Washington."

Angela was eagerly opening the bag, pulling the tape out of the black rental container, on which was printed: "Be kind. Rewind."

"What *is* it?"

"I know the guy at the store. I get like pirate stuff. Things not out yet."

"That's why no title." She looked up, puzzled, then wary. Angela Davis Dillard was a strikingly beautiful young woman. She was often said to resemble Lena Horne, not least because she had large eyes which flashed and darted with volatile energy. Even confusion came off her like a challenge to others to be alert. "Hey, brother. Two years ago it was Pee-wee Herman for you. Last year, Mom wrote me it was slice-and-dice. She said they was afraid you was gonna be the Black answer to Charles Manson." She held up the tape with two fingers, as if it might be contaminated. "Is this some sick little joke? *Texas Chainsaw?* Illegal snuff stuff?"

Karma felt diminished, hurt. "Hey, I get you *Batman* while it's still in the theaters for eight bucks a pop, months before it'll be on the open market, then I fight off a crew of muggers to hold on to it, just for you to sit on your fat ass at home to see it. And this is the gratitude I get?"

Karma had struck a chord. His sister was wearing a halter top and spandex bicycle pants and the bigness of her butt relative to her otherwise lissome figure was indisputable. In Beijing, she had taken to wearing a single long braid down her spine and she pulled at this while she tried to wriggle more deeply into the sofa. She tossed Karma the unmarked cassette. "Okay, Mr. Wonderful, slip it into the machine."

Angie had been watching *Hollywood Squares*. While the tape engaged, a doughy-faced young woman was introducing herself to Joan Rivers and Shadoe Stevens and ALF, who occupied the center square: "I'm Denise. I'm thirty years old. I have a six-year-old and husband and I love them a lot." The tape replaced Denise on the screen. Karma waited for the familiar Prince score to carry him away to the dark fascinations of Gotham City and the Joker. On screen, there were the usual FBI warnings, no titles. As the film began, the camera was panning over a crowd, a sea of young white American faces, laughing and cheering, in living color. In the audio background, crudely overdubbed, voodoo drums, gunfire. Then silence, buzzing. The screen split between two simultaneous images. On the left, in color, a young red-headed woman wearing jeans and a bikini top rose from the crowd assembled in the grass ampitheater and started an undulating dance. An unctuous voice-over cried: "Groovy!" The girl shook her head in slit-eyed ecstasy, her thick unkempt locks spilling across her features, "L-O-V-E" stenciled on her forehead. Close-up of the waving serpentine arms, the hands. The hands reaching behind her and unsnapping the top. Breasts milky white against her tan, small nipples erect. On the right of the screen, in black and white, an earnest looking fellow wearing a tie and a white short-sleeved shirt making a speech about "progressively demystifying a false democracy."

"That ain't no Batman," said Angela. "That's *Mister* Jane Fonda."

"You been away. The *former* Mister Jane Fonda."

The split screen images faded into a single two-shot: a solid-looking well-dressed black couple. Angela gasped. "It's Mom and Dad. What you tryin' to pull on me, Karm?"

Harrison Dillard was standing on a dais. His patented big-toothed grin. Silently, he gestured to his wife with one hand, stroking his goatee with the other. Close-up of Ruth Dillard, close-up of the candidate. His lips were moving, still smiling, but the dubbing was way out of synch: "I used to eat so much pussy my beard looked like a glazed doughnut." Gales of laughter, more jungle drums, more gunfire.

"This is *gross!*" cried Angela. "*Your* ass is . . ."

"Wait," said Karma, holding her arm. "The voice. That's Dennis Hopper. From *River's Edge,* remember? We saw it on tape before you went away."

"Who gives a fuck? Mr. Trivia Whiz. This isn't funny . . ."

But then Dennis Hopper himself was onscreen, wearing a coat and tie, looking sincere, mouthing flabby words about the spirit of love and peace which infused the sixties. Quick cut to a shot of President Kennedy and his wife, Jacqueline, riding in the back of a limo. Split screen with the Dillards riding in a limo. John Lennon at a studio keyboard, dissolute, in blue-tinted granny glasses, singing "Imagine." Yoko Ono in wraparound pitch-black shades playing a smaller keyboard a few feet behind and to the left of her husband. Offscreen, the sound of machine guns, agonized screams. Fade to the Kennedy limo. Kennedy's head snapping forward, then back to the left. Walter Cronkite intoning a forensic explanation of the phenomenon of the head going back and to the left. Jackie's pink suit splattered with blood. Reaching for her husband, then trying to climb over his maimed body, onto a rear fender of the car. A loop of maniacal laughter.

The Dillard children sat stunned, speechless, in their impeccably furnished living room on Garden Place. There were fresh flowers on the mantelpiece; the central air-conditioning functioned silently; the copies of *The New Yorker* and *Connoisseur* were stacked neatly on the coffee table. Civilization was holding its own.

On the screen the dancing girl in the crowd at the rock concert pulled off her jeans. She took the hand of a naked boy, a white boy with a spotty beard, about her own age.

Together the couple walked into a pond, joining other naked couples cavorting about. A joint being passed from hand to hand. Much blissful eye-closing. A close-up of Harrison Dillard, then a cum-shot from a porn flick: a black penis ejaculating in slow motion, gobs of sperm dripping off the pockmarked face of a white woman of uncertain age. A nude hippie male, back at the rock concert, standing in front of a bus painted in psychedelic designs. Rain falling. More flying semen. The hippie, wearing a cowboy hat: "The fascist pigs have been seeding the clouds. Why doesn't the media report *that?*"

"Turn it off," murmured Angela, deep in the sofa, but neither she nor her brother moved.

The footage was now of hippies, naked, rolling in mud. Mud—lava—flowing from an erupting volcano in an old newsreel shot. Mrs. Dillard in close-up, looking at once pleased and embarrassed. Jimi Hendrix playing "The Star-Spangled Banner." Setting fire to his guitar. Three-year-old John John Kennedy, in long coat and short pants, saluting; the Capitol in the background. Harrison Dillard, in his military officer's uniform, saluting. John John Kennedy, age twenty-seven, entering a downtown club, screaming teen-agers with autograph books restrained by a cordon of bouncers wearing Dead Kennedys T-shirts. The soundtrack began playing Creedence Clearwater Revival: the rich hoarse voice protesting about not being a senator's son. The Who onstage: Pete Townsend smashing a guitar, Keith Moon drumming maniacally. Split screen again. Two erect penises, parallel. Two mouths. Black on white. White on black. Two penises ejaculating. A Buddhist monk calmly setting fire to himself, burning up like so much tissue paper. The volcano. The lava flow. The naked hippies in the mud. The Hendrix guitar, the A-bomb erupting, the screen filling up with mushroom cloud. Harrison Dillard saluting. The voiceover like a stuck record: "Military-industrial complex, military-industrial complex." Jane Fonda demonstrating aerobics on a workout tape. A Spanish-style stucco house on fire. A lonely motel; a city burning. Mick Jagger, bare-chested, prancing about a stage in long johns and an Uncle Sam hat, shouting about being bled on. Bleeding prisoners in tattered uniforms. Fade to Harrison Dillard in a publicity still, looking awfully pleased with himself. "Won't get fooled again," someone intoned on the soundtrack.

The homemade movie sputtered to a close.

Angela was grim. "This is some welcome mat. Wait until Dad sees this."

Karma hopped around the living room. His jaw ached:

"Maybe he shouldn't see it, Ange. Let's forget about it."

"I'm not covering for you."

"But I didn't do it. I swear."

CHAPTER 5

MEGAN MOORE PROTESTED: "I can't do this anymore, Frank. Why do we have to move to Brooklyn anyway? My apartment in the City is plenty big enough for both of us." She stood on the corner of Court and President streets, looking resplendently show-biz Banana Republic in her khaki culottes and military-style shirt. Her hair flowed to her shoulders from beneath the Indiana Jones fedora.

The thunderstorm that had passed over so quickly had failed to cool things down. DeSales kept on walking, wiping his brow with the windbreaker he wore in spite of the heat to cover up the .38 he carried in a holster under his left shoulder. Then he stopped, turned back to her, folded his arms over his chest, and leaned against the window of the Luna Bakery. The seventier wedding cake with the miniature bride and groom on top towered over him from the rear. Next door, the glass sculptures commemorating in more permanent form the blissful moments of bridehood glistened in the bright light from the street, set off by the dark damp pavement.

He snapped: "There's one reason for starters. It's *your*

apartment. If we're going to get permanent about this thing, we got to start out on some equal footing: *our* place, not yours. Besides, that duplex we just looked at cost half as much, was twice as big, and is a lot closer to work than where we are now."

She said: "Closer to work for *you,* not me."

"Since when did you start working anywhere special? You never go to the studio anymore. You're always out covering a story. When you're on the crime beat, most of your stories are in Brooklyn. How long were you out here for the Amalfi trial? Months. Listen, your office is wherever there's a camera or a phone booth. You live out of that bag." He gestured with disdain at the heavy leather shoulder bag Megan carried, bulging with papers and wires for assorted electronic equipment. "I got a whole operation I have to run. And it's at one address on Tillary."

"I've had bad luck in Brooklyn, Frank."

"You and three million other people." DeSales put his head down and began to stride north.

Megan fell in alongside, determined to keep up and make her point:

"Let's get down to cases, then. The apartment we looked at was indeed larger and cheaper than mine and it is certainly possible that living here would reduce our overall commuting time. But the place is dark, unbearably dark; the fat busybody of a landlady would probably declare war if we touched the Levelor blinds she uses to make it even darker. Ditto for the black wallpaper with the white embossed harps. And remember, I've lived not far from here before—remember when Sam the Sham needed to be near his kids, then left me holding the bag—and I have to confess that it depresses me to pass block after block each with five bakeries and three salumerias selling the same produce and the same gooey inedible matrimonial sentiments. Did you see the way Mrs. Biasi looked at little me? Unmarried, childless. To her I'm the Whore of Babylon.

You could club me to death and she'd testify that I *asked* for it."

For a moment, Megan saw his eyes go funny and she thought he might indeed club her, if not to death at least into some form of submission.

"Frank, I love you, right."

"Yeh?"

"So, hold on already. I'm not trying to be a snob or take away your masculine prerogative or anything. So can we drop it for today, Frank? We're not going to move right away in any case. Look"—she put her arms around his neck—"it isn't really *about* Italians. Or cops. It's about *me*. Now"—she kissed him lightly on the lips, feeling the pistol against her right breast—"I'll try to make it up to you. I'll eat spaghetti and meatballs until they come out my ears and tonight we can do a hot tub . . ."

But DeSales had stiffened. He had seen the kids with the doll's head first. They were kicking it down Atlantic Avenue past the Middle Eastern markets and the fruity antiques stores. The dog was fetching and retrieving. Once the girl kicked it into the street and traffic came to a screeching halt. The dog went after the head, thought better of it, and leaped at the driver of the nearest car, who quickly rolled up his window. Then the dog fetched. The kids whistled.

DeSales patted under his windbreaker for his weapon and crossed the street, heading the kids off. "Why," he said, confronting them, "aren't you lovely children in school? Is this Reverend Luke's birthday or something?"

One of the boys raised his eyebrows; the other showed his gold tooth. The girl snickered. The dog growled. Each expression in its own way asked the inevitable question: What kind of crazyass middle-age, middle-size white man was going to mess with serious Bloods in the street?

The girl said: "Hey man, you the motherfuckin' truant officer? Or what?"

"Who I am isn't the question, bitch. What I think about what you're doing here is. And personally I don't like it."

"This is a free country."

"You earn your freedom. You do all sorts of uncomfortable shit like go to school and work a straight job. You don't go around playing badass, giving regular people indigestion with a lethal weapon like that mutt." The boy with the gold tooth did a long slow smile and began to raise an arm when DeSales dug his fist into his solar plexus and the kid went down gagging. The dog bared his teeth and crouched to leap, but DeSales had it by the collar and the barrel of his Police Special was jammed into its frothing maw. DeSales held it there, squirming, trying to chew on the blue steel of the barrel, while he looked up coolly at the girl and the boy who was still standing.

The detective bared his teeth: "You want me to blow the back of Fido's head off? You can take him home then and feed him to your rats." But the kids were running already, in the direction of Smith. The boy who had gone down was the last to take off. DeSales released the dog and kicked it, whining, after its masters. He picked up the abandoned doll's head.

"Honky motherfucker," screamed the fleeing girl over her shoulder. DeSales dropped the head and went down on one knee. He took aim with the pistol in both hands, just like the movies, and the kids hit the street, rolling through dogshit and broken glass to avoid being hit. He stood up smiling, holstering the pistol. He picked up the head again and walked back across the street with an all-in-a-day's-work expression on his face.

Megan Moore was not entertained. "Is the Dirty Harry act for my benefit? So I'll know not to cross you the next time? Or are you just scapegoating those kids to release some of your hostility toward me?"

DeSales dropped the doll's head in a trash basket. He looked at it a long while, hands in pockets, garbage bees buzzing around the lid. Finally, he looked up. "Did I ever tell you about the Snake Woman of Canarsie?"

Megan shook her head, warily. This story could be an object lesson, a parable. She saw the telltale twitch in his cheek and decided to keep her mouth shut. Listen.

"There's five kids," he said, scuffing his shoes on the pavement, eyes downward, oblivious to the Arab markets they were passing. "They're wandering around Canarsie the other week. They don't have a dog; they got a snake, a python, about seven feet long . . ."

"Uh-huh." Megan nodded, inspecting a barrel of ocher powder. The spicy aromas and the heat had her thinking about a Cypriot merchant she had once picked up on a Greek holiday financed by her mother after the breakup of her colorless marriage to Brian Sadleir, the Customer's Man.

"A seven-foot python. You got any idea how it feels to have five black teen-agers appear out of the darkness, out of the neighbor's back yard, hold this snake in your face and you don't know if they're gonna just take your purse or gangbang you or maybe both and then leave you in a toolshed with the snake? So this nice lady from Canarsie screams and the homeboys run and one of them drops the snake and comes back for it and the cops from the local precinct get there and pick the young herpetologist gentleman up and he squeals on his friends and the lady is brave enough to prosecute so we arraign them."

Megan lingered at a storefront window, gazing intently at campy Art Deco furniture she wouldn't be caught dead sitting in. The gays were moving in on the Arabs on Atlantic, just to add some flavor to the ongoing social discourse.

"Yes?" Megan replied, too politely. DeSales lighted a Benson & Hedges from a box. She waited for him. He threw the match in the gutter. A derelict of indeterminate race and age approached. DeSales waved him away. The derelict, unfazed, said, "Thank you, sir. How about you, miss. Spare change for a Christian gentleman who fell victim to the demon rum?"

DeSales took her arm. "The D.A. sends this kid who's still wet behind the ears and we draw Judge Mercedes Roundheels, remember her?" Megan nodded. DeSales would be on a number of shitlists if Mercy Rodriguez or the Puerto Rican Alliance heard him. Bias-related badmouthing had become a big no-no in the department over the past few months. "So the A.D.A. is confused. Do we got a Robbery One, a Robbery Two, or a Larceny Four? For Robbery One, which I was yelling for, we need use of a deadly weapon. I got two, maybe three witnesses to the snake, but there's no snake. I make Kavanaugh send out a snake-hunting squad, but the serpent has split from the garden. Kavanaugh discovers that Canarsie is the worst place in the city to find a snake because it's full of these underground tunnels from where they filled in the swamp it's built on, not to mention the old dump. Snakes love high water tables.

"Anyway, with no snake, the A.D.A. says maybe it wasn't poisonous. I say maybe the lady *thought* it was poisonous or lethal in other ways. I mean if you hold a toy pistol up and the victim *thinks* it's real, you can prosecute as if it *is* real."

"I know," said Megan, heading for a newsstand. She hadn't picked up the day's tabloids yet. "I covered the Cape Man Copycat case last spring. The jury spent a week on was his umbrella a lethal weapon. So no Robbery One for the Canarsie damsel in distress. Next, Robbery Two."

"Once we're down to Two, the D.A. thinks we can't try our Brownsville snake charmers as adults. Besides, there's a question whether they actually *took* the lady's purse or she just *dropped* it when they stuck the snake in her face and it flicked its tongue at her new tinted soft contacts. This of course introduces doubt as to the boys' actual *motive,* right? Without the five elements, we're down to Larceny Four, which means only that they tried to take something that belonged to the plaintiff but wasn't necessarily on her person, so Roundheels looks at our poor deprived soul brothers and suggests we bargain it down to Larceny Four. The moral of the story is, they walk."

"And—I want to get the papers here—if you abuse the kids with the doll's head, you'd prevent another miscarriage of justice. Is that the point of all this?"

But Frank was not yet prepared to laugh about that scene. He shifted back into outrage gear. "Miscarriage, shit, it was an abortion. Right now poor Adina Cohen's out on Seaview Avenue shitting her pants, afraid to even go over to Kings Plaza to get her hair done because they're going to come for her with a king cobra next and Stanley Cohen the father of her children and a former contributor to the NAACP has bought himself an Uzi personally modified to fully automatic mode by his Mossad-trained rabbi. Also, he's sent to a mail-order house in Texas for two hundred rounds of dumdum bullets and signed up at the Jewish Defense League for martial arts lessons Wednesday night instead of bowling and these kids are out on Rockaway Avenue laughing their asses off . . ."

There was a skirmish at the corner kiosk. The beggar who had just accosted them came hurtling out onto the pavement clutching a slick sealed-in-plastic magazine. Two Arab news agents followed, in hot pursuit. One collared the beggar and pinned him to the ground. The other, wearing a dishtowel headdress of the sort associated in the public mind with Yasir Arafat, flourished a dagger near his prisoner's throat. Megan Moore took her first good look at the man on the bottom. His skin and hair and clothing were uniformly dark and tattered so that he looked as if he had recently emerged from a Victorian coal bin. The magazine was something called *Double Delicious* and featured on its cover an enormous set of disembodied female breasts, very pink. He swatted gamely at the Arab holding the knife. The Arab bared his teeth, swore rapidly, and pressed the weapon closer to the man's dusky flesh.

More Arabs emerged from the nooks and crannies of the kiosk.

Megan was about to implore DeSales to do something, assert his authority, show his badge, pull out his gun, when a couple of uniformed patrolmen trotted from around the corner and separated the derelict from his tormentors. One of the cops was tall and slender with a ginger mustache. He was breathing hard and had a high hoarse voice. "What is this, a fucking skyjack?" he demanded. His partner laughed. DeSales bared his teeth in that grin he had which suggested both pleasure and displeasure at the same time. Heavy irony. Scoundrel time.

The opposing sides began to bicker loudly. Occasionally one would lunge at the other and the cops would have to throw their bodies in as barricades. The news agents charged theft, and aggravated theft at that: *Double Delicious* was one of their most expensive magazines. The alleged perpetrator began to cry real tears: he had only been inspecting the magazine when the Arab had attacked him with a deadly weapon. The one with the headdress flourished the weapon, showing how it was a tool of his work, necessary for cutting the bales of papers. Two more cops appeared in a cruiser. "Let's take them all in," said the senior officer. A collective moan arose from the retailers of Atlantic Avenue, like the cry from a minaret in a walled city at nightfall.

At that moment, DeSales's beeper sounded. He went to the pay phone on the corner. Megan listened intently to the paralegal haggling of the accused and his accusers. DeSales was back.

"You were right. Or rather half right."

"About civil liberties?"

"About the Dillard campaign."

"Somebody shot him?"

"Somebody missed him. They got the campaign manager

instead. Arthur Kaputz. Remember him. Your favorite un-attributed source? Talking all the time. Catching flies. Well, he took some semiautomatic fire. In the mouth. Had it open again."

"Where?"

"Under the Verrazano Bridge. Dillard was foolish enough to make an unscheduled stop on his motorcade. Just about the part of the world where you predicted some shit would come down."

"You going there now?"

"Car picking me up."

Megan pleaded: "Take me, Frank. I've been on this campaign from the beginning. I put off following the motorcade today because you wanted to house-hunt. I lose the whole story if I don't get there like five minutes ago."

"Sorry, Meg. That was part of the deal, remember. We never mix business with pleasure."

He was climbing into the squad car with the flashing red light.

"You prick," she yelled. He'd got her back after all. For not wanting to live upstairs from Mrs. Biasi. For not being amused by his acting out with the kids. For being a *woman*. He was an old-fashioned Italian sexist after all.

"Call a car service," said Francis DeSales, roaring away in the direction of lily-white Brooklyn.

CHAPTER 6

BEN ASTERISKY PACED back and forth in front of the classroom, rolling the nub of chalk between his thumb and index finger. He paused at the blackboard, scrawling the words "ghetto" and "white flight" next to the list of key words already in place: William Blake, Industrial Revolution, Karl Marx, Alan Freed, payola, race records, rootlessness, upward mobility, downward mobility, the Doors, Jerry Rubin, anomie, Death of God, Death of John Lennon, *The Catcher in the Rye,* Spiro Agnew, Ho Chi Minh, Batman, Harrison Dillard, "America's Funniest Home Videos." Out of the corner of one eye he watched Natasha Nabokov lean over from her seat next to the door, pneumatic breasts—the right newly decorated with a tattoo of a rose and a Harley Davidson logo—swelling out of her flimsy black tank top, fish a cigarette out of her purse. He turned to face the class and, coincidentally, get a more direct view of Nabokov. Her move for the cigarette was also an indication that the class hour was drawing to a close. He had to summarize the lesson.

"Today we have been considering an historical example of the sort of phenomenon you can relate to your own lives. In the mid-1950s, when I was your age, popular music reflected a significant change in American culture. After World War II, the old order was deconstructed. Soldiers returned home, new highways were built, a strange sort of trailer-camp prosperity began to reign in the Levittowns of the East and the new towns springing up out of the deserts and beaches of the West. People were on the move. At the same time the nation was still tainted by racial segregation. People were escaping by the millions from the *Lumpenproletariat,* but access was denied to minorities. Officially. Something had to give."

Asterisky paused for breath, wagging a finger in the air. He went on: "Then came the music. Chuck Berry sounded like a white country-guitar player on 'Maybelline'; Elvis like a black blues-moaner on 'Mystery Train.' Conventional stereotypical distinctions were blurred. There was new black pride rising: Bo Diddley asserted, 'I'm a Man,' then, 'I'm bad, don't mess with me.' The kids were listening on their car radios. White American culture had become rootless, drifting from the rust belt and the Bible Belt to the materialistic sacrament served up by carhops dressed like cheerleaders and prom queens. It was a drive-in culture without a conventional deity. The new Holy Trinity of faith became Disneyland, the climate-controlled motel with TV, and the car radio. On the car radios of the nation, as we buzzed on our parkways and freeways, we heard rock-and-roll, which was neither black nor white, but a marriage of black rhythm-and-blues and white country-and-western with a spritz of good old Jewish-Italian lounge balladeering. The stage was being set for a new social order: not only a freed-up geographic movement, but a new integrational spirit. Civil rights, student protest on the horizon. The lines were drawn and they were neither ethnic nor religious nor economic—at least to the degree they had been. They were generational. The young fellow and his girlfriend in their Corvette, tuning in their favorite deejay as they raced down the Jersey Turnpike in the wee wee hours, were harbingers of the second American revolution."

Asterisky wiped the sweat from his brow. In spite of the heat, he wore a tweed jacket with patches on the elbows over his tie-dyed Nehru shirt and blue jeans. The alarm wrist watch of Ng Ng, the inscrutably tireless Asian smiler in the middle of the room, went off, waking the Rastafarian who usually sat next to him, the only black student registered for this course on American Popular Culture at the Institute for Urban Studies, which had been founded only twenty years before with a mission to educate the Negro underclass of New York's most populous borough. The Rasta man shook his dreadlocks to clear his head and slouched back in his seat, eyes narrowed, distrustful. The Jewish fraternity boys with the muscles and spandex bicycle pants who whispered and snickered through class in the back row began to put away their untouched notepads.

"Of course, one might have been hard-pressed back in the fifties to predict the changes heralded by the rise of rock-and-roll." Asterisky was winding down. "But certainly each of you can observe something in your own personal environments—political, ethnic, artistic, sexual—which is a signifier of more social change, different kinds of social change. Gentrification, perhaps. The new fundamentalism of certain religious groups suggesting a reaction against the terrible beauties of the freedoms spurred by rock-and-roll, freedoms emblemized by the possibility that the largest city in the world will finally have a man of color as mayor, a man whose campaign is run, by the way, by a founding faculty member of this very people's institution which you attend, a man who has devoted his career, as many of us have, to redressing ethnic imbalances, deflating elitism . . ." Asterisky coughed, looking momentarily far-off, distracted. He pulled on his grizzled ponytail. His voice turned scornful, almost sneering. "Of course, there is a downside. For example, the commercial mainstream exploitation of nostalgia—like the current Woodstock-twenty-years-after craze . . ."

The bell rang; doors opened; the chaos of the halls infiltrated the room. Asterisky, silenced, sat at the old card table in the front of the hall and began to gather his effects. Only the fraternity jocks in the back row remained seated; they collectively held their books on their knees and, thick necks resting against the backs of their seats, gazed blankly at the ceiling, at the air-conditioning ducts which had never worked, since the renovation of the building had been brought to a screeching halt during the city's fiscal crisis of 1976.

The world had shifted on its axis, and not for the better, in only a baker's dozen of years. Asterisky glanced around briefly, taking in the thoughtless, uncommitted, conspicuous consumers his own generation had spawned.

His morbid reflections waned: Natasha Nabokov had stood up and was contemplating her reflection in the blank screen of the defunct TV monitor which had been installed, but never activated, before the budget crunch: She held her unlit cigarette aloft and stretched as if warming up for the ballet. Asterisky knew from her first assignment—the mandatory autobiographical essay—that she had arrived from Minsk only two years before and had already tanned her sultry flesh on beaches in the Carolinas, Florida, the Caribbean, Mexico, Texas, California; skied in the Rockies and gone hang gliding in the vicinity of Sugarbush, Vermont; and was currently in love with a Cajun musician from New Orleans, encountered during Mardi Gras the previous spring.

Nevertheless, as she made as clear as she could in her patchy articleless English prose, the bulk of her free time was spent with the Brighton Beach biker gang to which she had attached herself soon after her arrival in the Land of Opportunity (her father and his brother leased a Mobil station—repairs twenty-four hours, no credit—from an Israeli gangster in a neigh-

borhood near Kennedy Airport where drag racing was con-
ducted openly on the streets). Too much English in a given
day, she protested, gave her a migraine. She was brown as a
nut and, always bare-midriffed, displayed the most conspicuously sensual navel Asterisky had ever seen, in a considerable
career of navel nosing. Asterisky had been fantasizing since
he had met her that he would invite her, when the opportunity
presented itself, to try sunning herself with him at his cottage
in Amagansett. Oil. They would speak of the Finland Station,
cold nights in Minsk, perestroika, oil. The very sight of her
name on the class roster brought the taste of Hawaiian Tan
lotion to his tongue.

Asterisky forced his eyes away from Nabokov. Someone
was hovering over his makeshift desk. Miss LaRusso, a bulky
girl with a rooster tail of moussed raven hair and open-toed
sandals which showed that her toenails were painted purple.
Miss LaRusso was not someone he generally looked to confer
with, but now it was unavoidable. It was one thing to give
one's all to those to whom basic educational skills had been
denied because of economic deprivations or racial discrimi-
nation. Or, as in the case of Miss Nabokov, one newly emi-
grated from a repressive regime. But Miss LaRusso was a
fourth-generation American; her parents' combined income
was certainly greater than Asterisky's; they were active supporters of big business and conservative politicians; they
owned a substantial house in Mill Basin with a two-car garage.
When Asterisky contemplated the Miss LaRussos of Brooklyn, with their high-voltage hairdos and painted-on pants and
go-for-it manicures, he was well aware that their deprivations,
such as they were, were not of the sort the Institute had been
founded to excise from the body politic.

But he had his job to do.

"Yes, Tami?" he asked.

"You said at the end of class that that colored guy's campaign manager used to teach here? Is that for real?"

"Yes. Arthur Kaputz. We worked very closely together. Why do you ask?"

"Cause he got blew away at lunchtime. Down by Shore Road. They said somebody was trying to shoot whatsisname Dillard and hit this Kaputz by mistake." She fingered the headset hanging around her neck. "I heard it on my Walkman during class." Suddenly the girl looked startled: she had inadvertently betrayed herself by confessing to a deliberate inattentiveness, a literal tuning out, during Asterisky's impassioned presentation. No wonder she never understood the assignments. She scurried out the door without waiting for a response to her communication.

Asterisky laid his head down on the card table. In truth, there had been little love lost between him and Artie Kaputz, but they had shared ideals, had each in his own way continued to pursue the goals of social conscience. Jerry Rubins they weren't. And now one of them had died for the cause.

The Movement.

Asterisky felt his bowels shifting and grinding like the transmission of a vehicle ready for the junk heap. He needed to talk more about the emotional significance of this chronic inflamed colon in his therapy group.

Artie Kaputz was dead.

Asterisky arrived at the staff-room door to find Seth Pritikin awaiting him. As he opened the door, Seth took him by the arm and leaned forward in the conspiratorial manner he usually reserved for his lobbying binges before department elections.

"You heard the news?" he stage-whispered.

"About Artie? Only that it happened. How? Where?"

"In the mouth. In that park where they have the cannons commemorating the Revolutionary War. Battle of Long Island. In Bay Ridge. What do you think?"

"It's terrible, but at least there's a certain amount of nobility."

"How so?"

"He laid his body on the line for Dillard. That could be seen as heroic."

Seth blinked and sucked in his cheeks, so his lips resembled a tropical fish's. "That's what the media is saying, but look at this."

Asterisky took the piece of paper, a computer printout. He switched on the light and led Pritikin into the staff room, which was in fact the former Equal Opportunity office. Asterisky was the only one left there from the old days. Joe Verb had been killed by the police after he had gotten mixed up with the Black Revolutionary Army and been driven underground; Tim Desmond had gone establishment and was living in Europe on a grant; Greenstein had gone touchy-feely in California. Now half the space had been converted into a xerox room for the dean's secretaries; another quarter was taken up by stacks of boxes of old academic robes and four-cornered hats, left behind by a bankrupt rental house after some long-forgotten graduation ceremony. There were two large filing cabinets from those bygone days of rage and commitment which Asterisky had been loath to throw out: seventeen copies of an early draft of Joe Verb's never-to-be-completed dissertation on Bakunin, Greenstein's Iron Butterfly albums, and Kaputz's poster of Huey Newton-with-weapon-in-white-wicker-chair. Wearily he sat down, putting his feet up on the desk. Pritikin leaned against one of the file cabinets, crossing arms and ankles, and maintaining his look of simpering arrogance.

The printout was a class roster, of a sort that had been obsolete for some years. The class was called SS (for Special Services) Minus 9: Writing Across the Culture. The instructor's name, underlined in red, was Arthur Kaputz. Then there was a list of ten students, with Social Security and class and curriculum numbers. Asterisky skimmed the names: Raymond Martinez, Betty Robinson, and so on.

"Look familiar?" asked Pritikin.

"I guess. It's from the EOA program. Some of these kids were mine, I think. It's got Artie's name on it. What do *you* have it for?"

Seth took the roster back and waved it in the air: "*I* have it by default. As acting chair, I get undeliverable mail. *Dead* letters, as it were." He laughed softly at his pun. "This came in the mail last week, addressed to the Equal Opportunity for All program. Since the program is defunct, I wasn't sure if I should send it to Kaputz or to you or to anyone at all, since it didn't seem to be anything but an artifact of meaningless red tape."

"And it means something more now?"

"Ben, you surprise me." Pritikin raised an eyebrow. "You who finds significance in everything. Look closely. This is from a writing class. Did Artie teach writing?"

"No. Artie was the administrator. He didn't teach at all, so far as I remember."

"So, who taught the class?"

Asterisky pulled at his ponytail for a long time, as if making sure it was still there, eyes closed. Then he took back the roster. He looked at it very hard, thinking not so much about who had taught the class but whether his intense scrutiny might bring the names to life, produce flesh-and-blood testimony that Writing Across the Culture had provided a leg up for at least some of this motley crew of dropouts and subliterates and outcasts from the American Dream. Finally, he looked to the grimy ceiling, then, his vision blurred, at the library of mint-condition, free examination copies of freshman English texts with which he was swamped by publishers each semester and which he found himself unable to either use or discard. The titles blurred, as had the faces of the eager kids in SS Minus 9.

Ben Asterisky had realized what Seth Pritikin was getting

at. He said: "In spring 1969, I was the only EOA faculty member teaching writing. They were my kids. This was my class."

"Why is Kaputz listed as instructor?"

"We weren't very well organized. We never knew who was coming in. Since Artie was nominal director of the program, and the schedules had been submitted so late—none of the students had been officially admitted to the university until the last minute—his name must have been entered as instructor by default."

Pritikin smiled icily. "So he could have been shot by default too. And not because he was in Dillard's line of fire."

"You mean you think this roster was sent here as a warning. And that I . . ."

"That maybe the person who sent it meant to get the instructor of the class and assumed Kaputz was the instructor."

"You mean somebody may be gunning for *me?* Isn't that a little melodramatic?" Asterisky wasn't feeling nearly as casual about this as he was trying to sound.

"You should sit in there." Seth gestured toward the department office. "In the chair of the chair." He gave the awful smile again. "I get at least one a week who threatens to get one instructor or another."

"For flunking them? I didn't flunk people in those days."

"How about for *not* flunking them? I had to handle a protest last week that could turn into a major lawsuit. A West Indian woman. Says she lost her job because they found out she couldn't read or write even though we gave her a diploma. Woman is fit to be tied. Homicidal in fact."

"One of mine?"

"Not that I know of." He pointed at the roster. "Not one of those, at any rate."

"So what do you suggest I do?"

Pritikin shrugged. "Dunno. Reckon I'd call the police. Or

check up on how these former kids are doing. Hell, they must be in their forties. Now that you mention it, I reckon I'd do both. Cover my front and rear, so to speak."

Pritikin left the office, saying over his shoulder: "You can keep that roster. I've made a copy."

Ben Asterisky shuddered, letting the printout fall to the surface of his desk. He had been the instructor of these ten lost souls. Asterisky wished he were still in an earlier phase of life, one from which he could withdraw without penalty. Artie Kaputz had uttered thousands, millions of ill-timed phrases and been withdrawn from life. With the ultimate penalty. For the first time Asterisky tried to visualize the incident: the curly-haired schmuck from Jamaica Estates, Queens, beloved son of Beatrice and Sheldon Kaputz, the orthodontist who made his son's teeth almost as much of a conversation piece for Beatrice as his verbal skills, shot in that beautiful mouth. The back of the head blown off, Artie's revered brains, the brains which created the words, spilled over the green grass of the park overlooking the Narrows through which his and Asterisky's and Pritikin's and, presumably, Miss La-Russo's ancestors had sailed on their way to Ellis Island. Land of the Free. Home of the Brave. Asterisky was not feeling particularly brave. He tried to recall the name of the detective with whom Tim Desmond had been involved back when Joe Verb had taken his bullets. The superstar. Supercop. The Saint. Saint Francis. Francis DeSales.

It was against Ben Asterisky's principles to deal with the cops, but he had better cover himself front and rear. He picked up the telephone and dialed.

CHAPTER 7

FRANCIS DESALES and his chief aide, Detective Bernard Kavanaugh, stood in the shadow of the Verrazano Bridge, in a patch of grass and trees and monuments known as John Paul Jones Park, and watched the ambulance bear most of the remains of Arthur Kaputz in the direction of the morgue. Behind barriers set up on the Fourth Avenue and One Hundredth Street sides of the park, a horde of reporters—Megan Moore included—clamored for the detectives' attention. Inside the barriers were a large cannon and a constellation of three-foot-high stacks of cannonballs; it was the dark surfaces of these which the forensics men were scouring for the rest of Kaputz and any evidence of the shooter—his location, method, weapon. The rain had blown over, cooling things somewhat, but the sky was sunny again, the whitecaps in the harbor bright and lively.

DeSales walked Kavanaugh away from the din, circumnavigating a fifty-foot obelisk dedicated to the joint ventures of American and British forces in World War I: the Dover Patrol. They passed a rough stone which announced that this was the site at which the British army had first been resisted in New York State in 1776. There were big tankers entering the Narrows from the Atlantic, framed in the span of the bridge, and DeSales took note that this was indeed a convenient spot to unload on an invading enemy. Or on a boatload of huddled masses.

"How'd you let him get down here?"

Kavanaugh's head was bent over, his thick neck indistinguishable from his shoulders. He seemed not to have heard. But he looked up briefly, nodding across the Narrows. "Look," he said mournfully, "you can spit and hit Staten Island if the wind is right. All I had to do was get him over there and he was their problem."

"But he got down here instead. Kings County. And now he's *our* problem."

"So let me backtrack. You gotta see the bigger picture."

"Make it quick. The M.E.'s boys are sealing up their ziplock bags."

"The motorcade had a theme—'Back to the Future'—remember?"

"Vaguely."

"The New York Marathon is this weekend, and Dillard—or, rather, Kaputz—decided they could get a lot of free publicity by driving the route of the race *backwards* and saying the trip stood for the Dillard ticket going back to the beginning of the real modern age of liberal politics and at the same time starting something entirely new and different. Like twenty years ago, when the Marathon started and Lindsay was mayor. So they had to take off from Central Park, where the race ends. This is where the bullshit began. The commissioner wanted to have each individual precinct in charge of security, but that was unmanageable, so he had the borough presidents designate sections. Midtown North got Manhattan; Earl Campbell's boys from South Jamaica got Queens; Fort Apache got the Bronx; we got Brooklyn. It was supposed to be an honor—the elite groups, whether they were precincts or special squads or task forces, like us, got to take charge. If we needed manpower, all we had to do was pick up the phone. So I end up with ten of our guys and a hundred of the mangiest flatfoots ever hustled for overtime . . ."

"Yeh." DeSales was smoking, impatient. To the east of the park was the Fort Hamilton army post, all fenced in and armed—an unlikely escape route. To the north was Harbour House, a high-rise apartment building for blue-haired ladies with a doorman and a bunch of waiters standing outside the glass facade of the ground-floor French restaurant. A thousand eyes would have been watching the street. Anybody wanting to get in and out of range of Dillard and Kaputz standing on their cannonballs would have had to head west—Fourth Avenue, Shore Road. Or go by boat.

Kavanaugh gathered his thoughts and resumed. "Anyway, it was a quiet trip down here from the city. I was in a car monitoring the radio until they crossed over from Queens on the Kosciusko Bridge, and then I got in the back-up car. A little of this, a little of that: lavender protests in Central Park; free Larry Davis in the South Bronx; Polish power in Greenpoint; the Hasids in Williamsburg throw a raspberry or two and go back to the baby carriages and the torahs; Reverend Luke has a few of his publicity hounds in Bed-Stuy. We sail down Fourth Avenue after the Academy of Music. The Puerto Ricans don't even look up in Sunset Park, so I say to myself: he's on the bridge and I'm rid of him; I just gotta be sure I don't get a panzer brigade of Guidos in white Caddies coming down Eighty-sixth Street from Bensonhurst. Eighty-sixth is crowded but everybody's shopping and not exactly interested in Dillard one way or the other.

"At this point, from what Caruso tells me—Caruso was in the lead car—Kaputz begins to agitate. He doesn't like the low turnout: He doesn't like it that there aren't a hundred TV crews hanging on every fender. He's worried that the statement he wanted to make isn't being made, and it's certainly not going to be made in an empty toll plaza across the bridge. Not that anybody in Staten Island would listen anyway; they moved there to get away from the colored. So it's gotta be here, not exactly a hotbed of Dillard supporters either, but by this time rationality has blown out the window. Dillard has to speak to the people, *any* people. So Artie K. tells Dillard's driver not to go up the ramp at Ninety-second but to go to the end of Fourth, where Dillard will make a little speech looking over the harbor. This will give the motorcade and the speech historical significance.

"I stopped the parade and drove up to argue, but Kaputz and Dillard are determined. I look around. There's retired guys in Brooks Brothers suits and rich college-grad coke dealers in BMWs and tennis whites and old Irish sports and some former seamen, Nordic types on their pension. The Chinese got their heads in the fried rice, the Koreans in the cantaloupes. There's the white widows, of course, and Greeks from the diners counting their money. There's nobody with a tattoo or a haircut or an attitude within miles. The most dangerous sharks around here are the women real estate agents . . ." He paused for breath, coughed.

"Yeh," said DeSales.

"It happened real fast. Dillard took a loudspeaker and climbed on top of one pile of cannonballs. Kaputz and some of the other guys from the campaign got on the other piles of cannonballs. They made sure there was a cameraman or two from the TV stations. They even helped one get a good angle by lifting him and his equipment onto the barrel of the cannon. I had twenty men in uniform to form a cordon around them to keep out, what? Fifty or so people, mostly the retireds, who stopped to listen. And the next thing I know . . ."

"Ack-ack-ack."

"I swear to Christ, Frank. That fast, that light. But there

was Kaputz down and the rest of them hiding behind benches. We pulled the cordon tighter and assumed our positions. But that was it."

"What did Dillard do?"

"When there was no question Kaputz was dead, he got in one of our cars and beat his ass out of here. Home to make sure his family was okay, he said."

"And you don't know where the shots came from?"

"If he was up in the Harbour House, to the north, the trees would have blocked a good line of sight. He couldn't have been over at Fort Hamilton."

"Unless this is a CIA plot, like a lot of people say Jack Kennedy was."

"He couldn't have been down in the park, which leads to the Belt Parkway and the water, because he would have been too low. The preliminary medical report says the bullets entered from about the same height as Kaputz or slightly above."

"Which leaves Fourth Avenue. Those co-ops? The ones that look like Jersey shore motels?"

"Maybe. But we scoured them immediately. They have common gardens in the back and lots of windows, so it isn't easy to hide."

DeSales said: "You fucked up, Bernie. You went soft, letting him deviate from the route. But I still have confidence in your other judgments. Did the shooter skip or do you think he's holed up in one of the buildings?"

"We're still going over every bit of space with a fine-tooth comb and questioning everyone we can find, but nothing's turned up. One witness—an old seaman who'd been drinking—says a short kid ran down into the bushes of the park right after all hell broke loose, but . . ."

"But?"

"But I don't know about him. He says the kid was carrying a violin case."

"Too many James Cagney movies."

"He also says the kid looked like something out of a horror movie."

"How?"

"You know." Kavanaugh crouched like an ape. "Long arms, overhanging brow, big lower jaw sticking out."

"Sure. The witness'll be in Downstate in a week."

They had circled the obelisk. DeSales sat on a bench and put his head back. He massaged his temples, lighted a Benson & Hedges, looked around, trying to take in all three hundred and sixty degrees. Flocks of pigeons exploded through the yellowing leaves of the oak trees. The tankers lay offshore, frozen in the now crisp air. Staten Island glimmered like an undiscovered country across the water. The streets surrounding the park were peaceful and clean. In the French restaurant there were peach curtains in the windows and peach cloths and napkins on the tables. Only the hum of traffic from the bridge suggested the polluted and dangerous environment which surrounded the idyllic little hideaway at the southwesternmost point in all of Manhattan, Brooklyn, Queens, the Bronx.

"Could he have been on the bridge?" DeSales asked.

"No way." Kavanaugh shook his head. "Most of my men were up there blocking the regular traffic. Kaputz was facing the people on Fourth Avenue anyway, and the shots entered from the front. I know we can rule out the bridge, Fort Hamilton, and probably Harbour House."

DeSales stood up, stretching. "I don't want to see anybody down here, Bernie. I'll have an agenda by the time I get back to headquarters. You clean up here, fend off the media, do the dirty work. You brought this on yourself. I want all the reports at my office as they come in. I want Dillard before the afternoon is over. If you get a bullet, I want a record of all sales, if that's possible. Ditto the weapon. Anybody wants to talk, take a deposition."

"That's already done."

"I'm going to take a look in the bushes between here and the water."

"It's a nightmare," said Kavanaugh. "Twenty crisscrossing paths. Lots of stone steps appearing out of nowhere. The vegetation is very thick. And we've already combed it."

"I'll just take a look."

"I'm sorry, Frank."

DeSales nodded, patting Kavanaugh's broad back. He slipped around the obelisk and benches, across a cloverleaf access to the Belt, and entered a gravel pathway heading steeply through the woods to the playing fields below. There were cops all over the place, singly and in pairs. As he had penetrated the brush, he looked back. He wondered what the thousands of marathoners who didn't know Brooklyn thought when they first crossed the bridge into a borough world-renowned for its mobsters and crack houses and poverty and racial violence and found themselves striding through the cozy village of Bay Ridge, with its parks and white faces and low buildings and quaint shops and the blue-haired ladies of Harbour House schmoozing over peach napkins. DeSales smiled crookedly to himself and cruised the bushes, looking for . . . what?

Frankenstein carrying a violin case? Footprints. Perhaps a voodoo ceremony. It was all so ridiculous, the way crime happened in cities. When DeSales had been a kid, he had imagined that disaster struck and then lingered, the smell of death and destruction and fear lingering in the air, written in blood against the sky. Like the day his father left and his mother said he wasn't coming back. But here in the park it was silent and undisturbed. The traffic on the bridge hummed. On the Belt below, cars raced back and forth from Manhattan. Just before the highway there were tennis players with their shirts off, ball fields; in the soccer field, a young couple cheered as their baby took some tentative steps from his stroller. That was the way crime happened in the city.

DeSales heard a rustling in the bushes and then the sound of faroff sharp cracks, like drumming. He saw the outline of a figure backing into a secluded grove on a terrace above him. The figure was male and squat, and was holding near the side of his head a black box. Or a violin case. Clearly the man had backed off into a sort of secret retreat from the path, unaware that he could be seen from the decaying flight of steps which DeSales had chosen to follow back up to Shore Road from the playing fields below. A couple of tennis players jogged down an intersecting path, unaware of either the man with the black case or DeSales. DeSales took out his pistol and, crouching, slipped back down the steps so he could approach from the more traveled path to his right, in the wake of the tennis players. In order to do so, he had to face the harbor again. Everything was like a still-life in an empty museum. DeSales wondered if there was a life that could be lived in freeze-frame.

Like Megan frozen in orgasm in the light of her own graven image on the TV.

DeSales was pissed off at Megan, but he didn't want to think about it. There was too much thinking going on. Too much analysis.

Quickly he scurried from tree to tree, weapon drawn, hoping that he could get an angle on the man with the box. Now he was lost from sight. There were more cracking sounds. A woman was speed-walking down the path in the other direction. She was wearing a pink and black spandex bodysuit— something more suitable for social skin-diving. Bracelets jangled as she flailed her arms like a hyperactive chicken. She glanced with concern at DeSales, who in turn attempted to conceal the gun behind a tree and look innocent. The woman averted her eyes, looking casually to her right. Then she saw something in the clearing in the woods. Her face became grotesque. The scream died in her throat. DeSales raced forward. Took the position. Flashed the badge. Shouted, "Police!" The woman fell backward into a copse of shiny birch trees as DeSales plunged down the pathway worn by informal usage rather than a planner's intent.

Lines of desire, landscape architects called these spontaneous walkways scuffed into the earth by anonymous men and women.

In the clearing in the woods, a man was dancing his own pathway to desire. He was about DeSales's age, white, and had a shaved head with scars at the temples. His eyes were translucent, visionary. A latter-day Pan, he had cast his trench coat into the bushes and was wearing a leotard with a hole cut out at the crotch. There he stroked himself slowly as he performed his choreographed shuffle of sad ecstasy around the large black boom-box cassette player, from whose speakers roared Ton Lōc's "Wild Thing."

A flasher.

DeSales comforted the woman jogger and talked the fresh-air fiend back into his trench coat as a prelude to submitting himself peacefully to the appropriate authority.

At the top of the hill the press awaited him. DeSales deferred answering all questions about the shooting of Kaputz. "Still unresolved. Under investigation," he pleaded.

Megan Moore, at the back of the press corps, had her hand up. DeSales acknowledged her with a brusque nod.

"If you'll remember, Inspector," she began, "just before you were called to rush down here to this emergency, I was interviewing you about an incident involving an alleged theft and possible assault outside a newsstand on Atlantic Avenue."

DeSales nodded, wondering what she was up to. There was a hard edge to her voice.

"Just after you hurried away, Inspector, the alleged perpetrator collapsed with a heart attack and died, and the police officers on the scene have taken the proprietor of the stand in for questioning as a murder suspect."

"No, I didn't know that," DeSales muttered, shaking his head. "And just why are you asking *me* about it now, *Ms.* Moore?"

"I wanted to know how you would prosecute the case. Is this Murder One, for example? Manslaughter Two? Self-defense?"

DeSales squinted off into space, rubbing his chin. Finally, he said: "That, *Ms.* Moore, sounds to me like a clear-cut case of Brooklyn Three."

"Brooklyn Three?"

"Yeh. No matter how it comes out in the wash, the wrong guy gets screwed."

CHAPTER 8

THE BOY CALLED BONO drove the LTD slowly away from Bay Ridge down Eighty-sixth Street, past the golf course and the tire repair shops and the insurance agencies with their own parking lots, until he was under the El just past the intersection with New Utrecht and Eighteenth avenues. Here he knew he wouldn't find a regular parking place, so he simply double-parked alongside a couple of Toyotas near Nineteenth Avenue, shutting off access on the sidewalk side of the pillars of the raised train tracks. A man who looked like he should be an organ grinder with a monkey started to come out of the vegetable store to complain, but Bono gave him a look and he shrank back inside to his piles of artichokes and fennel stalks.

Bono slipped the "Official Police Business" sign on one side of the dashboard and the "Clergy on Mission of Mercy" with the black cross in the middle on the other. He lifted the elongated rackets gym bag from the trunk and entered the stairwell with the marquee that said "Perfect Program Fitness" on one side and "Palms Read" on the other. At the top of the stairs was a juice bar. There was aqua pile carpeting all around. Bono nodded at the woman reading *Muscle Monthly* at the receptionist's desk and opened the unmarked door into the locker room. At his locker, he stripped down quickly to the leopard-spotted bikini brief, copyright Hang Ten, hung his clothes neatly, and then attempted to maneuver the bag with the rifle in it into a manageable vertical position in the locker.

A familiar voice behind him said: "You look totally cut. Finally into the chemical warfare, I bet."

"All I do is pump," said Bono.

"Sure, and you got those eyebrows and big feet at the Boris Karloff fire sale."

"I was born with them. Ask my mother."

"Get outta here. You ain't got no mother, Junior. Remember. I lived down from you on Seventy-sixth Street. I never seen brows and feet on somebody put together like you except they was shooting megadoses of hGH. At *least* hGH."

Bono looked over his shoulder. The guy speaking to him was Anthony Cardinale, a business associate with a loose mouth who also happened to be a cousin of Sonny Grosso, whom he resembled. It was something that went with the territory: loose mouths, Sonny Grosso types. Bono regretted that his next major deal to go down featured Anthony up to a point, but that was the reality of the thing. Anthony had a double weakness: Dianol and LSD. When he wasn't hyper he was tripping. Bono said calmly, readjusting the barrel of the rifle inside the satin gym bag: "I'm in a hurry, Anthony. I got to do all my squat reps in a half-hour, then see a man about an investment. You need me for anything before our meeting later, call my beeper."

Bono slammed the door, twisted the combination lock three times to the right, and swaggered into the weight room. In the doorway he paused, counting with his fingers the pills he had secreted in his hand. Five. hGH. Parabolin. Nice names. It was easier to go on the syringe, but it took discipline and privacy, which he didn't have that much of. When he saw Anthony go into the bathroom and made sure none of the people working out was watching him, he swallowed the pills and washed them down at the water fountain. Then he headed for the machines, where he began to execute one-armed pulley curls from behind, feeling the deltoid muscles expand. He wasn't only getting cut good, he was positively ripped to the bone. There wasn't one of the punks from the old block would mess with him now. They could only stand back in front of the candy store and whistle.

He did his repetitions, sweating freely, feeling the power come over him. He finished the delts, the lats, played around with the new hamstring curl the trainer had suggested the week before. He did some seated cable rows, then one-arm dumb-bell rows to get to the traps. The enlargement and definition of his muscles was palpable, like a big hard-on, like a whole system of big hard-ons. He thought about money. If he had time after he filled out his arsenal, he would buy the Mega-bench he had seen in the ad and put it at home in his studio, only that would make less room for the tapes. Problems. Training was supposed to bring an inner peace.

The clock on the wall said it was 4:00 P.M. Time for his appointment. He went back to the locker room and stripped off the leopard-skin brief, carrying it into the tiled shower area and hanging it on a hook on the wall. The switch outside the steam-bath door was turned on. He opened the door and stepped quickly into the heat, the wet, almost impenetrable. He could just about make out the silhouette of the fat man sitting on a white towel on the upper bench in one corner. Bono sat in the other corner, on the lower bench, as they had arranged as a signal if everything was cool. The fat man's voice had a rasp to it and wasn't always easy to make out over the hissing of the steam.

"You don't look bad, kid," he said. "Your balls start to shrink yet?"

Bono did his best not to sound annoyed. Today of all days he needed the fat man. "I told you a thousand times I'm clean."

"I guess I gotta believe you. Can't see your balls and you ain't growin' the bitch tits. And I guess you can't help the way your head's shaped. You understand my position?"

"Sure." Bono had heard this story before.

"I rely heavily on middle management. I put a kid like you into an important distributorship, I need guarantees he's stable. Look at Carmine Cozzi."

"Why? He got nothin' to do with me. He's from Seventeenth Avenue, I'm from over past Bay Parkway."

"Carmine Cozzi had a position like yours in my organization, but he became one of his own best customers. Started like they all do with the Building Boxes and Synergy and Metabolic Optimizers. Next thing I know he's shooting Equipoise. That's supposed to be for horses, right? People around here started to call him the Experiment. Then he discovers he can't get it up anymore, can't cut the mustard. Edgy all the time. He had this girlfriend, Anne-Marie Adverso?"

"I didn't know her. Before my time."

"Made the Ms. Olympia contest. Thigh adduction that wouldn't quit. Perfect coordination of the brachialis and biceps and forearms. You know how these dumb broads overdo the biceps, right? They're like children, think that Charles Atlas pose is the works."

"Forget about it."

"Carmine got her into the horse medicine too. So he wants to fuck all the time like he used to and he can't get it up, not to mention the 'roid rages. Anne-Marie's up to her ears in testosterone and she don't want to fuck—at least like a woman is supposed to want to fuck. So Carmine loses it. He offs her with an ice pick and then OD's. In his fucking mother's kitchen. His mother was in the sodality at St. Francis with my wife. This was very bad PR for my business, you can understand?'' The fat man began to laugh. The steam had started to rise off the floor. The pale tiles on the ceiling were dripping. Bono could make out the belly shaking like jelly.

"What you laughin' about?"

"Anne-Marie and Carmine. They said when they found them she was better hung than he was."

"I get the point. Now, I got a deal to talk about myself. I need some high-quality juice. None of that Mexican shit. A thousand syringes of Deca-Durabolin; another thou of Parabolin. Maybe some Xylocaine. And rhesus monkey hormone if it's cheap."

"What the fuck? You got the concession for the '92 Olympics?"

Bono shrugged. "Does Macy's tell Gimbel's?"

"You're not your own store: You work for me, kid."

"On commission. I need some freedom to deal."

"What if it's the Feds? You take a fall, they got me."

"The guy who was distributor at Northern Athletic Clubs got killed on the Jersey Turnpike last week. If they like our product, we're in a position for some serious expansion. They got the best suburban locations—Lodi, Valley Stream, Yorktown Heights."

The fat man gathered the towel over his thighs. "This is all you want to do? Hand me a Christmas present so early?"

"I got needs. I have a big purchase to make. Nothing to do with you or steroids. I'm working on a project. These people I know got the product I need and they require cash. Tonight. If you advance me a thou, then I can take care of my own thing before I pick up the steroids tomorrow at the warehouse for the Northern people. They pay cash on the line, you get the loan back along with your profit, not to mention an advance on the long-term contract from them, all within a day of fronting me the thou."

"There'll be the usual vigorish."

"Of course."

"And I'm still worried about security."

"There's no problems for you here, I swear on the Virgin."

The fat man stood up, shook out his towel, touched his toes. Finally he got the towel back where he wanted it and was sitting again. He made a gesture with his hand like he was flitting away bugs. "Okay, *paisan,*" he croaked.

Suddenly Bono was standing over him, hissing like steam into his face. "Don't ever call me that again. Fucking *paisan.* I'm not one of *you.*"

"Hey," the fat man protested. "You got a name like your father's and you swear on the Virgin, I call you *paisan,* it's natural."

Bono took a deep breath. This was no time to blow the whole scene. He was getting manic from the steam. Or the pills he'd eaten.

"Sorry," he said, backing off. "We're talkin' big numbers here and that name makes me feel like a kid. Please don't call me that again."

The fat man laughed. "Okay, kid. Delivery tomorrow morning. The usual place. You pick up the cash from the receptionist when you go out. Don't forget to sign the voucher. I hope it gets you what you want."

"It will. It's a project I've invested a lot of thought in."

"Anything I ever heard of?"

"I doubt it. Wasting mushrooms. Saving the planet. Endangered species. That sort of crap."

"Well stick with it, kid. I didn't know you was into social work. Just watch your balls don't start to shrink."

Bono took a quick shower. When the European liquid soap didn't come out of the dispenser, he pulled the plastic piece of trash off the wall and broke it into sharp little pieces which he scattered on the floor. *Paisan.* Maybe the fat fuck would cut his feet and bleed to death. He put on the clean polka-dot brief from his bag and looked at himself in the floor-length mirror, flexing this way and that.

By the time he hit the street, he was cool. He drove his car to the parking lot at Ceasar's Bazaar. The wind was whipping in off Gravesend Bay. He put on the Stones' tape *Let It Bleed*. He got out his appointment book. This would be the most complicated piece of business he had ever done. He needed to write things down in sequence so he didn't forget anything. He would get the pure cocaine he had contracted for with the thousand bucks in his pocket. Then he had to go to Jersey— over the Verrazano Bridge and through Staten Island was best for traffic, he figured—and trade the coke with the Cubans in Union City who had the designer crank, worth twice as much as the coke if you knew your market. He would then deliver the crank to the stupid speed-freak rich kids in Jersey who thought they were serious bikers because their daddies had bought them motorized vehicles on two wheels and let them walk around in leather jackets with skulls and shit. With the profits from the crank delivery he would go to the Arab grocery store in Queens, where he would seriously enlarge his basic inventory of plastic explosive—enough to put him at least on par with a Third World nation in terms of military strike force. Along with the rocket launchers they'd promised to throw in when he told them he might like to try a little duck hunting when the season opened.

There was no hurry with the Northern Athletic Clubs. He wanted to begin tonight to wire the block, one house at a time, so he could be finished by the week after Thanksgiving, when the Gianellis next door would have the ceremony where they turned on the Santa and sleigh and eight tiny reindeer on their roof. Bono wanted to help them lift everybody's spirits.

He thought of the neighborhood, of Mrs. Mazzoli and Father Cabrini and Anthony Cardinale and the fat man, and then he realized he was watching the people coming out of Toys R Us with their kids' Halloween masks and early Christmas presents in shopping carts and he was listening to the Stones on the tape and he could see the black guy going down from the Hell's Angel bullet at Altamont, the long-barreled Colt waving in the air, the end of an era, and he realized he had his own weapon in his gym bag and he could waste a little antipasto right there in the parking lot. End of another era. Italians Anonymous. With the wind, you wouldn't even hear anything, like having a silencer.

He hadn't needed a silencer for the ex-do-gooder from the Institute. And the getaway was a joke. Down the path, into the lot, and out onto the Belt. Just like that. Hit and run, stick and pedal, was his motto. Besides, he was saving up his firepower for the big hit. Soon. It was all a question of choosing the right moment—when they were all tucked into their beds, St. Francis of Assisi parish and at least half of the Virgin of Padua, for starters, visions of sugarplums dancing in their thick heads along with the Saint with the fucking birds on his fingers and the cuntless lady in the blue gown and the crowns of thorns and the sauce like blood cooking all day on the stoves of every kitchen from Avenue X to Fort Hamilton Parkway.

Then he thought of Remi and the promise he had made to him and felt confused. He had forgotten whether he planned to waste the superstars or save them. It was all that geography he had to deal with. Bensonhurst and Gravesend, Jersey, Queens, back home before dawn. How was he going to fit in a little visit to the club on the Lower East Side of Manhattan? He swallowed some more pills and washed them down with a caffeine-free Diet Coke out of the six-pack he always kept on the floor of the back seat.

He thought about front squats.

Mind curls.

Training brings an inner peace.

What goes around comes around.

Remi would get his treat.

Who doesn't need someone to bleed on?

CHAPTER 9

BERNIE KAVANAUGH WHEELED the video monitor and VCR into DeSales's office at the Violence Task Force headquarters, near the Brooklyn side of the Manhattan Bridge.

"I thought you were bringing me Dillard," said DeSales.

"He says he's too upset. He's secluded himself with his family. He sent these instead." Kavanaugh held up two videocassettes.

"What are they?"

Kavanaugh shrugged. "His people said one's a statement from the candidate and the other Dillard thinks is a piece of evidence that was sent to his house today. Just before the shooting."

"A *statement*?"

"I asked the same question. They said a lot of the law-enforcement agencies are videotaping confessions, even the testimony of the arresting officers. So they just send tape through the system instead of trying to transport live bodies around the city. It's one of Dillard's campaign promises—to

cut down on waste in the police department. Like arresting officers spending entire days in court to give a minute's
testimony. Like overtime costs. So why not a politician's
statement?"

"You can't ask a tape questions."

"Dillard says get back to him when and if you have any.
Tomorrow. Says he's managing enough stress today as it is."

DeSales picked up the tapes, marked "Exhibit A" and "Exhibit B," and turned them over in his hands, as if he might
be able to warm life into them. He slid one into the machine.

The tape was running. A tall slender Negro boy with a light
complexion and round rimless spectacles appeared on screen.
He fidgeted with his ear lobe, in which was embedded a tiny
jewel. Then he coughed and stared at his feet. He seemed to
have realized too late that he was wearing a T-shirt that read
"Die Yuppie Scum" on the chest and now he folded his arms
over it to obscure the message and whatever were its impli-
cations. The screen indicated that the time of filming was
midafternoon on that same day, only a couple of hours before.
A title read: "Stokely Carmichael Dillard: Testimony."

DeSales sighed. The boy, in halting tones, identified himself: address on Garden Place, graduate of St. Ann's, freshman
at Yale. He explained that he had rented a videotape that
noon on Fulton Street, gave the address and the name of the
clerk who was his friend. He described, very briefly, the sequence of attacks upon his person near his home: first by three
disorderly black youths with an attack dog, then by a young
white man with a big old car.

A voice off-camera, murky but still recognizably that of the
boy's father, the candidate for mayor, asked impatiently: "Can
you state with any certainty that these black youths were in
any way acquainted with the white youth?"

"No sir."

"So this could have represented either conspiracy or mere
coincidence? Inconclusive, in short?"

"Right."

"Go on."

Young Dillard described pulling himself together and going into his home to play the tape, explained that he had not notified the police immediately because he had not been physically harmed and because nothing, so far as he could tell, had been stolen. He then hesitated, as if he were going to say something else, but instead mumbled that the "tape was still in the bag, so what could I do?"

The offscreen voice became more prosecutorial: "Let's not speculate about what you *could* have done. Am I correct in asserting that there was still a videocassette in the bag which resembled the one you had rented, and that you and your sister had elected to divert yourself for the afternoon by reveling in this passive entertainment, and that without so much as a phone call to a member of your family about the attacks on your person you proceeded with said planned entertainment?"

"Yes sir."

"And that you found said videocassette to be something entirely different from what you *thought* you had rented, yet you and your sister watched it through and, in spite of being profoundly disturbed by its contents, you maintained your silence about this shocking switch both vis-à-vis the authorities and vis-à-vis your own family or representatives thereof?"

"Yes sir."

"Until, that is, you were made aware of an attempt upon your father's life and finally intuited that this tape may have been related to some threat to harm your family or members or representatives thereof . . . at which point your sister called campaign headquarters."

"Yes sir."

"Do you have anything else to say?"

The young man shifted from one foot to the other. His mouth seemed dry and the words sounded cracked and old:

"I'd like to swear that I had nothing to do with the making of this tape and that I am not aware of any information regarding the source of the tape. It seems that someone put it in my bag without my knowledge in the confusion this afternoon." He held a black cassette box toward the camera. "I hereby submit it to the police as Exhibit B. It is so marked."

The camera began to pan across the comfortably furnished room. It hovered over the figure of a man in a deep chair, then settled on his talking head. Harrison Dillard's head. His customarily natty suit and tie were disheveled; his eyes had the same murky quality as his voice. He said: "There you have it for now, gentlemen. That is the sum and substance of awareness of the Dillard family on this matter. I have already submitted a personal statement regarding the tragic end to my motorcade in Bay Ridge. I submitted it to the uniformed officer who accompanied me as we sped from the scene of the assassination. I saw nothing and heard nothing extraordinary until Arthur Kaputz was lying martyred by my side. The police are well aware of all the threats made upon my person preceding the events of today. There is nothing I have to add to that considerable archive. The exhibit which we are now submitting for your analysis is all that is worth adding for the moment. Thank you."

DeSales spat into a wastebasket. Kavanaugh laughed. "Well, you got your questions."

DeSales propped his sharp chin on his fist. "They were his questions, not mine, anyway. What control, what a power trip."

"You would have asked the kid something else?"

"Lots. But not until I see this mysterious tape. Roll it."

Kavanaugh ejected the Dillard family submission and loaded the second cassette. The two detectives sat in the gloomy room and watched the rock-concert footage, the hippie footage, the various juxtapositions of the Dillards and the Kennedys. When it reached the point where the close-up of

Harrison Dillard at his campaign best segued into the first hard-core sex, DeSales leaned forward and hit the rewind button.

"Hey," said Kavanaugh, "this was just getting hot. When did you turn into a prude?"

DeSales shook his head, tapping a cigarette out of a box and looking at it laid out like an exclamation point against the lifeline in his palm. "At a moment like this, Bernie, it does us absolutely no good to go any further without expert consultation. Indeed, I think we'd be in deep shit with the commissioner and mayor-to-be, for starters, if we didn't bring in Dr. Jive up front. They imported him specifically for moments just like this. Is he in the building?"

Kavanaugh picked up the phone, dialed an extension, and waited. DeSales had lighted up and exhaled the first drag by the time a voice came on the line. Kavanaugh asked: "Is Oublier there?" Another silence. "Send him up. Now."

Kavanaugh covered the mouthpiece with his hand. "There's a guy wants to see you. Friend of Desmond's from that Institute in Coney Island. Name of Aster something. Says he has some important evidence about Kaputz."

DeSales was grinding his butt down to the filter in a glass dish. "Tell him to send me a videotape."

"He's waiting outside."

"Tell him to keep waiting then, but I can't guarantee I'll be able to see him today."

The door opened. The outline of a very large man with very black skin filled the doorway. He was wearing a suit which would have been appropriate for a Third World diplomat at the United Nations but not at Violence Task Force headquarters in downtown Brooklyn. He spoke in a deep baritone with a thick accent.

"Inspector DeSales. Detective Kavanaugh. This is an honor, I assure you. I am not often invited here to the inner sanctum."

DeSales said: "Dr. Oublier, I presume. Welcome to our heart of darkness. We find ourselves with a puzzle on our hands, one possibly relevant to your professional interests."

Oublier nodded in the direction of the screen. "This is the artifact I must examine?"

"Yes."

"And it pertains to the psychology of sex, race, and political oppression."

"It could."

Oublier slipped quietly into one of the softer chairs in the corner of the room. "Let's see it then."

Kavanaugh started up the tape. DeSales tilted back in his chair, feet on the rubble of his desk. Oublier took out a notebook and scribbled intermittently, when he wasn't emitting grunts of recognition. Three times—at the first instance of fellatio; at Mrs. Kennedy's attempt to climb onto the back of the speeding limo; and at the newsreel clips of lava flowing—Oublier asked Kavanaugh to rerun the scene. Once, as Jimi Hendrix was igniting his guitar, he requested that the detective hold the moment in freeze-frame as he contemplated it.

By the time Jane Fonda was being overtaken by the burning house and the Rolling Stones, DeSales was pacing about the edges of the room. The tape ran out. He rolled up the shades noisily and stood poised in an attitude of interrogation, hands on hips, over Dr. Oublier's chair.

Oublier looked up. In the daylight his skin was more purple than black. He wore a dull-gold tie clip which matched the frame of his pince-nez. He said: "I assume this has something to do with the shooting today. May I inquire as to the source of this film?"

"I'd rather you didn't," said DeSales, "for the time being. I'd like to get a . . . um . . ."

"I see," Oublier filled in. "An untainted response."

"That's it."

"You want me to treat this clumsy attempt at montage as

a kind of Rorschach, a mental fingerprint if you will, of the person who made it."

DeSales was back at the desk, tilted back in the chair again, lighting up. Here he was putting up with analysis again. Somebody else's.

"Smoking tobacco is the worst thing a man your age can do for his health," said Oublier.

"*That*"—DeSales exhaled—"is none of your fucking business."

Oublier shook off the rebuke: "And you hope that this will help you to delineate a kind of profile, a silhouette, of the maker of the film."

"Right."

Oublier sat back in the chair, resting the small of his back against the edge of the seat. He hitched up his neatly pressed gabardine trousers from the thighs to the crotch. He looked at the ceiling, where the plaster was already beginning to crack.

"First of all," he said, "I suspect our *auteur* is a male who has trouble forming a lasting relationship with a woman. Indeed, he may be at least a technical virgin; perhaps impotent. Rage, you see."

"Go on."

"I focus in a case like this on the recurring images: the black penis ejaculating on the white face; the wife abandoning the husband in the open car . . ."

Kavanaugh interrupted. "Hey, Jackie O was under fire when JFK was hit. Parts of him were all over her dress, as a matter of fact. What would you do? What would you have your wife do under similar circumstances? This is *abandonment?*"

Oublier made a pyramid with his hands on his chest, lowered his head, and peered over the apex at Kavanaugh. He let out a short laugh. "You take me too literally, sir. In this case we are not examining the shadows on the screen as they were in real life, but merely as images conjured and selected and ordered by a particular mind. In the displacement of the semen onto the mature white woman's face, I see a resistance to the vaginal—in plain terms, to the possibility of insemination. The woman has aroused the man and brought him to climax, but in the end she has chosen not to accept his 'pledge to fortune.' "

"A convention of skin flicks, Doctor," said DeSales. "The jerk-offs in the theatre *want* to see the cum."

"Like your colleague, you are missing the point. The person who made this film is not analyzing filmic conventions; he is expressing his own sublimated pathology. We have the non-accepting, nonvaginal woman; then the abandoning woman; then the recurring volcanic eruptions and fires, through which flow rivers of molten lava. Menstrual symbols; no pregnancy again. Such ambivalence! I see this film as a world in which sexuality is everywhere, but the filmmaker feels so alienated from it, so abandoned by women, as it were, that he cannot even be born into this world. Moreover, the sexuality which is envied is largely black and violent—a not unusual psychological circumstance in this society of yours, of course. The blandly naked white children are set ablaze by the towering inferno of black phallus and black guitarist. The flag is burned, figuratively, as the guitar which plays the national anthem goes up in flames. The white maternal symbols of water and earth cannot put out the conflagration."

"So what could this have to do with Dillard? Or Kaputz?" asked DeSales.

"I don't know about Kaputz. In the case of Dillard, what is at least superficially evident is the envy of the Noble Savage, the black man as existential sex symbol and subverter of established values at the same time."

"So if the person who made this film is the shooter, he's jealous of black sexuality—of any successful sexuality—and he tries to kill Dillard in consequence."

Oublier nodded knowingly. "Dillard has figuratively fucked his mother, and fucked her very well indeed. Our perpetrator is the wounded suitor in a kind of Oedipal psychodrama fueled by racial energy. Someone has taken his mommy away and left him with white Western masochism in exchange."

"Masochism?"

"The prancing fellow near the end of the tape—the one who was trying so hard to look and sound black? I believe his words implored his audience to bleed on him, didn't they? Pity me, cries the filmmaker, and then tries to shoot the black man, the scapegoat for his own insecurities about his manhood." Oublier pulled back a monogrammed cuff to consult a gold Rolex. There were deep scars, old scars, torture scars, engraved in his wrist: "I'm afraid I'm going to be late for an appointment. Sorry. Obviously there's more to the film that I've not been able to touch on, but if you like, I'll be able to view it again later in the week."

"You have any advice on who to look for?"

Oublier harrumphed. He stood up, smoothing his sleeves and trousers. "A boy who's lost his mother. A boy whose masculinity is on the line. A boy who identifies strongly with the ruling class—as he understands such a concept—and sees the black man as a threat. But"—he had his hand on the doorknob—"there is always a caution I give in cases like this." He wagged his finger.

"What's that?"

"This is also a boy who is terribly confused. Erratic. Who can know what his next target will be? The one sure bet is that all bets are off."

"You're sure this is a boy, a kid?"

"Put it this way: He *thinks* he's a boy."

The door closed behind the broad back. There was a long silence in the room.

"Oh, shit," said DeSales finally, "I just remembered something about Megan."

"From the porn-flick?"

"Up your ass. About a date. If I meet her on time, I can't see this guy with the name like a flower."

"Important evidence, he says."

"She's really on the fucking warpath. We had a little set-to at lunchtime."

Kavanaugh tried to keep the solemn look on his face by sticking his tongue prominently in his cheek. "Well, *sheeet*," he said. "If the TV personality goes on the warpath, all us bad boys better fold up our tents."

"That's a mixed metaphor, Bernie," DeSales said, but at the same time he was dialing the phone. Kavanaugh heard him ask for Lois Lane to be paged. That was a joke they had between them. Lois Lane and Supercop. Then DeSales was saying, "But Meg, you got to understand. This is a heavy day for me. I'll be late. How late exactly I don't know. Before dinner is . . ." DeSales held the receiver at arm's length, wide-eyed in feigned innocence.

"How do you like that, Bernie? She hung up. I guess I have no choice but to interrogate the next witness."

CHAPTER 10

MEGAN MOORE SLAMMED the phone in its cradle, then looked up with embarrassment at the maître d'. Tony was a very short man; in his suit with the big shoulders and his sable-colored toupee, he resembled more than anything a churchgoing Roman Polanski. But his cartoon courtliness could be reassuring in an age when one was usually greeted in fashionable restaurants by affectless post-adolescents with asymmetrical haircuts.

"Something wrong, Miss Moore?"

"Nothing exceptional, Tony. I'd just like to put a contract out on somebody. No offense, I hope."

"Your cop?" Tony had been listening in. "No problem." He winked conspiratorially. Three mobsters had been gunned down in the garden of the Villa Lucretia the year before, and the media had played up the location of the headquarters of the rival Amalfi family directly across the street. Since then, the place had come back into fashion, after years of decline. The room was so crowded that Megan thought she might need a diagram to get back to her table. She put her hands on her hips and contemplated the lurid mural of the Bay of Naples which covered the entire facing wall, swearing to herself. "Listen," she said, touching Tony's sleeve. "Change my drink order, please. I want booze after all. Stoli on the rocks." She made a V-sign with her fingers. "Only two rocks, okay? And a *nice* glass."

"You got it, Miss Moore. Hey, I saw ya on the TV last week. The baby crack addicts? Great show."

"Thanks, Tony."

Tony snapped his fingers. When the drink was poured, he took Megan's arm and began to escort her back to the corner table, balancing the drink on a tray. "What are we gonna do about these ghetto people?" he asked with considerable indignation. "They're animals, right? Do these drugs, then they're sex-crazed. Don't even care about the *bambini*. And how about this Reverend Luke character!" He squeezed her bicep. "Know what I mean?"

"I know just what you mean, Tony." Megan passed through the caramelized imitations of Roman pillars that separated the front from the rear section of the restaurant. She watched herself in the myriad framed mirrors that graced the other walls—a habit she had picked up out of necessity when switching from radio to TV some years before—and saw that several strands of her hair were sticking out in the back. Trying to live with Saint Francis DeSales could do that to you. She combed the hair back with one sweep of her fingers as Tony helped her into her seat.

Glenn Moulder was sitting upright with his pristine white linen napkin in his lap and his Perrier-and-lime untouched before him. He raised an eyebrow at the vodka and at Tony helping Megan into her chair.

Megan leaned over and whispered: "It's Frank. The shit says he'll just be a bit late, but I recognize the tone—he's seriously considering not showing at all."

Moulder had astonishing eyes. They seemed never to blink. Along with his baby face, the appearance they lent him of unflinching sincerity had made his TV career. DeSales, who had even less time for Moulder than for her other colleagues, had once said that he looked like a little boy in school who always had his hand up. Now his gaze encompassed Megan's. "If he doesn't show, he misses the best piece of business in years."

"What's the time frame on this story?"

"ASAP. If the Feds up here are willing to leak to me, then there are Feds all over the place leaking like sieves."

Megan responded: "If you're including me in on this, you'd better do it right now, even if I don't have the Saint to offer up as my side of the bargain. You don't want me sitting here not knowing my ass from my elbow. It would ruin your party."

Moulder looked thoughtful, the Bay of Naples reflecting off his baby blues. He sipped the Perrier delicately without removing the stirrer from the glass. "Okay," he said finally. "This is the scenario. You know I went to South America and did that series on drug kingpins last month?"

"Do I know it? My producer has decided everybody on the local beat has to put their lives on the line at least once a week as a result of the attention you got. If you'd been shot up we'd probably have to get shot ourselves. The Moulder Effect. Instead of the National Press Club award we're going to go for the Purple Heart."

"It's nice to be appreciated by one's peers." Moulder seemed genuinely pleased. He went on: "In Medellín, you know, nobody talks, but one of the lawmen I met suggested I go to a certain bar on the coast and I might hear some conversation which would be of professional interest. So I go to Cartagena. Nice beach. Also a local hanger-on who puts me onto a source in Barranquilla. But the source has disappeared when I get there, so I put the word out I'm looking for him and a week later he catches me at the Bogotá airport just before I'm flying home." Moulder's Adam's apple bobbed above the Windsor knot as he swallowed. "Claims he's an old friend of the Drug Enforcement agent who's going to meet us here tonight—Pancho Torres."

Megan took another drink and made a face. "I know Pancho."

"This source tells me he hears that there is a significant drugs-for-weapons deal about to go down, but the principals are worried about Mr. H. Dillard."

"Why?"

"They've heard through one of *our* government snitches that Dillard, in anticipation of becoming mayor, has already been talking to the DEA, among other Feds, along with some Banana Republic military strongmen who are *not* into the drug trade and resent the guns and butter being afforded by those who are. The new crowd in Panama is prominent in these rumors. Dillard even has a Panamanian shrink. They call him the Witch Doctor."

"Very funny," said Megan, not smiling. "Boogie jokes are very in this fall."

"Have I caught you on a bad night, Meg? PMS?"

"None of your business. Go on."

"Anyways, this aforementioned source claims—a month ago, mind you—that there are people in Colombia who have reasons for wanting Dillard not to ever get to live in Gracie Mansion. Reasons having nothing whatsoever to do with race, the motive which most of us liberal media monsters have been guessing is behind today's shooting."

Megan Moore sat back in her chair. She parted her hair with her hands, then ran her fingers through it down to her shoulders, wondering if she had tamed the wild spot—the mirrors were behind her. "And you kept this a secret?"

"Tell you the truth, I didn't believe it. I *still* don't believe that Dillard even had the time, let alone the inclination, to be playing footsie with those people—or that they'd bother playing with him. But the way I read it now is apparently someone did. Believe it, that is. Maybe my source was reporting a false rumor, but if he had heard the false rumor from the right—or wrong—people, or if he spread it to some such heavy people, then it didn't have to be true. Dillard would be a marked man in any case."

"Mmm. If that's your angle, Glenn, what do you need from me? Not to mention DeSales."

"Remember, the concluding message of my reports from Latin America was that the Medellín cartel was prepared to send death squads up here if anyone made a serious attempt to put them out of business. Well, I'd like to look at the shooting today as my prophecy come true. In fact, I'd like to use it to get a new series going. But I've got to do the usual fact checking before I go any further. I was going to see Torres anyway, to get a take on his Bogotá friend's reliability, but another source—a very local source who shall remain nameless—called me this afternoon and said that your friend DeSales was sitting on a videotape that was sent to the Dillard family just before Bay Ridge, and that the videotape may have been sent by the murderer as a warning, and that in any case a knowledge of the contents of that tape would go a fair distance toward encouraging or discouraging me from pursuing my plans to do the pieces I've been talking about."

Megan tapped her long fingernails on the tablecloth. A waiter was hovering over her almost immediately. She waved him away, sucking on the residue of ice at the bottom of the long-stemmed wineglass in which her drink had been served.

She spoke through the ice. "And where do I fit in? I don't know anything about any tape. And you know Frank doesn't talk shop with me."

Moulder picked up his menu and stared intently at it.

"C'mon, Glenn, you know you're going to ask me to split a puttanesca with you for starters, and then you're going to worry about veal or chicken francese."

Moulder put the menu back down. "First of all, Meg, you know I love your work and I respect the hell out of you."

"Sure, and we're in business to help the homeless."

"Wait, I'm sincere. I admit I wanted you because you could bring me DeSales and he could at least maybe give me an idea of what's on this tape. But I would be giving as much as I'm getting. I would do DeSales the favor of telling him about my source from Colombia before he has to hear about it on the eleven o'clock news, not to mention getting indigestion when he finds out that Pancho's boys are on top of the Dillard-Medellín connection when the Violence Task Force hasn't a clue. That's a fair trade, no?"

"I'd let Frank worry about that. What's in it for me, is what I asked."

"You're local, I'm network. And even though we're on different stations, I consider us colleagues, not rivals. There's room for both of us on this story. If the Colombians did it, I get to segue straight from my triumphs on the road last month, while you can cover the local angles moving outward from City Hall."

"Let me put it another way," Meg continued. "What do *I* have to offer? You want DeSales for the tape; you want Torres for a confirmation of the Bogotá rumor . . ."

Moulder snapped his fingers. "The missing link is all! A technician at your station was fired last month. For stealing videotape. Some blank, some not so blank—tape of regular shows on the air and tape that couldn't be shown, either because it would have been editorially indiscreet or because the significant persons on the tape were behaving indiscreetly. I understand this tech was already in hot water for his penchant for working overtime making his own little movies by editing station-owned tape with station-owned equipment. Not to mention selling some of this tape under various *noms de guerre*."

"And?"

"And the official name of this technician is Kim. *Ernesto* Kim. A.k.a. Che. Euphonious name. Che Kim. Great for a *Post* headline: 'Che Kim Kills Kin,' say."

"Or 'Kaputz's Kaput.' "

"Right on. Kim was born on the coast of Colombia—Barranquilla, in fact—to a Korean father and a Colombian mother. One of his cousins is serving time right now in a U.S. federal facility for smuggling cocaine into Miami."

"You think he may be the assassin who sent the tape to Dillard?"

"I merely think he has an interesting background and should be looked into. If DeSales confides in us about the tape we'll have a better idea of Kim's relevance, and that's something else I have to offer him in exchange for him helping me out."

Megan Moore pursed her lips and narrowed her eyes. "The dawn begins to break . . ."

"Right. You go up to your office and find Kim's address. They're sending him severance pay, I'm sure. I can't find him through conventional channels."

"You want me to break into my own employer's office and provide you with confidential information."

"You wouldn't have to break in. You'd just say you want to send old Ernesto something he left with you."

"I'd rather break in. And what if DeSales won't play?"

"I told you, I love your work. I still want you on the local angle with me. We can track down Kim together and I'll share with you anything out of Latin America that impacts on the local situation."

"You want me to rob my employer and play games around my boyfriend's case."

"In the crudest terms, yes."

"I'll have to think about this, Glenn."

"Yeh. Let's just keep the idea alive. I have the sense that DeSales is treating you like shit these days and this would be a perfect opportunity—if he's unwilling to give you a career boost—to let him go fuck himself." Moulder was watching the door, and now his eyes doubled their wattage. He began to get out of his chair. "Here's Pancho anyway. Let's hear from him first."

Megan turned to see the people coming in the door off Mulberry Street.

"Oh my God," Megan gasped. "He's got *two* bimbos tonight."

Moulder tightened the knot of his tie even further. His eyes bulged dramatically. "One of them is for me," he said. "Interesting girls. Actresses. Mine is working now as the on-camera coffee pourer for John Jerome on that new breakfast talk show on ABC."

CHAPTER 11

CLUTCHING THE ARMS of his chair with his stubby hands, Benjamin Asterisky looked like an Egyptian Buddha. DeSales was completing his examination of the roster sheet from 1969. Finally, the detective dropped the printout on his desk and asked: "What do *you* make of this?"

Asterisky hesitated. "I don't know, exactly."

"You must have brought it here for a reason."

"I had reservations, but Tim Desmond said you were a good guy in spite of . . ." Asterisky realized he was about to be indiscreet. These days, as the eighties wound down, many of his deeply held convictions didn't fly as well as they once had. He put his fingers to his lips, as if some litter had become entangled there and was impeding his speech.

"In spite of?"

DeSales had an interesting face for a cop. There were angles there of complex proportions. Cat-and-mouse angles.

He decided it would be healthier to confront any insinuations head-on, rather than trying to dodge the rodent holes into which he assumed people like DeSales were intent on propelling him. He coughed into his cupped hands, looked up, and declared: "I'm a man of the sixties, Inspector. I became an adult, started in my profession, and flirted with a kind of ecstasy in the political ferment of those days. Included in this package, or what remains of it"—he indicated his ample girth—"is an innate distrust of law-enforcement agencies. So my first inclination was to put this piece of paper in the wastebasket and forget about it. But at the same time I'm afraid that this piece of paper, and the killing of Artie Kaputz today, are *about* the sixties. I've got these bad vibes that the past is finally coming back to haunt us."

The tightly wound intensity the detective gave off made Asterisky feel himself pitched on the deadly incline of long-windedness about vibrations and such. But a bright light of interest shone behind DeSales's dark features, a chiaroscuro effect.

The detective said: "I think you may be on to something. But you better draw the whole picture for Bernie and me. We're probably not as tuned-in to this stuff as you are."

Kavanaugh was whistling quietly in the far corner, trying to get the Mr. Coffee to work.

Asterisky warmed to his explanation. He had rehearsed what he would say on the D train all the way from Stillwell Avenue to DeKalb.

He told the policemen about open admissions and the EO program and the SS courses. He explained how Kaputz's name had come to be listed as instructor when in fact he, Asterisky, had taught the class. He told them how the printout had come onto Pritikin's desk the week before and why, reasonably enough, Pritikin had delayed in announcing its arrival.

DeSales was thoughtful. "Do any of these names on the roster ring a bell? In the sense that one of these people might be vengeful, dangerous?"

Asterisky smiled. "I've been working on that question since Pritikin showed this to me. Those were strange times. Today all but a few of my students are white—or Asian—and they are sickeningly career-oriented. They all want to be accountants, I think. In an EO class in 1969, there were kids who had never even *thought* about going to college, let alone having such a thing as a career. There were Black Panthers wearing gun belts with live ammo strapped across their chests. There were people on methadone maintenance. There were devout Southern Baptists and Pentecostals." He paused to savor the memory. "You really felt you were opening up new worlds to them. And most of them were into it—they tried, they were *alive*. They wanted to change the world, just like we did."

DeSales raised his eyebrows and waited, not an unusual reaction these days when the subject of improving the lot of humanity came up. Kavanaugh blew air out of his nose as he watched the coffee drip into the pot.

"But none of them seemed to resent *us*," Asterisky went on. "We were not—to paraphrase Eldridge Cleaver—part of the problem; we were part of the solution. Of course kids dropped out who might have been unhappy or carrying a grudge, but none of those names is on there. See, that's the last printout before final grades, dated late in the term. The washouts were already gone."

"I was wondering how an introductory public university class could have only ten students."

"Originally there would have been eighteen or twenty students. We needed additional federal funding to keep it even that small. So maybe half dropped out by midterms. That was about par for the course. These were American citizens totally deprived by the system. To salvage a third of them would have been considered a triumph."

DeSales was reading the printout again. Kavanaugh poured coffee into his mug and offered some to Asterisky, who shook his head. DeSales said: "And how about the grades, once they were in? Is it possible someone failed who didn't think he should have?"

"I looked that up in the department files before I came. It was a pass-fail course, and everybody on that list passed."

DeSales's dark eyes peered from over the mug. "And how about the next semester? And the next? You mean these people actually went on to get college degrees?"

Asterisky blushed. He dug his elbows into the arms of the chair and raised himself up. "I can't answer that."

"Why?"

"Because the program wasn't fully designed. It was a groundbreaking kind of thing and we never got far enough along to have formal evaluations and recordkeeping. We didn't follow the students after they completed their freshman year. Technically, that is, beyond twenty-four credits."

Asterisky saw that Kavanaugh had stopped in the middle of the room on the way back to the coffee machine.

"Not credits, exactly," he corrected himself. "Contact hours. Some of the courses were no-credit but they still counted toward eligibility for financial aid."

The burly Irishman swiveled his head on his neck so that his double chin lay in folds over his collar. His eyes were pale and critical.

"Look," Asterisky stammered, "we fucked up. Face it. We were just getting around to the self-evaluative phase, the linear progress charts, when the budget crisis came. I got tenure because I was publishing articles. Artie Kaputz wasn't interested in scholarship; he was headed for greener pastures in politics. The program folded before we could implement any long-term goals. Sometimes I have nightmares."

"That you got ten kids a start to a higher education they otherwise wouldn't have had a chance at? Isn't that what you just said you did?"

"No. That we raised their hopes, their expectations. And then hung them out to dry. Someday I'm afraid a beggar is going to approach me in the subway and it's going to turn out to be some kid I had once convinced that the world was full of limitless opportunities. Sometimes I imagine opening a tabloid and finding out we nurtured a mass murderer."

"Like maybe tomorrow morning?"

"That's why I'm here in spite of myself."

"I understand," answered DeSales without warmth. He spread out the roster between them. "Let's take them one at a time. Maybe it will help if you give me a little bit of what you remember. Bernie will get on the computer and plug into the National Crime Network. We got Social Security numbers, names, and addresses as of twenty years ago. He'll type in the name and number as you read it out loud and see if it jogs your memory. If the person has a criminal record it'll be accessed from the database. Do you mind reading the names out loud? From the bottom up."

Asterisky was suspicious again. Why from the bottom up? Perhaps they had him secretly wired to a kind of lie-detector apparatus and they could measure his emotional reactions as he read the names. Reading from the bottom was designed to put the reader off balance, to upset his emotional preparation. Grammar-school teachers did it to kids who tried to memorize answers in advance. It was a typical Establishment exercise.

For at least the fifth time that day, Ben Asterisky felt the overheated embrace of paranoia as he read out the names:

"Tyrone, Ishmael.

"Robinson, Betty.

"Perez, Leon.

"O'Hare, Scarlett . . . That's O'Hare like the airport.

"Martinez, Raymond.

"Hill, Rosamund.

"Holmes, Earnest Joe.

"Garcia, Sheldrake.

"Braithwaite, Lord.

"Bongiorno, Giovanni."

"Bring back any memories?" asked DeSales.

"Betty Robinson was a black girl who had just come up

from down South and was woefully unprepared for city life. She also had medical problems—she was in the early stages of sickle cell anemia. And had serious housing problems— lived right near the Institute in one of those slumlord tenements. The heat and hot water were constantly being turned off. It was a miracle we got her through." Asterisky shook his head. "A miracle." The edges of his eyes crinkled.

"Well," Kavanaugh barked from the corner, "*she* couldn't be holding any grudges, then."

Asterisky kept looking at the floor. He had other memories of Betty Robinson that he wasn't quite prepared to share. In any event, there was no reason to believe they were relevant to the case at hand. "Raymond Martinez I think was gay. I don't know where he got the Spanish name. Strictly urban black. He was a wonderful artist, not much of a thinker. He spoke very well. I remember counseling him to go to some art or design school."

"And did he?"

"Never saw him again. Earnest Holmes had family problems. He turned in papers that were total messes. Then one day I made him sit in my office and complete an assignment. It was superior, truly superior. Trouble was he couldn't work at home; everybody in the family was stoned or drunk and they mocked him for trying to better himself. I *did* see him a few years later. He was still in school but he hadn't accumulated too many credits. He had a job nights with the post office and seemed to be taking care of himself."

DeSales put a finger on the name at the top of the list. "Giovanni Bongiorno? An Italian? I thought this was an all-minority program."

Asterisky smiled. "Before we were finished, we had every conceivable group represented. It was like Noah's ark. Giovanni was called Johnny—Johnny B. Goode was his nickname. He was a kind of fluke. You're right he didn't belong in the program, although it was a poverty program, not a racial one."

He looked up warily. "There *are* poor Italians, aren't there? Anyway, Johnny's address was technically in a poverty-designated area, and when he applied for financial aid the registrar automatically sent him over to us. The system had a lot of trouble spreading the wealth equitably in those early days of reform. There were abuses, not just mistakes. At one point we found a lot of prosperous third-generation middle-European kids giving their grandparents' addresses back in the ghettos they had immigrated to just so they could get free benefits. But you know, what's funniest to contemplate is that Nixon was President. Isn't it? Nixon as President and the country was actually trying to give some of the people who had been shut out a fair shake. The sixties was a decade of paradox. Johnny Bongiorno came from not exactly the right side of the tracks, but not the wrong one either. More like *on* the tracks."

DeSales interrupted, impatient, sounding as if he were sorry he'd asked the question. "So if this Italian kid didn't belong, why did he stay in the program?"

"He *wanted* to stay. He qualified for a regular scholarship, but he wanted to come up with 'the people.' " Asterisky held his fingers in the air to indicate quotation marks. "It's hard to imagine in the eighties with the Me Generation and the yuppies, but people were idealistic back then, even people like Johnny who were essentially blue-collar white ethnics and weren't supposed to have ideals. Today"—Asterisky looked out the grimy window and made a face in the direction of Flatbush Avenue Extended—"they're killing people who have different-colored skin and waving watermelons." He looked out the window again for a long moment. "In any case, Bongiorno is one I do *not* have nightmares about. A talented musician, an opportunity to go into the family business. He was just passing through the Institute anyway. Wrote beautifully, had his own band, long hair, one of the real counter-culture people. He and I became friends. We . . . uh . . .

socialized together on occasion. When I last saw him that summer of '69 he was heading for California. We all—Joe himself, Artie Kaputz, Desmond, me—we all agreed he didn't need college. He would transcend the Establishment . . ."

DeSales gave Asterisky an angle, then looked meaningfully at Kavanaugh, who was peering at the screen of the computer. "Any of the names coming up with priors Bernie?"

"Not so far. This would be only felonies, of course."

DeSales stood up and went to the monitor. "What do you teach at the Institute now, Mr. Asterisky?"

"American Popular Culture."

"Rock-and-roll and the sixties and so forth?"

"Among other things. Why?"

"If you would give us a few minutes of your valuable time, I'd like you to look at a videotape."

"Sure." Asterisky lived alone; he had no papers to grade that week; and he had long since not had to prepare for classes. His academic subject was his own life. Tonight he had his weekly group-therapy session but that wasn't for three hours.

DeSales ran the tape again. Asterisky watched attentively but did not request any reruns or slo-mo or freeze-frames. He sat quietly with his hands folded in his lap. DeSales said: "Well?"

Asterisky cleared his throat. "I could give a conference paper on this film. But I'm sure you would like something a little more pithy. You want an analysis of meaning, a literal reference guide, a—"

"Whatever you got. This is a crucial element in the Dillard case."

Asterisky shook his index finger. "In memory of my departed colleague, I'd like to mention that it was Kaputz who died, not Dillard. Why does it have to be the Dillard case?"

DeSales shrugged. "I was asking about the tape."

"Taken literally, the rock concert footage is of Woodstock.

Weekend of August 15, 1969. It's from the documentary that was made. It was released in two parts. The first was 1970; the second was a year or so later. Except some of the Jimi Hendrix stuff. That could be *Monterey Pop.* You could say *Monterey* was the *Ur*-rock-concert film—the first rockumentary. The Tom Hayden political speech, the Lennon session with Yoko, they're from one of those countless documentaries on the sixties and the Beatles and flower power that have been running this year."

"Not hard to get?"

"Hardly. You turn on Channel 5 or 11 or MTV or whatever and push the record button on your VCR."

"How about assembling and cutting the material into this tape?"

"I'm no expert, but I think you can buy your own home video-editing machine for a couple of thousand dollars. And this is pretty crude. If you know anybody in TV with access to a professional editing system, you could see in a minute how it's done. They may even be able to identify the level of the equipment used here."

Kavanaugh gave DeSales a knowing leer and mouthed Megan's name silently. DeSales ignored him. He asked Asterisky: "Anything else about the film clips themselves?"

"Well, the Kennedy assassination footage is from the home movie that came to be known as the Zapruder film. Dillard, John Kennedy, that recent stuff probably comes off TV news."

"The A-bomb, the volcano?"

Asterisky laughed quietly; he held up one hand, then fiddled with the ponytail. He was in his element. "*Time Marches On?*" he asked.

DeSales played with an unlighted cigarette, swiveled in his chair, put both his feet solidly on the floor. Finally he wrinkled his brow and ventured softly: "How about the fire at the end?"

"Oh that? I forgot. Very important. That's the house Patty

Hearst wasn't in when the Symbionese Liberation Army got torched by the L.A. cops. Nineteen seventy-four. Something curious there."

"What?"

"Patty was watching the live footage of that torching on TV in a nearby motel as it was going on. There's a certain disassociation implied in this film when we see the lonely motel *not* on fire as the rest of the city burns."

"You know your stuff," said DeSales. "I'm impressed."

"Thank you. You could say it's the history of my own times that we're looking at. I *should* know it. Anyone who doesn't must have been living in a cave all these years."

"Not me," said Kavanaugh. "I been in Bay Ridge."

DeSales went on: "So if this is your own times, Professor, what would you say about the guy who made the film? Is it *his* times too?"

"A good question." Asterisky went back to pulling at his hair. "There's something funny—a nostalgia, a sense of fond memory. Somebody who's into the extraordinary power of those moments. As if he'd like to bring it all back, even the bad parts. The person in the motel watching the city burn from a safe vantage point. It makes for the sense of apocalypse, too. When the film ends, you almost expect a personification of plague to walk right out of the screen and take you by the throat. For example, the contemporary sound and footage. The bouncers at the club with the Dead Kennedys shirts juxtaposed with the little kid saluting his father's coffin, who grew up to be at once too beautiful and too human. The line about eating pussy—that's Dennis Hopper's voice. I can't remember the film—he makes so many these days—part of the recycling of the period for purely commercial gain. Anyway, that line next to Dillard laughing isn't only vulgar, it's very *now*."

"How so?"

"The kids these days grow up on MTV. Have you ever watched it? They do montages of news clips and sound. They think they're being witty when they're being gross. No subtlety. No feeling." Asterisky put his chin on his chest and closed his eyes. When he opened them, they were bright with awareness. "And then there are the blowjobs."

"What about the blowjobs?"

Asterisky winked. "I actually think I can give you a specific reference here. Slick video porn has no attraction for me, but of course in my field of popular culture one has to keep up with everything. This is probably from the racist room episode in *The Devil in Miss Jones IV*. It was made within the last few years. The premise is that Miss Jones is being guided through hell—a rip-off of Dante, rather quaint. The racist room is where racists are forced to endure endless copulation with members of the races they discriminated against in life. The man at the end of the long white penis wears Nazi tattoos, so of course he's got a series of black women mounting him. The mouth on the fat black penis belongs to an actress playing a Southern belle who of course couldn't bear even the presence of a darky. But what I always say about film porn is, no matter where it comes from and no matter what the context, there's a sameness, a dreariness, that makes sexual acts and organs indistinguishable from one another and actually tends to reduce arousal in the viewer. The impact, or lack of impact, is the same. But still, the selection of a scene with two penises and two mouths gave me an idea."

"What's that?"

"It's almost as if the film were made by *two* people. One who was in his prime in the sixties and one who is coming of age right now."

"Not one black and one white?"

"I guess that's possible too."

For some minutes after Asterisky left the office, DeSales sat silently at his desk while Kavanaugh continued to use the computer. Kavanaugh shook his head. "Nothing here. You know, I think Asterisky looked awful nervous when he was talking about the black girl with the disease. Like maybe he caught a dose from her or something."

"DeSales raised one eyebrow, then the other. "Could be." He picked at a fingernail. "Call it a night, Bernie. We can write up a report in the morning. So far we know we're looking for two people, preferably Italian, or black and white, who have lost their mother and are at the same time violent racist peace-loving hippies who are disassociated from their surroundings."

"Sounds good, Frank."

"Now I have to catch Megan. She'll be steaming, if she's still there."

"Take her a present," said Kavanaugh.

"Flowers?"

"No. The tape. She'll think you're cutting her in on the action. You can swear her to confidentiality until we're ready to go public with it, and in the meantime she gets her jollies being on the inside. Besides, she can help."

"How?"

"You heard Asterisky. He said someone familiar with video equipment could probably guess the level of machinery and expertise it took to make the tape. Megan works with that stuff all the time."

"Good idea." DeSales swung his feet off the desk and reached for the cassette, doubting his own judgment. He was in no mood for compromise. He would do as he goddam well pleased when the time came.

The phone rang. Kavanaugh picked it up and spoke briefly into it. Then he listened. The room was silent. "Frank?"

"Yeh?"

"It's somebody named Teresa Colavito. She says she has an idea about who shot Kaputz."

DeSales waved dismissively at the phone. "Never heard of her. Tell her to leave her number. No more witnesses today."

Kavanaugh grinned, his meaty palm covering the receiver. "Well, she's heard of you, Frank. She says, 'Remind him I'm the little girl he seduced out of her innocence on her Aunt Marie's back porch on Seventy-first Street near Bay Parkway in the spring of 1957.' "

" 'Little girl,' shit!" DeSales was smiling, reaching for the phone. "She was at least sixteen and she was built like Sophia Loren."

"Don't forget Megan and the tape," said Kavanaugh.

CHAPTER 12

In the Ceasar's Bazaar parking lot, the new white Cadillac convertible pulled up alongside Bono's vintage LTD. The Irishman from Marine Park they called the Fish was driving. He had dirty-blond hair combed straight back from his forehead, with lots of gel, and a peach-fuzz mustache. Anthony Cardinale was riding shotgun. In the back seat, noses pressed against the glass, were Anthony's two prized attack dogs, the rottweilers he called Zippo and Lola. Fish rolled down the window and squawked: "Follow us."

Bono fell in behind, across the Belt and then a right on Cropsey, heading toward Coney Island. They were about to recross the Belt and go over the bridge to Coney when the Fish hit a sharp left, then another left, then two rapid rights, until they had passed the old Department of Sewers building and were on Avenue X with the car yards on one side and the Marlboro Houses on the other. The high-rise houses were faded yellow brick and outside them there were piles of green trash bags, most of them cut open and their contents spilled on the ground by the bums looking for food and nickel-return cans. Groups of blacks leaned in the entranceways to the houses, some of them already taking notice of the two fine sets of wheels. Each apartment in the project had its own terrace, and more blacks, mostly women, were sitting behind the bars which enclosed the terraces top to bottom like they were exhibits in a zoo. The projects had been built for poor Italians—there were still some left even now, mostly old and invisible—and the terraces had been open. But as the blacks moved in the terraces were enclosed. Too many jumpers. The gutters were deep with broken glass, bottles and car windows. It wasn't a block on which Bono would choose to do any extended fresh-air dealing. Maybe Anthony and his boys had decided to cut the Jamaican posses in on the action instead of fighting them anymore.

The Fish and Anthony got out of the car and stretched as if they were getting ready to take a nap. Bono got out of his car and walked up to them. You could smell the ocean and the sewage in the dead creek and the garbage from the projects and the chicken shit from the Puerto Rican slaughterhouse with the big sign that said "Vivas Gallinas." Bono didn't need a weatherman to know which way the wind blew, and that he wasn't far from his own house. They were in the no man's land where the elevated trains began to pull up for their last stops, abutted on all sides by different neighborhoods: Bensonhurst, Coney, Gravesend, Brighton Beach, and every kind of mob from every corner of the earth. You could get a bullhorn and say the words for "free money" in Russian, Chinese, Italian, Spanish, Hebrew, Indian Indian, West Indian, even English, and rocks would turn over in every direction and all the scum of the earth would scramble out with one palm open and the other holding tight onto a weapon.

It was a nice place to think about all that shit coming down.

As Bono approached the Caddy, Anthony's dogs went into a frenzy, growling and barking and attacking the windows. Anthony was carrying their leashes; he slapped them across the roof of the car and the dogs settled down in the back seat, silently baring their fangs.

Anthony said: "You wasn't too nice to me this afternoon at the club, Junior."

"Business," muttered Bono. Anthony sometimes had a fantasy he actually belonged to a real Mob family and there were codes of honor people should live by.

The Fish had a whiny voice that cracked a lot. He was known to be very dangerous if he thought somebody was making fun of him. He said: "Forget about it. You wouldn't know no business if it came up and sat on your face."

Anthony thought this was very funny. The Fish looked pleased with himself. Included in Bono's master plan was a time when Anthony and the Fish would laugh until they hurt. Mortal-wound time.

Bono said to the Fish: "I didn't know they let your kind into the projects."

Anthony took Bono's arm, steering him away from the Fish and the subject of the Fish's origins. "Hey, we was just kiddin'. Look, we picked you up at Ceasar's we was remembering the good old days at Chuck E. Cheese. Too bad they ripped it out. Remember. We had the only indoor amusement park in Brooklyn. And right upstairs from Toys R Us. Those were the good old days, huh kid?" He slapped him playfully on the shoulder. "Listen, we only stopped here to make sure nobody was following, see. Now we go over this new place I got. Me and the Fish and our women gonna fix it up. Get in our car now."

Anthony got in the back with his dogs, who were all over him, licking his face. Every now and then he would give a command and they would freeze. Sometimes he cuffed their faces or pulled hard on their ears, without eliciting so much as a flinch or a whimper or a growl. "See," Anthony crowed, "these dogs is *trained.*"

The Fish drove up to Avenue U and they had to sit in the

traffic jam caused by the people shopping at all the more or less identical Italian stores within a couple of blocks. It was that kind of neighborhood. You did what everybody else did. They turned left under the McDonald Avenue El, then left again and another left and again it looked like they were going to cross to Coney at Stillwell, but instead they cut right and there was the shantytown where the carnies lived, and then the greenery of the old park, and they had pulled up outside the house that the neighborhood kids used to think was haunted.

For miles around this part of Brooklyn most of the private houses were brick and stucco jobs with small fronts and narrow driveways separating them, but the haunted house was this big old wood-frame thing with gables and overgrown bushes up to the first-floor windows. The windows were mostly broken and there was a wraparound porch that made it look like something out of a deep South movie, a house with a crazy old lady or one that the Ku Klux Klan would burn down. Bono's old man claimed that Bensonhurst was once all farms, like the deep South, but that never quite grabbed Bono as believable. He also seriously doubted that Anthony and the Fish were that heavy into home restoration.

"Now," said Anthony, "me and you get out. The Fish drives around the block as lookout."

Anthony and the dogs and Bono got out on the pavement. The Fish laid rubber as he headed back toward Stillwell.

Anthony looked down at Bono, hands on his hips. He was wearing a cream-colored designer sweat suit and a porkpie hat. Anthony was prematurely bald. "You got the money?" he asked.

"Sure," answered Bono. "But I gotta see the goods before you get it. Gimme a taste of the coke and we can get this over with. I gotta hit the road."

Anthony rubbed his chin and looked like he was thinking real hard. "That could be a problem," he said finally. "See, I'm letting these niggers use the place until I get around to fixing it up. They're my main source. They only deal with me. They don't want no one to see them and they don't particularly want to see no one themselves. You know how spooky these boogies are. We got a system. I go in by the back porch, slip the money through the inside door with my calling card, and they slip the dope out to me. They got an eyehole they can see me from anyway."

"I want a taste and a look before I hand over a nickel."

Anthony rubbed his chin some more. The Fish cruised by, acting like he didn't know them. Anthony's eyes lighted up, as if he had received a divine revelation. "I got it," he said. "If you give me your cash, I gotta give you a deposit. Like security, right?"

"Sounds better."

"So you take the dogs." The rottweilers were standing calmly, leashed, by Anthony's legs. Their tongues were hanging out of their enormous heads, framed by the fangs; they seemed to pant in unison.

"Gimme a break."

"No, I'm serious. Here, I give you the leashes. You stand here with the dogs while I take your thousand smackers over to the house. You know what those dogs are worth?"

"I hear at the gym. Lotsa guys got them."

"These two got all the papers and they're already trained. Let's say a thousand *minimum* apiece. To me personally of course they're worth more, since I've got a *relationship* with them, but you go to a breeder and you want their pups, you pay close to a grand. It works out I'm leaving you holding what's worth, say, two grand total to me while I carry your one thou to get you your product. How can you lose?"

Bono looked skeptical.

"Here, take Zippo's leash. There. Now give him a command."

"Sit," said Bono. Zippo sat. "Shake my hand," said Bono. Zippo offered his paw.

"Now take Lola," said Anthony. Bono took the second leash.

"Lie down," he said to Lola. Lola sprawled on the pavement, yawning.

Bono held the two leashes in his left hand while with his right he pulled out the ten hundred-dollar bills the fat man had advanced him. He handed them to Anthony. Anthony crossed the street slowly, looking right and left. The Fish passed again. Anthony disappeared into a hedge and then could be seen turning the corner to go behind the sprawling wreck of a house. Bono looked at the dogs, who seemed unconcerned, one lying and the other sitting.

As each second passed Bono became less comfortable. Not only was Anthony taking too long, but this business of holding the leashes was unnatural to him. The truth was he didn't trust animals. The Fish had not returned either. He could see the projects looming out of the marshlands, dim copies from a distance of the condos for the old Jews on the nice end of Coney; he could see the old parachute jump at Luna Park. He began to cross the street to the big dilapidated house and felt the dogs tense. Then there was a kind of eerie wail, maybe a whistle, and Zippo was growling, leaping for his throat, knocking him to the ground, snarling into his nose with aquarium breath while Lola chewed on his arm. He bellowed, letting go the leashes, and the dogs were gone, racing toward Stillwell. Bono, bleeding from arm and ear and dizzy from the fall, struggled to his feet and dashed toward the haunted house, leaping over a fence and struggling through underbrush and loose bits of machinery. The back door of the house was padlocked. Without hesitation he kicked it in. He was going to pull off some toenails with his bare hands. There was an odor of burnt piss. Like death. He realized that the porch had recently been torched. He took a cautious step and a floorboard crumbled under him. The house was empty; except for bums and stray cats and rats, it had been empty for a long time.

He had been ripped off, fucked blind by Anthony Cardinale, the dumbest dago in Bath Beach, and the Fish, whose IQ was lower than the shanty he had been raised in. Bono saw the charred bits of floorboard where some bum had probably tried to keep warm one winter and then he saw in his mind's eye a crescendo of flames around the motel, the molten lava running in the streets, and he knew the time was drawing nearer than he had thought.

He looked through the shattered glass of the window to the street where he had stood with his thumb up his ass with the dogs. A white car passed, speeding. It could have been the Caddy; through tears of rage he thought he saw Anthony and the Fish give him the finger, laughing with their jaws gaping as wide as the stupid dogs in the back seat. He remembered how they had laughed at him at Chuck E. Cheese too, on the Sunday afternoons when the parents left their kids so they could go shopping at the Bazaar. Bono always wanted to take his turn in the room with the balls on the floor, the one where you left your shoes outside and tumbled and bumped and rolled on the balls—which were about three feet deep—with the other kids of Bensonhurst. But the other kids never let him in: "You stink," they taunted. "Your father's a hippie. He never takes a bath. He's a fucking nigger-loving liberal."

The boy leaned against one of the splintered walls and pressed his spine into it. He closed his eyes and breathed deeply. It was simply a matter of patience. He waited for Thanksgiving or he didn't. He used the Santa and the eight fucking tiny reindeer or he didn't. But he had enough to do a considerable job already. Muttering litanies of revenge, he ran back to the LTD, parked on Avenue X. A crippled J train clanked along the tracks toward the car barn.

Mushrooms would be wasted.

The planet would be saved for the righteous.

CHAPTER 13

As usual, the west side of Mulberry Street was lined with the Lincoln town cars and Mercedes limos—drivers leaning on fenders, chatting—favored by the Amalfi mob, whose center of operations was in the storefront across from the Villa Lucretia. On the east side of the street, also illegally parked, was a string of the closed vans and large Ford sedans with smoked windows favored by TV producers and reporters and law-enforcement types because of the privacy and roominess they provided for surveillance crews and their equipment. On both sides of the street this unseasonably warm night the restaurants and cafes had spilled over onto sidewalk tables inhabited by various talent scouts and talent. DeSales spotted Megan—part of the talent—sitting with Glenn Moulder— more talent—and Pancho Torres, the DEA's house Latino, who was always into some surveillance, professional and otherwise. There were also two girls, model types on the make. The party had probably finished dinner inside and decided to do coffee and dessert where it was easier to see and be seen.

DeSales pulled up a chair next to Megan. "I'm really sorry," he began, "almost didn't even get over to say—"

"Just in time for dessert." Megan cut him off. "We ordered you a cannoli from the cafe next door. They were running out and we know you have such *limited* tastes." She narrowed her eyes, then smiled by slightly turning up the corners of her mouth. "You know Glenn and Pancho. These are their friends, Tanya and—what was it?"

"Serendipity," piped the strawberry blonde. Tanya was a brunette with a silver streak like a skunk's down the middle of her head. The girls were tall and skinny. They wore ill-fitting imitation Jumble Shop jackets, hanging open, over Keith Haring T-shirts. No bras.

Torres was saying to Moulder, sotto voce: "So the Secretary of Defense calls this afternoon after they heard about the Dillard thing at the Pentagon and says, 'Sometimes I think that after we invade Colombia and Panama, we're going to have to send the marines into Brooklyn.' " Torres had a horse laugh that he always used to punctuate the punch lines of his stories.

Serendipity leaned on Moulder's shoulder. "This is so *awesome.* He gets calls from the Pentagon, you've saved New York from the drug menace, and then *we've* got a front-row seat to watch a real godfather at work."

Moulder looked at his watch, then furrowed his bushy blond brows and peered across at the social club. "He leaves every Tuesday night at exactly ten to make his rounds. Right now they're counting the money. You've heard the bugs, haven't you Frank? They fight like children over every crooked dime they've taken in and then go out on the town leaving hundred-dollar tips."

"They're in the entertainment business, Moulder. And you're their shill. They know we're listening. They know the brown van at the corner is the NYPD sound center, and they know the white van over there is your camera crew waiting for a nibble to toss into tomorrow's news. It gives them a sense of power. I'll bet it even gets them up in the morning to see if they're on the air."

Moulder was not without a sense of humor. "Not a chance, Frank. I know for a fact Gino Amalfi's wife programs each of their three VCRs every night before she goes to bed so no bites are missed by the media darlings."

Torres emitted a low rumble this time, and poked DeSales in the ribs. "Sounds like you got no *conviction* anymore, Frank!" He winked at the two girls.

DeSales looked grim. "And what have the Feds done for us lately?"

Torres made an effort to be serious. "Frank, my man, you know we're fighting an international war here. If we're successful, it will pay off for you locally in the long run. We gotta close the borders first."

DeSales was silent. He watched a red Chrysler convertible with Jersey plates and an Italian flag affixed to the aerial cruising down the middle of the street. The kids in the car had a guidebook and they pointed excitedly at Umberto's Clam House. Kids in convertibles from Jersey who pointed excitedly at Umberto's were usually doing so because they had read somewhere or heard on TV that this was where Crazy Joey Gallo got shot. Next they would be looking for the Amalfis. It was the new upwardly mobile suburban Italian-American pilgrimage, kind of their version of the Wailing Wall or Westminster Abbey. One of the girls in the back seat had coal-black moussed hair and a T-shirt that said "Italian Bitch."

"Do you think real ducks go to see Donald and Daisy at Disneyworld?" DeSales asked.

Serendipity didn't get it. She wrinkled her button nose and was about to open her mouth when Megan decided to save her the trouble and intervened. She put her hand on DeSales's knee and said: "Glenn met a snitch in Colombia who predicted today's shooting. A month ago. Pancho says the guy is one of his most reliable sources."

DeSales was already fidgeting in his seat, the videocassette in a plain brown wrapper on his lap. He had intended to stay for coffee and hear the deal Megan was so excited about uncovering, but he was having trouble even looking interested.

"And what do you and Glenn and Pancho think we can do with this information?" he asked.

When DeSales was a kid, his Aunt Sally had regularly brought him shopping on Mulberry. But that Little Italy was gone forever. DeSales looked up and down the street as Moulder launched into his spiel. There were still the mom-and-pop operations with the Caruso portrait next to the gleaming chrome espresso machine and pasta maker in the windows; there were the shabby-fronted groceries smelling of strong cheese with the mountain hams hanging over the sawdust floors; there was the plain unpainted storefront housing the Amalfi social club, with a bleeding-Jesus statue in one window respectfully laid out on a grimy tablecloth which hadn't been touched in thirty years. All of this remained. But now the spirit had gone out of the thing, the Old Country flavor, like air out of one of the balloons being peddled on every street corner. The Chinese were infiltrating from the south, the artists from the east, and the loft lawyers from everywhere else. Little Italy was an artifact and Mulberry Street was a stage set for the Mob and the media to do their little dance together. The remaining authentic Italians were all trying to make a buck selling the guidebooks with the stories about Matty the Horse and Carmine the Snake, a version of their own history that was something like selling Adolf Eichmann memorabilia in Germantown.

Megan said: "Frank, I don't think you're taking us very seriously. You have that distracted look in your eyes."

DeSales had finished his coffee. "Look, I appreciate your

tip. Seriously. Megan, if you get the names and stuff that's relevant to this lead, bring it home. I'll get to it in the morning. Right now, I've got some required reading I have to drop by the apartment." He held up the book-sized package. "And then I have to get back out to Brooklyn. I have to see a witness who wants to talk now, a witness who might clam up or be clammed up by morning."

Megan didn't like it. He knew she wouldn't. He was getting tired of anticipating what she wouldn't like. He didn't need a shrink to tell him why he had stayed single all those years. "But Frank," she protested, "you just got here, and two hours late at that. This is a hot story too, and Glenn wanted to cut you in so you wouldn't feel scooped by the media and made to look bad." She pouted. "We were trying to do *you* a favor."

"I already apologized. Nobody ever said a cop was an ideal dinner date."

"Or an ideal anything else," Megan said, eyes blazing.

Torres rumbled again with laughter. Tanya and Serendipity sucked in their cheeks and tittered. Moulder checked his watch, got up, and sauntered over to the van holding his camera crew. He knocked three times on the back window, presumably a signal that it was almost time for the Boss of Bosses, and strolled casually back to the table. DeSales started to get out of his chair. "So long, sorry," he said. Megan was studying the bottom of her coffee cup. DeSales headed back toward Hester Street.

"Hey, *paisan!*" He heard a familiar voice call from a black stretch limo with official plates. He walked over to the side of the car. Two men wearing blue Brooks Brothers suits were climbing out of the back, smiling.

It was the district attorney and a high-profile congressman from Queens who was rumored to aspire to next year's gubernatorial race. DeSales felt weary now. "Good to see you, Guido, Richie," he said. They all shook hands. The D.A. held on, making brilliant eye contact. DeSales could smell Guido

Pasquale's favorite Cuban cigars. The D.A. spoke his best Tuscan. He always spoke Italian to DeSales, at least until he ran out of vocabulary. He seemed to think it raised his stature in DeSales's eyes.

"Good to see you, Frank. But go soft on the Guido, huh? I got to change my name. What is it they're calling your old neighborhood, Guidoville?" He clucked his tongue. "They're terrible people, Frank, these Sicilians. Barely off the boat. I assume you're making progress out there with the Kaputz matter."

DeSales shrugged. "I'm working my ass off. Just broke a date to go out to Brooklyn now to interview a witness. But so far there's nothing concrete to link this to Bensonhurst. Matter of fact, there's lots that points other directions."

The congressman was a tall fellow who affected paisley bow ties and matching pocket handkerchiefs. DeSales had never heard him speak Italian, but he had been told that Richie Coma had been raised by his grandparents in Astoria and that English had never been spoken in the house. Richie now not only spoke English but he spoke it with an accent that suggested he had spent his formative years with the Cabots and the Lodges—playing bocci, perhaps—in Harvard Yard.

"Mark my words, DeSales," Richie Coma said. "It's going to come out of that mess down there one way or the other and we're all going to suffer for it. We're all being tarred by the brush of these watermelon wavers. I just got a call from my pollster and Dillard's numbers are climbing sky-high while my party's man is bottoming out. If Dillard keeps his nose clean, we won't have a chance next year in the big election."

Guido Pasquale leaned over, confidential. "So you've got the burden of your people, your *real* people, on your shoulders, Frank, to clean the scum out of that neighborhood. Otherwise we'll be back to the days when you couldn't get elected if you had a vowel at the end of your name."

"Sacco-Vanzetti lynchings," said Coma, nodding.

The D.A. smiled again, finally releasing DeSales's hand. "Well, you better be off to that witness. Don't see you down here much, Frank. The pasta's still good and these Tuesday-night godfather sightings are a show. Huh, Rich?"

The congressman chortled. "We have a ten-dollar bet whether John the Don wears the baby-blue or the aquamarine sweatsuit tonight."

DeSales headed for his car. For the first time in years he was looking forward to a visit to Bensonhurst.

He had even liked the sound of Teresa's voice on the phone.

Real Brooklyn. Real Italian.

CHAPTER 14

MEGAN TURNED THE BOLTS on the various locks on the inside of her door.

Glenn Moulder sniffed the air of Megan's Union Square co-op. "Is that DeSales's cologne?"

"Don't be a wiseguy. *Herbes de Provence* and garlic. I'm marinating a leg of lamb. We were supposed to eat at home tonight. Then Kaputz got shot. And, of course, you called."

"And I was supposed to be indulging myself in the sweets of Serendipity until you dragged me out of the restaurant."

"Do you want the tape or don't you?" Megan looked around the living room. "I don't see it here." She walked into the bedroom.

The bedroom was large for a Manhattan apartment, as large as the sprawling living room. Megan snapped on a bedside lamp and the lamp on the desk, illuminating the tangled sheets of the king-sized bed.

Moulder was peering into the bathroom. "In the Jacuzzi?"

He then sauntered toward the chest of drawers, fingering as he went the ornate surface of the oversized desk which took up most of the far corner of the room beyond the bed and the TV set. "This is out of place in your *très chic* decor," he ventured. "Cheap at any price. The wood isn't even *real*."

Megan was kneeling at the lowest drawers of the desk. "It's the only thing of his own he brought when he moved in." She looked thoughtful. "The spa was his idea, and with the shrapnel he's still got in his body it's something of a medical necessity. But the desk? It was his mother's or something. He doesn't talk about it, just insists it be here. In fact"—she looked up briefly—"he doesn't talk about anything."

Moulder lingered. "His mother's, eh? A sentimental side to the Saint? The plot thickens. My heavens. Is she dead?"

"All he tells me is she's sick and he doesn't want to talk about it."

Moulder addressed himself to the chest of drawers. Megan slammed the last desk drawer, swearing. She briefly fingered the pigeonhole section, where the openings were too small for a tape. "I don't get it," she said. "Maybe he took it to Brooklyn after all."

"Nothing here," said Moulder.

"But I can't see him carrying it around all night," Megan said. "If he didn't take it to Brooklyn, he must have hidden it."

Moulder sat on the bed, burying his head in his hands. "He's a detective. Put yourself in his place. Where would you hide something on a temporary basis? Wait," he said. "Remember Edgar Allan Poe, 'The Purloined Letter'? Look in the most obvious place."

"The most obvious place is the middle of the living-room floor for *this* detective."

Moulder was down on his knees, scrambling toward the TV. "It's a *video*cassette. Where do you put a videocassette? In the *VCR,* dummy." He pushed the eject button, and sure enough a cassette slid out. He handed it to her. "Look."

The tape was unmarked except for a white label with "Exhibit B" written on it. In another hand, someone had scrawled "Dillard."

"That's DeSales's writing," Megan said. "Let's *see* it!"

Moulder took it out of her hand. "Are you crazy? I have vivid penal-system fantasies if he catches us. Let's jump in the car, race uptown, make a quick copy on the video equipment at my station's studio, and rush it back down here so he doesn't know we have it. Then, and only then, do we go back to the studio and take our time analyzing the evidence." He cackled with glee as he consulted his watch. "It's still early. We can be ready to move on Ernesto Kim, if that's what the tape indicates and you can get an address, before DeSales gets back from Brooklyn. Watch, we won't only scoop the rest of the profession; we'll beat the cops and the Feds at the same time. Let's hit the streets!"

Megan allowed herself to drift out the door in Moulder's wake. At the last moment she felt a pang of guilt. This wasn't playing fair; it was not anything Frank would ever do to her. She often suspected him of resistance, indifference, male chauvinism, infidelity, but never of stealing or cheating in this sense. Then a truly awful thought cast a shadow over her entire being. Perhaps Frank had not been hiding the cassette at all but had merely put it in the machine as a gesture of atonement, an offering so she could be first in the media to see the tape from her own bed as soon as she got home. Maybe Frank had hoped to get home in time to be in bed with her so they could watch it together. Maybe he had finally decided to share something of himself with her.

"Wait a minute," she called. "I'm not so sure this is a good idea."

But it was too late. Glenn Moulder was holding open the elevator door, ushering her in, then out, then into his brand-new Lincoln Town Car, the one with the police-band radio and the CB and the two telephone lines, the one with the enormous back seat and smoked windows so that a camera crew could work almost comfortably without detection, the one which looked exactly like the vehicle favored by John the Don as he made his businesslike rounds.

CHAPTER 15

BEN ASTERISKY surveyed Dr. Kitzbuhl's office with some distress. He had determined that on this night he was going to take the plunge and share with his group his innermost feelings about something at once more sensitive and threatening than his irritable bowel syndrome. However, before he could utter a sound a full-scale battle had broken out in the room. Mel, the jeweler, had not only blatantly violated the no-smoking rule by lighting his cigar in the waiting room, but Nina, the feminist psychotherapist, felt that he had blown the smoke directly and deliberately at her.

Barely had the five adult white middle-class female clients and three adult white middle-class male clients—four of the eight professional therapists in their own right—and the group leader settled into the motley assortment of thrift-shop chairs and sofas and the one black vinyl chaise longue, which each of them studiously avoided sitting on, than Nina pointed at Mel, voice quivering, and declared: "I wish you had the balls to *voice* your hostile feelings to me rather than act them out with that atrocious phallic substitute you insist on sucking on while you pollute the environment at the same time."

Mel raised his eyebrows, looking at once hurt and astounded. "Jeez, Nina, it was a mistake. I had a hard day at the store and I guess I was preoccupied. Hey"—he held his hands out, flashing his most disarming smile—"gimme a break. I'm *stressed!*"

"Don't give me the sweet little boy–bad mommy act. You're a sexist pig."

Mel's retaliation was quick. "I'd suggest that anyone with your thighs might be cautious about calling somebody else a pig."

Momentarily, she was taken back. Mel had led her into a trap. Virgilia, the lady lawyer from the old Tidewater family and Bryn Mawr, seized the opportunity to get the group on its proper track. "Listen, you two," she drawled, "we're not here to call names. We're here to talk about how we *feel.*"

Mel was just warming up. "I'll tell you how I feel! I feel like punching this fat bull dyke's lights out!"

Nina squealed. "See! Now we're seeing the *real* you! The macho thug behind the guileless facade."

Asterisky felt faint. Mel's was not exactly an empty threat. The group, over its eight-and-one-half years of meeting, had thus far escaped any real bloodshed, but Dr. Kitzbuhl's office was really the living room of a residential apartment in one of the newer high-rises on West Seventy-ninth street and the space was oppressively small. A tall powerful man like Mel could easily reach out and smack Nina—or, for that matter, in a not inconceivable outburst of unfocused rage throttle to death most anyone in the room, without even leaving his seat.

Now, as Lars, the phlegmatic Scandinavian object-relations specialist, began to explain for the one-hundredth time to Mel—not professionally, of course, but out of the depths of his own experience—the likely significance of the withholding of the mother's breast in this ugly transaction with Nina, Asterisky tried, as he usually did, to escape his own fretful anxiety in the face of such strong emotions by tuning out.

Half the space on the walls was devoted to photographs and the other half to reproductions of great paintings. Asterisky's eyes strayed from a triptych of photos of starving Ethiopians to Munch's *The Scream*. But even fine art provided no solace. He could not erase from his mind's eye the hopeful faces of the students in the old EOA program, the ones he had forgotten for so many years, juxtaposed against the videotape DeSales had shown him, the recurrent looming image out of his imagination of Natasha Nabokov lying naked whistling James Taylor's "Fire and Rain." Then he watched helplessly as the lifeless and equally naked form of Betty Robinson floated out of sight like driftwood on a river of thick white fluid.

Abandoning his reverie, he looked about at the group members. Virgilia, without any apparent provocation, had just burst into tears, and Mel appeared to have fallen into a trance. Moreover, most fearful of all, Asterisky saw that Dr. Kitzbuhl was about to intervene and speak directly to him.

"Benjamin," she said in her timid, little-girl voice, "you seem agitated. Could you share with the group how all this makes *you* feel?"

Up until this point, Asterisky had managed to avoid making eye contact with his therapist. She was a petite woman, wan and expressionless, who always sat in one corner, barely moving, on a straight-backed chair with her stocking feet propped up on a white vinyl hassock. Although she was not old—probably, like Asterisky, in her late forties—or manifestly ill, she always gave the appearance of someone who had been wheeled in from an intensive care unit for the express purpose of calling attention to her clients' own mortality. Asterisky stammered, closed his eyes—the EOA people and DeSales's tape had disappeared from his vision—then blurted out: "I think I've committed a terrible crime."

"You probably have." Nina, her arm affectionately draped over the back of the chair in which Mel was snoring loudly, was giving the shark's smile which she used to evoke an air of clinical reassurance.

"I think I'd better start from the beginning," Asterisky said.

The group—even Mel had come to—looked alert, prodding him with their eyes.

"Please," said Dr. Kitzbuhl.

So Asterisky started at the beginning and haltingly made his way to some approximation of the end.

Mel was leaning forward eagerly now. "You've gotta go for it! Pluck the fruit when it's ripe."

Lars mumbled something about Natasha being a "symbol of the unattainable affirmative."

Asterisky wasn't sure that they had heard him right. Natasha was a significant but minor component in the matter at hand. "What about the unfinished business?"

Virgilia made a sweeping gesture with her blue-veined hand. "Toss out the garbage from the past."

Dr. Kitzbuhl's eyelids fluttered. "Amen," she intoned.

Asterisky meandered up Columbus Avenue to his apartment, his head buzzing, wondering what he could have said or done that had elicited such unanimity from the chronically discordant group. He passed facades of ersatz Southwest adobe, each restaurant offering a more lethal chile pepper to attack his digestive system. He passed a sparsely furnished unisex clothing boutique with whitewashed walls and a single mannequin which appeared to have been constructed out of the bumpers and radiator grille of a 1951 Buick. He passed a pseudo-Milanese club whose walls were equally whitewashed and whose all-male clientele looked like real-life window-dressers' dummies. He passed surfer bars, dark and ropy. He passed dozens of Korean greengrocers, grim proprietors standing under identical awnings with their arms folded against their chests, ever-vigilant against light-fingered fruit-loving adolescent members of the few remaining pre-gentrification families.

Asterisky paid almost nothing for a cavernous seven-room rent-controlled apartment between Columbus and Amsterdam in the Nineties. He had taken over the lease by default when his second wife, Mercy, a bluestocking Quaker from New Hope, Pennsylvania, had deserted him in April of 1969, a few months before Woodstock. Most of the place was now a clutter of artifacts of popular culture—baseball cards, cigar-store Indians, 45-rpm records, thousands of unsorted books and magazines and newspapers—but he had kept two rooms reasonably neat and systematic. One was his study, where he slept and wrote and watched TV; the other was the room in which Mercy had done yoga on a gym mat and created and practiced her pacifist modern-dance routines. She had left behind both the mat and her drawing table and they had not been moved since. On the drawing table still rested the note she had left for him explaining that she needed to be free, that he shouldn't feel guilty just because he had married a woman who felt an irresistible urge to ride horses, alone, in the surf in Baja California. On the mat he had added the empty florist's box, addressed to Mercy, he had found in the garbage that day twenty years before, the one with the little white card which asked, in an assertive masculine scrawl: "How would you like to be one of the beautiful people . . . ?"

In this large corner room, the only one in the flat with good light, Asterisky had added a businesslike bank of files along one wall. Here he kept his tax records and significant professional papers.

There was a drawer devoted to current affairs. Here he found Natasha Nabokov's address and phone number in Brighton Beach. There was also a drawer devoted to the EOA program. Throw out the garbage from the past, he said to himself as he removed this drawer and set it on the mat next to the florist's box. He sat on the floor cross-legged, reminding himself, against his will, of Mercy's self-satisfied smirk as she assumed her lotus position. In the EOA file from the spring of 1969 he found a copy of the term paper he had judged best, and most worth saving: Giovanni Bongiorno's scandalously funny account of student life at New Utrecht High School in Bensonhurst, Brooklyn. There was also the instructor's copy of the same Institute roster that had been mailed to Pritikin. There was a grade book. Asterisky opened it and a photograph fell out. It was a color three-by-five-inch snap of Betty Robinson and Raymond Martinez embracing, mugging for the camera. Betty was caramel-colored, with a large Afro halo and a winning smile. She was tall, taller than Ray. She was wearing a miniskirt and had kicked one long shapely leg into the air. Ray had glossy straightened hair, a very dark complexion, a black apache-dancer's costume, and a cat-that-ate-the-canary grin.

Somehow, they didn't look at all as Asterisky had been remembering them. A sensual presence invaded his being: dark flesh, dark lace underwear, the smell of pomade, the sour taste of his own cowardice. Distinctly un-sixties, this stage-Negro image of the ex-students, a hangover from another age. Sepia darkies, minstrel shows. He put the photo back in the grade book and the grade book back in the folder and hurled the lot into the corner.

The group had insisted he pursue his interest in Natasha Nabokov, the New Hope of the New World. Asterisky stood up on the mat, made sure he had put her address in his wallet, and headed for the door, for Brighton Beach, the end of the D-train line, at the same time knowing he had hedged his bets by also hanging on to the roster with the addresses of the 1969 EOA class.

CHAPTER 16

MEGAN MOORE, BREATHLESS, escaped from her apartment for the second time in one night. She had almost wiped the cassette for fingerprints before replacing it in the VCR in the bedroom, but then decided that that was just a tad melodramatic. If DeSales was dusting for prints around their bed, it was better they split up anyway.

She got back into the waiting cab at Union Square West and told the driver to take her back uptown. Riding up the noisy valley of Sixth Avenue between the mountains of gray lofts and glassy skyscrapers, she remembered why she had come to prefer Manhattan over all other places in the world. One lived in shadows and almost nobody could afford to raise a family.

She made a mental note: Maybe she could make a bargain with DeSales. He gives her marriage and kids; she moves, without a discouraging word, into his residence of choice in South Brooklyn.

Bambini. It was the first time she had allowed herself to say the word out loud. But she hadn't said it out loud, for real.

So she did: "*Bambini!*" The cabbie misunderstood her exclamation for a question.

"You bet," he called over his shoulder. "Five of them. All beauties, all brilliant, and they're all *nuts*. Especially the boys." He shook the palm of his hand. "Thank God for their mother. She's a saint."

Megan did not pursue the conversation. When she reached her office building she signed into the security officer's book in the lobby and took the elevator to the fortieth floor, not the thirty-ninth, where she had a desk and where she had declared it her intent to go. What she had to do was potentially job-threatening but simple. She had to walk directly into the payroll office, head straight for the files, and be prepared to lie through her teeth if anyone found her in there, after hours, with her fingers doing the walking through pages where they shouldn't go.

But it was a cinch, after all. The security woman in the reception area was a big Megan fan—indeed, she was watching the late news on her portable TV at that very moment—and waved the star on when she mumbled something about the thirty-ninth-floor ladies' room being cleaned. The door of the payroll office, around a corner and out of sight, was ajar, and the files were not locked.

The floor was silent except for the drone of the TV around the corner and the sound of charwomen gabbing on the thickly carpeted floors of the executive suites. Through the window, facing south, the twinkling city looked outer-spacey, an opulent *Star Wars* set. The file drawer squeaked. Megan began to flip through the tabs identifying the various job categories and panicked momentarily. She wanted to kick herself because she realized that she had not ever got it clear exactly what Ernesto Kim had *done* at the station, and if the categories were finely segregated she might have a hell of a time finding him. And what if the records of terminated employees were sent to some morgue in the basement, like old news stories?

Her fears were unfounded. In a minute, she had a Brooklyn address—an unfamiliar one. She scribbled it in her notebook. She also had an old ID card photo.

Moulder had removed his jacket and draped it over a director's chair in the corner of the studio at his station. There were half-moons of sweat in the armpits of his blue-and-white-striped shirt with the white detachable collar. He was standing at the controls wearing a headset while Jimi Hendrix silently ignited his guitar on the bank of monitors, the multiplication of the single image of the black man with the fuzzy hair and headband making the whole scene somewhat hallucinatory. Moulder grinned like a fool, pointing at his ears, and said: "Let me run this by you again."

Megan shook her head. "Once is enough." She had found the tape profoundly disturbing, the work of a pervert. A murderous, racist pervert. Watching it was like peeping through a hole in the wall and finding yourself face-to-face with Dread.

Moulder took off the headphones. "Don't worry, you don't have to watch the porn or the bloodshed. I've found something right here. I put the original in the source deck, right, and put the blank tape into the recording component. That's how we copied the tape so you could take the original back to your apartment. After you left, I ran the copy through the source once, to see what I'd missed, and I thought I *heard* something."

"There's plenty to hear."

"This was something you wouldn't necessarily notice right away. It's not one sound so much as the quality of the mix."

"How so?"

"Just as the film editing is awfully rough in parts, if you listen closely you find that the audio transitions are even rougher. At first I thought there was some kind of feedback problem or a time lag in the equipment. Then I could see that in most cases it happens when Kim is mixing in audio which

is separate from the original tracks. Like here at the end."
Moulder pushed a button and Jimi Hendrix's ear-splitting ag-
ony and ecstasy faded into the A-bomb erupting, and the
voiceover began to intone "military-industrial complex" as
Dillard's face reappeared.

"Okay," said Megan, "I hear the lag. Just means it's an
amateur's job. But why do you say 'Kim is mixing'? We don't
know that yet."

Moulder flashed his million-dollar smile. "Because Kim is
a *pro*. He was a tech at this station, right? I say to myself,
why else would he lag here? So I separated out the audio on
the deck and slowed it down. Here, listen."

Megan put the earphones on. She heard the mad keening
of the guitar. Slowed down, prolonged, it was an intolerable
assault, like a nail dragged methodically the length of a mile-
long blackboard. Then came the break, then the quite different
quality sound, scratchier, probably transcribed from a TV
rather than hi-fi equipment, of the ominous voiceover.

Moulder pointed at the earphones, then at a button and a
dial on the control board. Megan heard the audio track re-
winding as she watched the picture of the A-bomb in freeze-
frame. There was the caterwauling guitar again, even slower.
Then, faintly, in the rift between the guitar and the scratchy
voice, another voice, dim and clumsy. Moulder played it again,
turning up the volume. Between "The Star-Spangled Banner"
and "military-industrial complex," just at the point where the
tape had seemed to go silent with the mushrooming of the
cloud, a childish male voice was chanting, as if in an echo
chamber or from a long way off.

Megan took off the earphones. Moulder was sitting with his
feet up, looking smug. "What did you hear?"

" 'Save the planet. Waste a mushroom.' "

"Right."

"And that means something about Kim?"

"Of course! Remember what the Colombian dealers in

Queens used to call the innocent bystanders who were gunned down in the street wars?"

"I've never covered the drug beat, Glenn."

"Actually"—Moulder looked almost dreamy, ecstatic with success "—the Jamaicans picked up the same lingo."

"*What* did they call the innocent bystanders, Glenn?"

"Mushrooms! Get it?" Moulder pretended he was aiming a rifle: "Pop! Pop! Pop! Just insignificant bits of vegetation that pop up in the forest. I remember they caught this guy from Medellín, Sanchez, liked to call himself Scarface? He'd just riddled a little girl with an Uzi, cut her to ribbons, and one of the beat guys asked on the air: 'Scarface, why'd you do it?' And he shrugged his shoulders and said: 'She just a mushroom, man.' "

"Lovely."

"So Ernesto is Colombian and Ernesto is giving us a message from the kingpins."

"Kaputz is a mushroom?"

"Right. They don't want to eliminate Dillard; he could turn out to be a *friendly* mayor. Just want to give him a little warning, so it's easier not to crack down on their import business."

"And Dillard was supposed to hear this when it was delivered?"

"This shows how subtly clever these people are. You know tomorrow DeSales takes this to the lab, right?"

"Right."

"So the *cops* hear the subliminal message first, after Dillard has a couple of days to sweat it out that he almost died, that he was a target. Now the cops come running to tell him it was just a warning. Now he *really* takes heed of the warning."

"Maybe it's just late, Glenn, or maybe it's because I'm a fragile female and my brain starts to malfunction after a certain number of hours on the job. So"—she raised her arms in mock surrender—"I'll buy your scenario. For now."

Megan held out the slip of paper on which she had copied Che Kim's address.

Moulder was pulling on his blazer. "By tomorrow, DeSales may be coming to some similar conclusions. We gotta get there first. Let's go."

CHAPTER 17

I T T O O K B O N O three phone calls to get the night's location for the club called Disaster Area.

Now he was circling Tompkins Square Park, checking out the tent city of squatters. He saw no sign of any exceptional police presence. As he drove further east, toward Avenue C, there were only civilians not even pretending to be contributing members of society. The buildings were mostly abandoned, boarded-up shooting galleries, and from the few windows that remained intact you could see individuals of all races and genders looking out glassy-eyed. This was the local Establishment. In the vacant lots, there were fires in oil drums and lean-tos and little groups of bums and various criminals talking trash, drinking out of bottles in brown paper bags, and exchanging the inevitable glassine envelopes and vials and rocks and maybe even reefer and blotter acid. The song of the sixties had ended, but here the melody lingered on.

That was something his father liked to say.

He turned a corner and parked. He had passed the building which should have been the address of the club—if it had had a number outside. There were limos pulling up all the time and quite a number of bouncer types hanging around outside, even though the entryways seemed to be sealed with sheet metal and the stonework on the grimy tenement facade was crumbling.

He opened the trunk of the LTD on the dark wasted side street and took out the Tec-9, making sure the thirty-six-cartridge magazine was full. He put the pistol from his belt underneath the pile of tire irons he liked to carry in case he was traveling with friends. He removed the silencer from the assault gun and tossed that into the trunk too. He squeezed the short-barreled gun under his jacket; the cartridge extended down below the jacket in front of his crotch. It was beginning to become clear to him that he hadn't quite thought this maneuver all the way through.

Bono sauntered toward the black hole at the side of the house. The heavy dudes in and around the entranceway were packing heat. Only the customers getting out of the limos appeared unarmed. There were men in black tie and men in denim miniskirts; there were women with shaved heads and women with roses in their hair wearing spike-heeled boots; there was one woman writer he had seen on a TV talk show who looked like nothing but a hairdo with feet. Many of the limo riders were speaking foreign languages. These were the ones Remi called Eurotrash. Bono wished he had brought his camcorder so he could take Remi a tape. He wished he had scored the rocket launcher from the Arabs. He wished he had brought his antipersonnel mines and grenades. Then he would have felt real tight with the Beautiful People. The jet set hits the Ho Chi Minh Trail.

For the time being he hung out in the shadows, trying to get a focus. It was the 'roids. They gave you strength and focus for a while and then they took parts of it away so that the whole package wasn't exactly together anymore. One thing was for sure—his firepower was neutralized. He returned to the car and put the Tec-9 back under the tire irons. He would try to sneak into the club unarmed.

Just then a silver stretch limo with smoked windows and rental plates pulled up. The driver, a squat guy in a gray uniform, hopped out of his seat and around to the back to hold the door for his employers. The woman called Reno Sheeny got out first, running her hand nervously through her platinum brush cut. She reached into the back seat and yanked on the arm of her companion until he more or less tumbled out after her, his knee scraping the curb. Then he righted himself. It was Buzz Derma. He and Reno were wearing matching black leather bib overalls, both bare-chested under the bib, and those clog shoes without any backs on them.

A smile creased Bono's heavy features. Not exactly your escape-oriented footwear.

Then Bono had his brainstorm. Nobody had to do any chasing. They could come to him. As the couple was ushered down the old cellar stairs into Disaster Area, he set his sights on their limo, casually following it as it cruised slowly down Avenue C to find a place to nestle itself, awaiting its passengers, among the other limos double-parked in front of the bodegas and burnt-out slums and sidewalks littered with trash and derelicts.

Reno slapped the photographer who had been hanging around all night waiting for one of her boobs to pop out of the bib, but she didn't slap him too hard, only enough to raise the energy and get the bouncers over and focus the columnists' attention. Not that there was anybody worth the time anyway: only the little Andy Warhol imitator with the Instamatic from *Downtown Trix* and the other boy in the outsized black suit with the boutonniere and the Addams family haircut who did freelance for the fashion rags. Now she had to get Buzz home before he became immobile or threw up on somebody. She made a mental inventory while going through the motions of

swearing and making obscene gestures as people tried to separate her from the photographer. Buzz had had a couple of
bloodies and some wine over late lunch at Indochine and then
did a few Percodans and some lines of coke, and she had
managed to get him to wash up and dress for the evening
without much resistance. Then, at dinner at the Horned Toad
Cafe, he had had seven margaritas, leaving his gumbo untouched, not to mention what he dropped or snorted or
smoked on his frequent trips to the men's room. Here at
Disaster he had drunk beer while swaying in the packed basement to the house music. She had also seen him smoking a
joint with one of the bald girls who were sometimes rumored
to be cousins of Princess Diana and sometimes rumored to be
in direct line for the throne of Bulgaria. Or was it Belgravia?
Buzz's intake was not unusual for him, but it was also not
unusual for Reno to have to take him home before things got
out of hand. His career, as well as her own, was entirely in
her hands. Women had their trials. Ivana had The Donald;
Reno had The Buzz. The Donald had projects; The Buzz *was*
a project.

So she pulled him by one of the straps of his overalls and
led him to the door. They made their grand exit in the glare
of flashbulbs. The car was waiting in the street, with its smoked
windows. The long sexy chassis glistened under the streetlamp.
Reno decided that she would spend tomorrow acquiring a limo
of their own. Certainly it would be more convenient and
cheaper than renting every night. The driver didn't get out to
open the door for them. Typical. As the night went on, these
rental people got surlier and surlier. She always imagined their
boring lives and boring families and boring ticky-tacky houses
in Brooklyn or Queens or Staten Island or New Jersey, and
congratulated herself for having managed to stay in the fast
lane. She opened the door herself and climbed in, Buzz dropping in behind her. Before she could tell the driver to take
them home Buzz was sleeping like a baby, his head on her

shoulder. The driver nodded when she said "Home, guy." He put the car in gear. Reno began to calculate the interest lost on tying up the fifty grand or so in the car against depreciation against the cost of renting. Then there was the IRS; would they allow more of a deduction for renting or owning?

She looked up, finding the streets they were traveling unfamiliar. It appeared that they had continued downtown to the old Lower East Side. Delancey Street was not exactly her home turf.

Impatient and imperious, she asked the driver: "Where do you think you're taking us?"

The driver mumbled something about a wrong turn. Reno resolved to order a taller driver next time. This one could barely see over the steering wheel.

"Do you want me to tell you how to get to Central Park West?" she demanded.

"Nope," he said, cutting sharply into another side street, and another, until they were heading west on Delancey. Reno closed her eyes again, resuming her calculations. Then the car did a U-turn and before she could object they were on a deserted patch of waterfront under a bridge.

"Where are we now?" She was disgusted. She would buy a car and hire a personal chauffeur tomorrow.

Then the driver turned in his seat. It was not the fellow with whom they had started out the evening. This one was much younger and had a forehead that was *de trop*. He was training a fearsome-looking gun with a threaded barrel right at her head.

"We're under the Williamsburg Bridge," he said. "And if you don't do what I tell you, I make your face look like a bagel."

CHAPTER 18

THE SIGN OVER THE BAR SAID: "No One Under Twenty-five Served." An open bottle of Leroux Blackberry Brandy stood near the cash register. Dean Martin was singing "That's Amore" on the jukebox. Bernie Kavanaugh, squatting on his stool with a glass of beer and a shot of Seagram's at his elbow, looked pleased.

"I'm glad I got through on the beeper, Frank. A ton of shit fell on the office right after you left."

DeSales counted the change the young bartender had left. The Dewar's cost a dollar seventy-five, less than half the going rate in Little Italy.

"Glad you caught me, Bernie. I needed a decompression chamber between the City and Gravesend."

"You picked the right place. The real estate people haven't even come up with a name for it yet. Between Sunset Park and the cemetery. How about Sunset Stiff?" He snorted into his beer. "Gravesend where you meeting this Teresa?"

"She works in a spaghetti joint on Avenue U. I'm picking her up after her shift."

"You can get the bends dropping from your Vassar TV star to a waitress."

"She's the manager. And the bends you get going up too fast, not down. Anyway, that's the basic idea. Here's to the Kavanaugh brood."

The two men drank. Kavanaugh wiped his lips with his sleeve. On the TV a Geraldo rerun featured a cadre of battered lesbians. There was a newsbreak: Hindus were slaughtering Moslems in India; a militant Protestant group had blown up some Catholics in Northern Ireland; the liberation of the ethnic states in the Soviet Union had resulted in new waves of anti-Semitic violence perpetrated by the formerly oppressed minorities.

Kavanaugh said, looking up at the screen: "They picked up that line you gave Megan at the briefing in Bay Ridge. About Brooklyn Three? All the local TV stations and the radio ran it. Maybe we should up the charge."

"To what?"

"*World* Three."

DeSales said: "What came down at the office?"

"We got a tentative identification of the car driven by the guy who saved the Dillard kid from getting mugged this morning, the one who could have planted the tape. Very interesting."

"Yeh?"

"Neighbor on Garden Place was watching out her window. A green Ford, a big old one in mint condition. Bumper stickers with dirty words. And she actually wrote down the plate number but she can't exactly remember the dirty words."

DeSales's glass was empty. He held it toward the barman and pointed a finger at Kavanaugh's two glasses. "You ran the plate through the computer?"

"Of course. Registered to a rabbi in your old neighborhood on Ocean Parkway. Belongs on an '83 Datsun the rabbi reported stolen last summer. Not much of a car. Must have been a chop-shop job."

"What model was the Ford?"

"I sent Vinnie over to interrogate the lady in the Heights. She didn't know cars. Vinnie showed her some pictures and we're guessing '69 or '70. The big sedan, the LTD."

Desales whistled. "Fits Asterisky's profile of one of these sixties hippie nuts."

"I don't think hippies drove big new Ford sedans. Didn't they all have VW buses painted with peace slogans?"

"Whatever," DeSales said. "If this is the car, then we also come back to Italians. Mob. Chop-shop means underworld."

"Not if it's just a car thief who knows where to drop off his spoils. He keeps the plates, they don't want them. I hate to say anything offensive to your people, Frank, but every tribe in the city's got chop shops. It's a major industry. One hundred thirty thousand cars stolen last year in the city, for the perfectly good reason that an old Datsun reduced to its parts is worth five times what it is whole. You got no right to claim this brilliant economic analysis entirely for your meatballs."

Nat King Cole's "Mona Lisa" was playing on the jukebox. There was a guy in a vest and two-tone plastic framed glasses who looked like a high school principal. He was slow-dancing alone, holding on to air, gliding a modified two-step across the floor. When the song ended, he clapped and staggered a bit into his chair. With his glasses sliding down his nose, he drained his martini and called for another.

"One more, Dennis," assented the bartender.

A group of kids, well under twenty-five, stood up the bar from the two detectives. They had a pitcher of rum and Coke and were talking about trips to Fucking Galway and Fucking Weight Watchers. The big boy with the Boston College football shirt said that the Fucking Pubs in Fucking Galway were Fucking Awesome. One of the girls, a blonde with lots of mascara, got off her stool and lifted up her sweater, demonstrating to one and all the belly hanging over the belt of her jeans which Fucking Weight Watchers had done nothing Fucking About.

"You daydreaming, Frank?" Kavanaugh asked.

"I was thinking about the upward mobility of the Irish," DeSales answered. "Sure. How about ballistics?"

"They think the spent cartridges are AK-47, type 56."

"Any further trace possible?"

"Forget about it. They design them in Russia, manufacture in China, and smuggle most of them in. It's like the car parts. Disappeared into the underground economy. When these things—"

"And people."

"And people, right. When these things and people resurface, they're coming out of nowhere. They're off the books, invisible."

DeSales drank, then lighted up. "Mack the Knife" on the juke. Dennis of the hound's-tooth jacket and briefcase was into it, eyes at half mast, cigarette dangling from lips, fingers snapping. He was moving quite unsteadily now, singing along with "Memories Are Made of This." The bartender picked up the phone and dialed, speaking quietly into the receiver. DeSales kept his eyes on the ceiling. Aloysius the proprietor had hung "Erin Go Bragh" beer mugs, collected on his church-sponsored tours to the Ould Sod, from the rafters. A younger Francis DeSales and Teresa Colavito had had a date on New Year's Eve the winter "Memories Are Made of This" was on the Hit Parade. Maybe, he thought, he was getting soft and sentimental. Like the wedding cakes on Court Street that Megan had been so snotty about. Maybe blood *was* thicker than water, like Aunt Sally liked to say. In any case, it had to come out somewhere. Wasn't that what the videotape was about? Jackie Kennedy's dress, the Rolling Stones playing "Let It Bleed."

He spoke reflectively, without the usual hard edge. "Figure it out, Bernie. The Guidos and the Mob guys and even the neo-Nazis with the camouflage jackets and swastika tattoos, they don't stalk their victims alone with semiautomatic weapons. Senseless killings are our business, not the Mob's. Theirs are *business*. No crimes of passion either. They want everyone to know *why*. Clear-cut and logical. We get the other stuff, don't we, Bernie—domestic violence and nut cases. Sometimes I think marriage, family shit, is a state of self-induced psychopathology—you lock yourself up in a closet with some other people for a life sentence, and something's gotta give." For a moment he saw Megan more clearly, the great ass first, then the refined disapproval shining righteously out of the deep-green eyes.

Kavanaugh said: "The media is predicting a race war. Reverend Luke is marching tonight. Somebody's said Bensonhurst is arming in self-defense."

DeSales was taken aback. He had not thought it could go this far this fast. Probably it hadn't. It was still hard to believe Artie Kaputz's death could light a candle, let alone a civil war. He finished the thought he had started earlier. "This close-knit neighborhood crap is just an extension of the same thing, a form of war." DeSales picked up his change, began to pocket it, then left a couple of dollars for a tip. "This could take a long time, Bernie. But what if the shooter has a list, an agenda? It may not be war but there'll be a long hot winter in the neighborhoods. First thing tomorrow we work up a profile of the perp and we send out all the men we can get. Door-to-door, if we have to. Get to the real people in Bensonhurst."

A horn was blowing insistently outside. The bartender stood on his tiptoes to see out the window. "Hey, Dennis," he yelled. Dennis was weeping into his empty long-stemmed glass. "The car service you called is here to take you home."

Dennis's eyes were a blur: "I didn't call a car service. I want another 'tini."

"Hey. Your memory is going, good buddy. Sure you did."
The Irish kids and some old Hispanic men at the end of the
bar all voiced agreement. Befuddled, Dennis tried to gather
his things. "Remember, you said you had to be at work early
tomorrow."

Dennis squinted, then nodded his head. "That's right, I did.
I mean I *do.*"

"I'll help him," DeSales volunteered, picking up the briefcase on the stool as Dennis struggled into his sportcoat and
scraped his money off the bar. DeSales led him gently toward
the door. At the door, the driver was waiting:

"Hey, Dennis," he said, "right on schedule. Gotta get home
before you turn into a pumpkin."

"Right," said Dennis with vigor, pleased with himself for
his self-discipline. The driver helped him into the cab.

As DeSales was leaving, Kavanaugh called out: "Close-knit
and family ain't *all* bad, Frank. You oughta try it sometime."

DeSales smiled ruefully. Kavanaugh went on: "And, hey,
what about this Teresa?"

"Just another freak report. Gravesend. Avenue U, the
Street of Broken Espresso Machines."

"Since when did you start making personal calls on freak
reports in the middle of the night? Getting an early start on
the door-to-door?"

DeSales was grinning openly now. "A blast from the past.
One of my hidden weaknesses. When I get the chance I like
to check out what my memories are made of. Like Dennis
there." He pointed out into the night.

"Since when?" Kavanaugh was hoarse. It had been a very
long day.

DeSales shrugged his shoulders. "Recently," he said.

CHAPTER 19

BONO HUFFED AND PUFFED. It had been two long hauls pulling Buzz Derma and Reno Sheeny up old Miz Raney's stairs.

Reno squirmed in her bindings and her eyes flashed bloody murder as her big front teeth gnawed on the grease-sodden gun rag Bono had ripped up and tied around her head to keep the gag in her throat.

Buzz was still unconscious. Some celebrities had no personality once you got to know them. Bono wondered if he should be worried about the big dude choking on *his* gag, tied in with a strap from the overalls. But only for a moment. Ashes to ashes; dead meat to dead meat. He leaned against the wall in the twenty-five-watt light on the landing and tried to think. The pills were still fucking his mind up; he was shooting blanks in the idea department. This whole performance was supposed to be a surprise treat for Remi. He couldn't just leave the special guest stars propped against the soiled mattresses waiting for Remi's discovery because Remi seldom left the room. Miz Raney would find them first and send Bono a bill for overnight accommodations. He finally made a decision while studying the distortions of Reno's jawbone and the way the shadow of her agitation against the mattress contrasted with the neat square-top haircut. He felt strength drift back, on the tail of thought, into his arms and legs. He breathed easier.

He could strip them down and line them up, alongside Remi's window dummies. Remi would wake up to find the real bodies of the real people with the tattoos exposed on real skin—a couple of larger-than-life dolls to dress up any old way he wanted.

Bono started to laugh out loud at the picture in his mind, then tried to swallow before it came out. The strangled sound that remained caused Reno to go all still and for the first time there was real fear in her eyes, pants-pissing time, in place of all that attitude. Bono took his guests, one at a time, by the feet and dragged them slowly over the wide-board wooden floor with the old carpet tacks and splinters and raised nails and you could feel the bodies flinch as if they weren't so well-cut after all. Buzz Derma's eyes flickered open, then closed. Now they were inside Remi's unlighted room next to the claw-footed bathtub and the overused toilet. As Bono's eyes began to adjust to the darkness he saw one of the mannequins, the black one, standing nearby, closer than usual to the sink. Remi must have gotten up the energy to get out of bed and do some designing that evening. The mannequin's hat had been removed and there was a kind of heavy pale necklace running in coils from the breastbone to the chin. African shit. Against the wall, Bono could just make out the lump of Remi under the covers. It would be nice if the man got into jewelry instead. Bono was tired of the hats.

He tried to prop Buzz up against the tub but Mr. Gold Medalist slid off the slick tile back down to the floor, making a thump. Bono wondered if Miz Raney and her boys were deep sleepers. Remi, no problem; he'd gotten a lifetime supply of Seconal in his Easter basket.

On the sink Bono found the sharp, hook-ended knife that Remi used to cut patterns. He went to work on Buzz first, shredding the leather and pulling the leftover strips out from under the ropes. Soon Buzz was wearing only his clogs and a pair of white Jockey shorts. Bono took the knife again and split the briefs right down the crack bunched in the ass, not unhappy with the thought that he might draw some blood.

The tattoo was there. Remi was going to love it: R-E high and wide on the left cheek and N-O high and wide on the right.

Now he turned to the broad. Bono had never exactly confronted a naked woman up close and personal before. In movies, sure. And there had been the live fuck shows he had attended around Times Square when he was a kid, before AIDS had closed them down. But this was something else.

He went after the leather overalls and had them in tatters in no time. The knife had nicked her here and there and there were interesting red lines now on the all-over-tan body. There was an X mark on one of the swollen boobs and he couldn't stop himself, curiosity really, from reaching out and copping a feel. It felt like frog's eggs. Silicone jobs. As overblown as the inflatable girl-dummy he had sent for after seeing Dennis Hopper keeping one around for companionship in *River's Edge*. Fucking a doll wasn't as easy as people might think. A waste of money, just like the Peter Pump he'd bought for himself or the Realistic Dildo he'd sent for from the back of the X-rated video magazine in case he met somebody special and had a performance problem. The dildo was still at home, still Super-Natural from its plump spongy head to its chicken skin balls, no two exactly alike; things were expensive when there were no two exactly alike.

Then he heard the grunt. Remi was waking up, he thought.

The surprise would be ruined; nothing was ready to be presented yet. But there was no sign of life from Remi's bed. It was Buzz coming out of his stupor. Bono, still on his knees in the darkness, put his head down, an ear near the man's mouth.

Silence.

Bono remained frozen, waiting to hear the sound again.

Then he took the hit on the ear.

It was Reno. She had managed to get a leg and an arm free and was karate-chopping the side of his head, the back of his neck. He heard a weird ringing and had a sense of diminished attention. Then he got his wits about him and elbowed her backwards. As she stumbled away into the deeper blackness of the room, Bono grabbed at the ropes that still bound her with one hand and pulled her back toward him, dropping her with a forearm shiver to the mouth. She went down but not out, rolling away helter-skelter. Bono, still grasping the knife, went after her. She got to her knees again and he kicked her in the stomach. Still, she managed to lurch forward, colliding with the black mannequin with the necklace. Then Bono felt something stir within him he'd never felt before, and he was on top of her on the floor feeling the blood pulsing in his veins and liking the way she wiggled in terror underneath him. He held the knife at her throat, just to give her a sense of real, and, looking down so close, his face pressed almost against hers, the plastic breasts rolling around under him on her chest like enlarged ball bearings, he realized the eyes popping out of her head were not looking at him.

They were looking past him.

Over his shoulder.

As if she was seeing a ghost.

Something had *not* happened. Strange—Reno had collided full-force with the dummy and it hadn't fallen over, it had only kind of swung away and back again. Bono felt an inner sweat, something like the moment when you're not sure if you've taken too big a hit of whatever you're into.

Slowly, keeping the pressure of his pelvis on Reno's and the knife at her throat, he drew his head back and tried to check out what was behind him. But the darkness had thickened in the room.

He stood up, pulling the woman from between his legs up until her head was twisted to the breaking point against his shoulder and he could smell sour wine and chili powder on her breath. Her hair had the sickening smell that he remembered from the beauty parlor when his father left him with Mrs. Mazzoli when he was little and she made him go with her to sit and watch the old ladies under the dryers, their noses sticking out and lips flapping, nobody listening to no one. He twisted Reno's neck one more notch, just to see if it would. Her eyes had gone blank. He carried her stiffly the three steps to the light switch, flicking it on and dropping her to the floor in the same motion.

His eyes adjusted slowly to the light, taking things in one at a time, from the ground up and out. His sneakers. Reno's toenails, silvery blue. Next to her shoulder was the fallen stool. Pink toes. Remi's black silk pajama bottoms. The dummy that was not a dummy but was Remi hanging from the light fixture, the necklace not jewelry at all but sailor's rope.

Bono could see the lynching tape he had bought way back when he had started his film library, the one the guy had told him was the original snuff film. The tongue protruding, the eyes rolled up into the black head that hung loose on the shoulders. Then he was holding Remi's body, weightless as a reed, against his own. So Remi had decided to take the easy way out. But other people had opened the door, pointed the way. Long ago. Bills were past due. As he had been done in by Bensonhurst, Remi had been tricked by the liberals, the Urban Studies Institute; Remi had been beaten down and finished off by the phonies in the city. The two outcasts had been soul brothers; now Bono was the sole survivor. He guessed it was a question of choosing your own poison. He could feel the scabs forming on the bite marks left by Lola and Zippo that afternoon.

He blurted out: "The fuckers beat me again!"

Buzz Derma's eyes fluttered open, the Sonny Grosso dog eyes. He stared at Bono without comprehension. Bono remembered that Reno had shaken loose part of her bindings. He re-cinched the knots. Hard. Now things were going to get really messy.

CHAPTER 20

DE SALES PARKED THE CAR on Avenue U near McDonald. He was having second thoughts about his reunion with Teresa. There was a stone monument in Lady Moody Square commemorating Lady Moody's coming from England to seek religious freedom in 1643 and founding the village of Gravesend. It was also dedicated to the many local Italian-American boys who had made the supreme sacrifice for the U.S. of A. military-industrial complex in its wars against fascist and communist true believers three centuries later.

DeSales was feeling that old bitterness again, the one that fed his sense of irony. Teresa Colavito would most likely be a disaster, both personally and professionally. A toothless grandma in an apron, hair in curlers, hallucinating satanist assassins from the South Bronx.

He wondered if Lady Moody had ever figured out that the same Puritan oppressors she had fled in England had established themselves already in the New World as champions of religious freedom—so long as it was their own—and that this process of hypocrisy and self-delusion had a tendency to repeat itself over and over again.

He wondered what she would think of the floor of the shining sea of Gravesend Bay if she could see it today, littered with Italian-American skeletons in cement shoes who had made the supreme sacrifice to the Mob rules of their own people.

He wondered what she would think if they had to build another monument to commemorate a race war.

He wondered what she would think if she were to come back today and find her modest farming retreat transformed into a helter-skelter subdivision of Bensonhurst, a sprawl of dish antennas and late-model Cadillacs and pizzerias and above-ground backyard swimming pools and martial arts centers and teen-agers smoking angel dust and spitting on the war memorial dedicated to their grandfathers and uncles and cousins.

He wondered what Teresa Colavito would really be like after all these years.

Francis DeSales strode across the street and through the smoked-glass and blond-wood front door of the Trattoria Siciliana.

She looked good. She was sitting at a back table with a cup of steaming espresso in front of her, watching the entrance. She waved, smiling. She was a blonde now, or at least part blonde. The tips of her midnight-black tresses had been frosted and then teased into something between spikes and curls. She had makeup around her eyes and mouth but had made no attempt to cover up the crow's-feet or the smile lines radiating from the upturned corners of her wide luscious mouth. DeSales sat down, touched her outstretched hand, and told her she looked half her age.

She said: "You're only seeing the wrapping on the package," looking pleased and nervous at the same time. She fingered the string of beads around her neck. She was wearing a tight scoop-neck jersey and DeSales remembered with pleasure the unexpected freckles on her chest.

He nodded his head. "I can only go on what I see." He wasn't sure whether he was indulging her or himself, but he had decided to take it slow getting to the interrogation part, soften things up before having to get to the hard facts.

"Same old Frankie, the Romeo. Remember what you told Ralphie Mack the time he got pissed off you were dancin' so close to me? 'I'm no fighter, I'm a lover,' you said."

"I could afford to. He owed me money. Ralphie never beat on anybody he owed money to. He thought they might call in the debt."

"You ever call it in?"

"I went away to school. Never wanted to be in a position that he didn't owe me money, anyway. It was safer to lose a few bucks. Hey, you mind if I smoke?"

"I *want* you to smoke. I'm old-fashioned."

Teresa sipped from the demitasse. Her perm fell across her forehead. She peeked out demurely. "How you been, Frank?"

"Now that you mention it, hungry. I forgot to eat. Is the kitchen still open?"

"If it isn't, I'll cook myself. You want pasta?"

"What you got?"

Her face lighted up. She put her cup down on the place mat with the artist's renderings of ornate pottery and ruined aqueducts. "Guess what the special is?"

"What?"

"Ziti con le sarde."

"With the fennocchio and the pignolias?"

"You got it." She whistled for the bartender. "Tell Joe my friend wants to eat. And drink." She raised a questioning eyebrow at DeSales.

He nodded. "A bottle of Salice Salerno. If you got."

"Hey, Frank, of course we got. Where you think you are? In the City with the phonies? First you worry about smoking, then whether we got wine from the south."

The barman served the meal. The pasta was the long macaroni they call bridegrooms, with the green sauce of stewed fennel mixed into a paste with the sardines. DeSales dipped into the heaping bowls of breadcrumbs and grated cheese and spread them over the ziti and pine nuts. He sipped the wine. It was cool, hearty, almost rough, just what it was supposed to be. He found himself thinking again about the days during the war, when the men were away and he lived with his mom and Aunt Sally. Every Friday they had *ziti con le sarde.*

When he had wolfed down half the plate, he stretched and said: "*Benissimo!* Just what the doctor ordered."

Teresa smiled like someone who has found the cure for a dread disease. "Everybody calls me Terri now, Frank. Where you been, you haven't been eating?"

"I live in the City now, but for a long time I was in one of the big buildings on Ocean Parkway. Near Avenue P."

"That's right around the corner. I never seen you around."

"I didn't come around."

"Where'd you get your salami? From the Jews up there?" She made a face.

"Sometimes. Mostly I didn't get."

"Wife?"

DeSales shook his head, thinking that even if Megan were his wife, she would resist the designation, even hang on to her so-called maiden name. Some wife, with no sense of where you belong, what you belong *to*. He smiled. Teresa didn't beat around the bush. Neither would he.

"Husband?"

"You don't know the half of it. I had two and I lived with a guy for a long time. One Italian, one Greek, one Irish. They were all the same, except the Irishman didn't wanna get married while his mother was still alive. Can you believe it? Maybe we're all the same under the skin. Hung-up bastards. You think so, Frank?"

"Sometimes."

"You're a cop. It's your job to think that way about people, right?"

"Yeh, I'm a cop, Terri, and a lot of things are my job. If I were just doing my job now, I'd be asking why you called me up. So, why'd you call me up?"

"Maybe it was for the memories. You were always my favorite boyfriend."

DeSales was eating. With his mouth full and the fork midway between the plate and his face, he managed a grin to answer hers. "Thanks. Me too, but let's get the business out of the way before we get to the memories."

She was pulling at her necklace again. "I never watch the news on TV. Too depressing. Always kids getting hurt. I can't stand to see kids get hurt. I got two of my own. One is with his father and the girl's grown up." She stared at the back of the blinking neon sign in the window.

There were old men crowding the bar now. One was singing a Neapolitan love song. The men wore dark caps and trousers and Old Country shoes. The bartender was trying to get the giant console TV better tuned to the soccer game. You could hear bits and pieces of the play-by-play in excited Italian.

"Anyway," Teresa went on, "then there was this business at Twentieth Avenue and everybody around here was all hot and bothered and I must've had to look at that dead black kid in the papers, on TV, a million times. It tore me, right here"—she touched the freckles over her left breast—"you know, he had a mother too. But so did the kids who shot him. So what do we think? What *can* we think? Two mothers, two kids. Shit, I don't know. I thought about how we're all so scared, we're killing people cause we're scared of them. Then you gotta think *why* we're scared of them."

DeSales thought of the kids with the Barbie doll.

Teresa hesitated, sipping her wine, then went on: "The assholes are the people with the watermelons. They weren't just Italians, Frank. They weren't even all white. I know Puerto Ricans were doing it. I even heard some of the blacks from the projects came over and booed the marchers from Bed-Stuy. They're scared too, but they're afraid to admit it, so they find somebody else to blame. What is it, a scapegoat?"

DeSales nodded, thinking of Megan's lack of appreciation for his treatment of the kids with the Barbie doll.

"Look at me, Frank. I'm rambling. I never did make much sense, did I? That's why I never heard from you when you went to the fancy college down South, isn't it?" She asked the last question without any tinge of self-pity or accusation. She was only setting the record straight.

"You always made a lot of sense, Teresa. Did it ever occur to you that you made so much sense to me that I couldn't afford to both leave the neighborhood and keep in touch with you?"

She just shook her head. "You mean I was part of some kind of contract? Not a prenuptial agreement, but a pre-scholarship agreement?"

DeSales reached across the table and held her hand. It was rougher than he was used to. "I don't think you got to the end of why you called me today."

"There's this kid on my block, Frank. I been saying all along he's gonna kill somebody, somebody famous. An assassin, not just a street-corner murderer or a hit man, you know? A loner, no friends, twitchy. Like I imagine the guy who shot Kennedy was. Or John Lennon. And he's been acting extra funny lately. Then I hear somebody killed this Dillard's assistant and maybe was aiming for Dillard, then just before I come to work I see this kid with a stack of guns in the trunk of his car."

DeSales held on to Teresa's hand. "What kind of a car?" he asked.

"A big old Ford," she said. "An LTD, real good shape,

about a 1970. I know because my first husband had one. The Greek."

"Where you living now, Terri? I think I better come over have a look."

She smiled, raising her eyebrows. "That's what I wanted you to say. You know how it is usually. You try not to get the cops involved in family or neighborhood business. But you're one of us, a *paisan,* and I don't want nobody else hurt around here. If this guy is into shooting at blacks, there'll be more marching—this fat reverend they got who rabble-rouses. Then even the nice people are going to start to get scared and they won't be so nice anymore. We'll be back to living like the TV people want everybody to think we live. Like animals in a jungle."

"Tell the guy I want the check." DeSales was pulling out his wallet.

"It's on the house."

"Cops can't take free meals anymore, Teresa. They watch us like hawks."

"Pretend you're already at my place, that this all came from my kitchen."

"Just this once," said DeSales.

CHAPTER 21

BEN ASTERISKY STOOD in a corner of the Black Sea bookstore, trying to decipher the Cyrillic letters in the titles on the racks. Overhead, the D train clattered back toward Coney Island. A handful of late-night commuters came down the stairs to Brighton Beach, Little Odessa, and disappeared. The movement on the dark puddled pavement outside intensified Asterisky's panic. He had called Natasha on the phone. After he had suffered through the noisy background recording of "Hare Krishna" on her answering machine, she had finally picked up before he could leave a message (she was on the other line, she explained—call waiting). So he got on with his convoluted excuse for calling: he was working against deadline on a paper for which he needed a Russian speaker to retranslate a text which had already been translated from English into Russian. The Black Sea bookstore, it happened, was the only bookstore in the city open so late which would have a stock of Russian-language texts. If Natasha, with her command of the American idiom and her highly tuned literary sensibilities, could render the Russian text back to English, then he, Asterisky, familiar with the standard English text, could interpret the significance of these cultural interpenetrations.

His knees went weak and his palms were sweaty, not just because the thought of cultural interpenetration had revisited upon him the vision of Natasha writhing beneath him. Now the excuse he had used to bring her out into the night seemed to him impossibly lame. He needed help, someone to stand, spiritually and linguistically, by his side. For the first time in his life, Asterisky wished his grandmother, long and mercifully dead, were present. She would not only interpret the titles; she would select the appropriate text to procure her Benjy a nice Russian-Jewish girl.

Even if Benjy wasn't entirely sure Natasha was Jewish, Russian of any persuasion would be closer to the mark than he had managed to land in any of his previous liaisons. In any case, Asterisky would from now on be ever mindful of the pitfalls of assimilation. As a consequence of his own total immersion in being American, in refusing as a child to utter so much as a syllable of Russian or Yiddish at home, in getting thrown out of Hebrew school at the reform synagogue his parents had embraced, he now found himself helpless at a time of crisis in his life. At least the clerk had been able to identify the anthology of the great English Romantic poets and found for him one short verse which he knew by heart.

At that moment, Natasha appeared in the doorway, a vision out of *Dr. Zhivago,* radiant in a low-cut formal gown. Asterisky had never seen her dressed in anything except biker-moll togs, and the startling mixture of innocence and warped provincial sophistication she gave off was something out of a David Lynch movie. The Harley-Davidson logo was missing from her bulging left breast. What he had taken to be further evidence of her commitment to a hip liberation from the straitjacket of iron curtain values had been easily removed with a bit of soap and water.

She beamed. "Ah, Professor, I am late. You see I dress for party. What is book you want me to read?"

"It's the . . . uh . . . Blake I assigned in class. "London," from 1794.

Natasha made a face.

"There's a problem?"

"I hoped you were over with your Blake. You want truth? *Bo*-ring. The man is either bourgeois individualist eccentric or anarchist *faux naif*. And all this about Industrial Revolution! Blake imagines heaven and hell, but no *supply side*. We live in *service economy!* You say so yourself. Industrial Revolution, like history, is bunk!"

Asterisky cringed, hoping that this difference of opinion would at least pave the way for an intense discussion in a darkened cafe after the reading. Some vodka, perhaps. His Cinderella would yet drink out of the glass slipper and give herself to him.

"It's just the two lines, see." He pointed at the third and fourth lines of the third stanza. A reading of these would lead naturally to a description of his many exciting experiences as an antiwar activist.

Natasha squinted at the page and translated: "The imperialist soldier dies of broken heart / Running dogs in the palace are bathed in blood."

"Aha," said Asterisky, warming to the task. His selection had been particularly fortunate. "Confirms just the point I wanted to make. In English, it is 'And the hapless Soldiers sigh, / Runs in blood down Palace walls.' "

Natasha shrugged. "Not so different. You should see Pushkin in English."

"But the Slavic resistance to fresh metaphor; the inability to resist the political . . . Look, Miss Nabokov. Let's have a drink and talk this over." He gestured to the clerk with the book and his Visa card in one hand. His fairy-tale fantasy might come true after all. But suddenly, Ben Asterisky didn't feel like Prince Charming. He had glanced out the window and seen not only the unflattering reflection of his own pump-kin shape, but the ominous stretch limo standing idly at the curb, the large masculine bicep resting on the bottom of the driver's open window.

"I'm afraid that's impossible, Professor. I'm engaged."

Asterisky barely heard her. First of all, her refusal sounded like a line memorized from an Edwardian play; secondly, Asterisky now recalled that he was conceivably under threat from the people who had killed Artie Kaputz. Mafia, perhaps, if one disregarded the tape DeSales had shown him. There were Russian gangsters, too. Perhaps Natasha was in with them, had been planted in his class by someone who wanted revenge from the ultimate disappointment of the EOA program. He tried to remember if there were any Russians in his classes: weren't they always sent to English as a Second Language? There had been a few Israelis. Perhaps they had come from Russia originally.

As if to confirm his worst fears, a formidably built young man emerged from the back seat of the long car, pulling on over a Third World sleeveless undershirt the dress shirt and jacket to what had to be a hired formal suit. The tux was a color Asterisky was not sure he had ever seen before—a kind of shocking orchid. The big fellow strode toward the door. Asterisky looked for somewhere to hide.

Natasha said to Asterisky: "Here is Serge. I was waiting for him to confront you."

The boy was in the doorway, snapping on his bow tie. "Yo, Tash! Les go."

"Professor, this word difference is enough for whole profes-sional paper?"

Asterisky closed his eyes. "Sometimes I read that poem and I think it contains the meaning of my entire life."

"Serge," she called to the boy. "I translate poem for pro-fessor from Russian to English that he knows from memory.

He says it's about him in English. But I think in Russian it's about unemployment and dead soldiers in days before democracy and central heating."

Asterisky insisted: "The last line, 'And blights with plagues the Marriage hearse,' is *not* about unemployment."

"I don't go in for reading much," said Serge. "I already got a job." He mused: "But this Tom Clancy's pretty good."

Natasha began to make for the door.

"Wait," Asterisky cried out. "I mean, are you going to a dance?"

Natasha pushed up her bosom in the dress and fluffed out the crinoline. Obviously, she liked the way she looked.

"*Private* party," she purred. "*Vurry* private."

"Sorry to be nosy."

"No, come. You see. Engagement, I told you."

"I'm sorry," said Asterisky, the dawn beginning to break. "I think something was lost in the translation."

Outside, under the El, the young man stood impatiently while Natasha displayed to Asterisky the bar and the TV and the bottle of champagne chilling in a bucket. The back seat was as big as a bed. Asterisky looked at Serge. His black hair was greased and combed into an Elvis pompadour. He stood at least a foot taller than Asterisky. And was about thirty years younger.

"So, now you have officially confronted each other. My professor. My fiancé." Natasha went on, "Is my big strong lover." She threw one arm around Serge and planted her heavily reddened lips on his. Her cheeks were flushed. "Professor, we wait so long to be engaged."

Asterisky half-whispered: "But I thought there was a Cajun . . . from New Orleans."

"Only a fooling love. And what I write not always true. You tell us fact and fiction not always distincted." She put a long fingernail to her lips. "I just wait for Serge to get his medallion."

"Medallion?" Now perhaps Asterisky was getting it. Serge was an athlete, an Olympian. Or was the medal Natasha mentioned a citation for freedom-fighting heroism. Afghanistan? Chernobyl? Serge looked capable of standing out in most any physical activity.

"TLC." Natasha raised her eyebrows.

"Tender loving care?" Asterisky tried to smile with avuncular approval.

"Taxi Limousine Commission. Serge don't use counterfeit medallion no more. He can go to *airport*. Now we settle down and get babies."

"Good luck," muttered Asterisky. Serge and Natasha climbed into the back seat of the car. Natasha leaned out just before the smoked-glass windows closed.

"So we go to airport. All night, back and forth. Maybe okay I don't come class tomorrow? We not sleep tonight!" She winked at Serge and giggled.

Asterisky strolled, slightly punch-drunk. He stopped and leaned against the Hot Ponchik and Knish emporium on Coney Island Avenue. *TLC!*

Serge had been granted a taxi medallion. Natasha had been biding her time in class, waiting to get married. The group would hear about it for sending him on this self-destructive mission. To keep his hands from shaking visibly, Asterisky put them in his pockets and discovered the roster he had carried with him. He looked at it again and walked over to the all-night newsstand on Brighton Beach Avenue, across from the baths, where he purchased a map of Brooklyn. He had not come to the end of his mission. The visit to Natasha had been a mere diversion, a last shot at missing the point.

CHAPTER 22

BONO SHOT UP ALL FOUR QUADRANTS. He felt his traps and delts take on that shining quality they could get. Then he went to work.

Before he hanged himself, Remi had strapped a cassette to his body. It was the tape Bono had assembled out of Remi's old home movies. This was a message. The poor bastard wanted somebody to see it. But Bono didn't want to see it, he had seen enough of Remi's glory days. The celebrities could watch. Maybe they'd be impressed by Remi's romps on beaches and beds with wimpy white guys wearing wadded bathing trunks or Jockey shorts; nothing hard-core, just a lot of eye rolling and waistband snapping.

Bono inserted the cassette in Remi's old VCR. He adjusted the timer he had made out of one of his explosive starter kits for the tape to go on a couple of hours from now, when he would be long gone, and then to shut off when it was over—exactly forty-five minutes after it started, as he had noted on the white stickum nametag on the side of the cassette.

The next problem was a matter of splicing some wires so

that the VCR timer would also set off the alarm clock he had attached to the fuse, igniting the battery and then the charge exactly forty-five minutes after the tape went on. This crucial ignition would be effected by the double flash-bulb device he had perfected. One flash would set off the Semtex; the other would advance the 35-mm still camera and provide the illumination to make a permanent record of the exact second when the memorial service came to a close.

Bono sincerely hoped the film would not be destroyed. He had all but the lens of the camera encased in the lead box he had designed for just such a purpose, and the flash attachment was separate. He also prayed to the Virgin that they would show the surviving snapshot on TV so he could see the looks in Buzz's and Reno's eyes at the moment of truth.

Just in case the picture didn't come out, he shot a couple of minutes of Buzz and Reno with the camcorder so he would have it as a record. Then, with the tools from the kit he kept in the closet, he made all the necessary adjustments. With an hour and a half of cushion before he had to continue his mission across the borough, he sat against the wall and considered his handiwork, running through the plan in his mind step by step. He was in an organizational groove.

Buzz and Reno were strung up against the wall alongside Remi, still hanging, and the mannequins, all facing the TV.

The camera with the big flash attachment stood on a tripod behind and to the right of the TV, as far away from the damage as it could go and still get the picture, pointing straight at its subjects.

Bono had peered long and hard in the viewfinder to make sure it was properly adjusted.

Bono checked and rechecked the various timing mechanisms: VCR, alarm clock, camera with flash.

He stood again and addressed himself to the clutter of wires and orange plastic explosive he had left on the floor at the feet of Buzz and Reno and poor Remi. All he had to do was hook up the fuse to the Semtex and that was it, not only for the Raneys' upper suite but for the whole house. Bono had had a vision, and now it looked like that vision might come to pass. His luck was changing.

One Thanksgiving his father hadn't allowed him to go to the Macy's parade, and he had imagined that one day he would blow sky-high those inflatable superheroes that floated above all the screaming kids down Broadway. Santa Claus would come later. The Miracle of Thirty-fourth Street, they would call it.

He looked long and hard at the Semtex, the fuses, Buzz and Reno. Remi's room on the wrong end of Boerum Hill might not be Broadway, but he had some legitimate super-heroes here in the flesh. The problem was he wanted it to be what you might call an exercise in internal detonation.

He reviewed his options. He thought about technology, devices; he wasn't about to run around to the corner deli at this hour and find proper equipment. He had to go with what was available. The time he had sent away to the porn magazine for the sexual performance enhancers they had sent him some extras that he had considered a little out of his ballpark and he had brought them to Remi.

This stuff was in one of the drawers. There he found it: the Dual Dancing Bullets, the Cock Cup, and the Anal Intruder. He picked up the Dual Dancing Bullets. One dancing bullet for each hole. Stick it in and it jumps and rotates around like no real organ you could dream of. Stick the other in a friend and you've got company.

Bono connected the battery-operated wire between the two balls to the detonator fuse. There was a quantity of K-Y Jelly in the drawer. Bono rubbed one of the bullets all over with K-Y. But that was the wrong way around. He needed to coat the bullets with the Semtex first, then the K-Y for proper lubrication. He decided to work on Reno first. After a little bit of digital reconnaisance, he managed to slip in Dancing

Bullet Number One. Easy. Reno had her eyes closed and she barely flinched. Tough broad.

Then he turned his attention to Buzz. He didn't know how flexible a guy like Buzz would be in this part of his body, so he considered starting with the Intruder, then had a brainstorm, thinking about togetherness. He discarded the pyramid in the corner and grabbed Bullet Number Two, attached to the other end of the wire that dangled between Reno's thighs. He shoved it into that part of Buzz where the sun didn't shine.

That got the superstar's attention.

CHAPTER 23

ASTERISKY WALKED TOWARD Coney Island on Brighton Beach Avenue, past the accumulated garbage, hearing the mud-slow Dixie drawls of hookers hawking sexual favors in corrupted Russian and Yiddish out of the mean streets of dilapidated summer cottages which ran at right angles to the commercial thoroughfare under the El. There were Hebrew signs in the storefronts and slick photos of succulent plates of smoked sturgeon in the windows of the restaurants. Then the tracks overhead deviated from the street grid, and Asterisky entered Coney Island from Ocean Parkway near the Aquarium.

Soon he had passed the safety zone of Trump condos and well-secured Zoological Society lands and entered the derelict universe of the American carnival. Surf Avenue, with its abandoned shooting galleries and Tilt-a-Whirls and soft ice-cream emporiums and forsaken Gypsy scams, spoke volumes about the death of a form of recreation in the Western world.

He now considered himself: an innocent and vulnerable

stray. The Wandering American Jew trying to reconstruct a heritage out of cotton candy.

But the carny stands stood silent and empty, unthreatening. He knew there were homeless people in the alleys leading to the boardwalk and sleeping in the fun-house cars at Astroland, but none bothered to greet or menace the solitary pedestrian.

At Stillwell he heard the calls of new hookers—same accents, more English and Spanish content—where Surf was nothing but blight. He was savvy enough to turn up Stillwell, where a pocket of Italian businesses had survived from previous generations. These streets were reputed to be Mafia controlled. How could you drop a catering business in the middle of Coney Island and line your pavements with bright red carpeting and have no one deface your building or your carpet if you were not Mafia? This was the constant given in Brooklyn logic.

Whatever the explanation, Asterisky thanked the force that allowed him to breathe easy for a moment, take refuge from the rats and broken glass and broken bodies of America's Playland, from the torpor-inducing ocean winds, and he leaned for a while against the window of a crowded restaurant in which two lobsters in a tank waved antennae at one another. Inside, a white-suited man played a mandolin and red-jacketed waiters bustled with plates of steaming pasta.

Betty Robinson's address was on Mermaid Avenue. It had been twenty years since that afternoon Asterisky had walked her home from school, and changes had taken place, changes he could glimpse from his office window or from the train on his three-times-a-week trips overhead. But confronting Mermaid Avenue at ground level after the Italian border had been breached was something else. That time with Betty in 1969, they had passed evidence of a culture that was certainly changing, where the Jewish butchers and synagogues and the flower-laden Italian balconies were phasing themselves out. But it was the twin oracles of black power and flower power that spoke of what was passed or passing and to come. He and Betty had—it seemed now—sped down Mermaid at least two feet off the ground.

Now he passed endless vacant lots full of empty Huggies boxes, treadless automobile tires, broken-down Castro Convertibles. And heard no whispers of hope. Here and there were remnants of cheap electric heaters that had probably started the fires that had caused the lots to be razed in the first place. There were skeletons of buildings, too, old synagogues and Catholic churches, Moorish and Mediterranean in style, that suggested through the empty eyes of their windows a once-formidable grandeur. There were blocks which seemed to have returned to the primeval—not forest, but field: acres of empty green fields, dotted with clusters of unfinished white clapboard houses. The imaginations of the various housing agencies charged with rebuilding the rubble had stumbled over the memories of postwar prosperity, the Levittowns, the instant featureless cities of California, and had been able to make no further leap. The new Coney Island, if it survived the ongoing destruction of the old, would be afflicted with the same anomie which had granted Nassau County and the Bay Area world dominance in the Olympics of senseless killing.

Asterisky conjured up serpents in the newly dug septic systems. He imagined crazed adolescents firing assault weapons in elementary school playgrounds of the most advanced design. He thought of Artie Kaputz. And of Betty Robinson.

On the left side of Mermaid, the vacant lots had flattened into piles of unidentifiable debris. On one of these blocks, inexplicably, a house had been left standing. It bore Betty Robinson's old address. Asterisky didn't recognize the building; he only remembered steps in a state of disrepair, a dank hallway, the convertible sofa in the living area with the linoleum floor and hot plate. Now, the building seemed to have lost part of the facade on the second floor, and a kind of porch had been formed there out of what was once an inner room, exposed, as it were, by force of nature. There was a baby crying on the porch. Asterisky assumed there was a grownup somewhere nearby, though he couldn't see anyone from the street.

"Excuse me," Asterisky called out. "May I ask you a question or two? A friend of mine once lived here."

There was no answer, only more baby squalling, so Asterisky put a foot on the stair. There was a sign over the cellar door, "Fantasy Island Candy," with a palm tree painted on it that had been defaced. Then a woman hissed: "One more step and I'll shoot your ass!"

From the voice he imagined the same smooth-textured flesh he had caressed on the unmade bed in the room with the linoleum on the floor twenty years before.

"Betty," he called, holding out his hands in surrender. "It's me. Ben Asterisky. From the Institute."

"Oh," she said, remaining out of sight. "I remember the name."

Asterisky pointed at the sign. "You're in the candy business?"

She laughed without humor. "Not hardly. My mom tried the candy business once but failed. No customers. Then we rented to some Jamaicans who tried to make a crack shop down there. Failed. Too much competition. My mom's the Betty you want. I'm little Betty."

"May I come up?"

"No. I'm putting a child to sleep."

"Yours?"

"You bet."

"You married?"

The same laugh. "Never. What would the Welfare say? Hey, what institute you from anyway? The Welfare Institute?"

"Institute for Urban Studies."

"Studies! Shit, I dropped out of school when I had my first child. Eighth grade."

"How old are you?"

"Nineteen. Born 1970. Hey, you're not my father, are you? My mom said there was a white man in her life once."

"I was in her life, but it never . . . I mean, how could I be . . . Can I see you?"

"Don't like to be seen. You never know who's looking. Here's my baby. You can see he takes some of my white blood." She held the baby aloft. "I know who his father is," she said. "My mother, your Betty, she only knew the fathers of half her children. Didn't know mine, or she wasn't telling. There's progress. Now she knows the father of her grandchild, anyway."

"Where is she?"

"Old Granma Betty, she went back down South. Land of opportunity."

"When?"

"When she retired. Three, four years ago."

"Retired? At her age?"

"Hey man, she was gettin' old. She's thirty-eight if she's a day."

"What was her profession?"

"Nothin' much. This and that. Besides the candy store, took care of white folks' babies while the neighbors took care of us. Then when I started to get my own kids, I took care of her younger ones along with my own while she still went to the white folks, cooked, cleaned, pushed the strollers."

"She never got her degree?"

"Degree? Shit, I don't think she never earned no credits."

Asterisky took the frayed roster out of his pocket. "She earned credits with me," he shouted. "*I* gave her credits. Three credits. Here's proof. Look!"

The girl on the porch was now laughing. "Hey. I bet she appreciate that. I bet she think of you and say: 'Now there's the only man ever gave me credit!' That's my mom!"

Asterisky was running into the newly seeded field across

Mermaid, hearing the sad song of his personal sirens, leaving footprints from his black leather Reebok walkers. The roster was crumpled in his hand. The freshly dug sewers beckoned. Instead, he turned onto Neptune and ran until he could run no more, parallel to the path of the foul creek which served as a moat separating mainland Brooklyn from Coney Island. Finally he had to draw up, gasping for breath, and he found himself leaning on a substantial new brick building. "Gospel Assembly Church," the marquee declared. A plaque was mounted on the wall: "To all who are weary and need rest . . ." Asterisky skipped to the end where it said: "This church opens wide its doors."

Betty had gone back home, down South.

Asterisky would head back to his own people too. Beginning with Giovanni Bongiorno, his Johnny B. Goode, the one who had not failed, who *had* to be out there waiting to help him raise a dawn out of the dark night of mankind that had fallen across the land past Coney Island Creek and the car yards, the place called Bensonhurst.

CHAPTER 24

"DANK COURT," Megan protested. "In Brooklyn? Where the hell is that?"

Megan and Glenn Moulder, followed by the video truck and crew Moulder had requisitioned from his station, were tooling down the broad expanse of Ocean Parkway, heading dead south, seeking out Ernesto Kim's address.

"Look," he said, jabbing a finger at the map spread out in her lap without taking his eyes off the road. "I learned my way around here when I was on the local beat. We can turn right off Ocean Parkway anywhere around here, go a few blocks, and then continue south on McDonald, under the F train. Where Eighty-sixth Street runs out and takes an angle that is Avenue X, at that point McDonald is no longer McDonald but something called Shell Road, which only runs a few blocks until it dead ends at the Belt Parkway. Across the Belt it continues as West Eighth Street, or West Sixth, depending on the angle you lean to. By that time you're in Coney Island. Or Brighton Beach. It's sort of the dividing line."

"Only the dead know Brooklyn, as Frank likes to point out. In this case, who would want to?" Still, Megan followed the directions with her eyes by the light of the reading lamp on the dash. On the police band of the short-wave radio there was cacophony. She rattled the map against the two phones and the CB apparatus, which stretched from the middle of the dash to the seat. "I'm still a little uncertain here, Glenn. We're not crossing the Belt, are we?"

"Nope, Dank Court is right between Avenue Y and Z, off Shell. It only runs for a block, a short block."

"You've been there?"

Moulder shrugged his shoulders, skidding right into Avenue T, past detached prosperous brick imitation Dutch houses, and then gunning the car to McDonald, where he barely caught the light under the El. He narrowly missed an ice cream truck with Vermont cows on the side. Now both sides of McDonald, as they slid back and forth over the old trolley tracks, were lined with auto body shops.

"Not that I remember," Moulder finally answered. "Look." He pointed at the sides of the road. There were more cars mounted on tow lines than on terra firma. Sounds of saws and drills; blazes of acetylene torches in darkened garages. "Chop-shop city. And that city never sleeps. Who says the work ethic has died in America?"

"You sound like Dan Quayle. What are we expecting to find on Dank Court? More industrious Americans with lethal technology in their calloused hands?"

"Look at the map again. You ever take geology? This part of Brooklyn, you have to think three-dimensionally. Not geography, geology. Solid geology. Seams and faults and veins. Layers, sedimentary deposits. Underground stuff. See, all the way from the harbor and Manhattan, running in this direction, the streets are mostly in grids. You can get on, say, Sixty-seventh or Eighty-fifth Street at the East River and drive for miles and miles and you're still heading southeast on Sixty-seventh or Eighty-fifth Street. Then, going at right angles to the streets, northeast to southwest, at least from Prospect Park on down, you've got numbered avenues, First to Twenty-first. You can even go to Twenty-third or Twenty-fourth Avenue, but by that time everything is foreshortened. Anyway, by the time you get down here, to Stillwell and where McDonald is going to turn into Shell, you're into a whole different kind of grid. The streets are at different angles and have new numbers and the avenues have letters, like X-Y-Z, you dig? DeSales has something, in his plagiaristic way."

Megan was silent and alert. She did not like the looks of the dark and littered little streets called courts which could be seen as tributaries of McDonald.

"Everybody knows that," Moulder went on. "It's no mystery. Brooklyn makes no sense, map-wise. The planners lost control almost immediately. In Manhattan, at least above the Village, the map can be learned without a degree in metaphysics. Here's the court with the Polish name, Cobeck. The next is Dank."

"And Dank is maybe Asian?"

"Dank you very much. Hey, who knows who's living here? That's what's wrong with all the emphasis on the backlash against Dillard, on the black kid who got shot, on it being Italian. *Everybody* lives here."

"Like Korean greengrocers."

"Exactly. They've already beat the shit out of the Italians in the produce department."

Cobeck Court was unpaved, a swampy mess strewn with rusted wrecks of automobiles. Dank Court, only fifty yards away, was a newly developed row of two-story town houses, each with a driveway and a garage, an entrance up a flimsy stoop, a facade of brick that looked as if it had been manufactured in Taiwan, a solid-looking door with a diamond-shaped window, and green metal awnings.

Moulder sighed. "Canarsie Colonial in its essence." He

pulled up across the street from Kim's address, threw the car into park, and leaped out, waving down the video crew and directing them by hand signal to stay across Shell in the driveway of a darkened car lot.

On the next block down, before the parkway, Megan saw there was a tennis bubble. She found that strangely reassuring. She imagined she was saying to herself: "They play tennis; they *must* be nice," then realized it was her mother's voice she had managed to replicate in her own mind's ear, the voice she secretly hated and whose echoes in her own speech set Frank's teeth on edge. The Ponte Vedra–Nantucket connection.

Moulder climbed back in the car. It was after midnight. The newly house-proud residents of Dank Court, their lawns mowed and stoops swept and toy trucks taken in from the driveways, were tucked into their beds.

Megan asked: "And what do we do now?"

Moulder replied: "We wait." He began to fiddle with the police band on the radio, then with the CB. He was talking code numbers to the video truck. Megan leaned back against the headrest and closed her eyes. She thought of DeSales, where he might be now. Conceivably he was nearby; hadn't he said he had an interrogation in Bensonhurst? It had been a long day. Since they had made love on awaking, in the light of the TV. She could feel him inside her; could feel herself in the steamy shower room outside him, the tips of her fingers probing oh so gently the scars and wondering where it was he really hurt.

"That's him!" Moulder hissed. He began barking instructions into the CB. Megan had been almost asleep. She opened her eyes, thinking Moulder was talking about DeSales, then brought herself back to reality. A man wearing a black jacket and baseball cap, his straight black hair trailing over his collar, was striding out of the basement of one of the new houses, heading toward Shell. He carried a plastic shopping bag that said in stark black letters "Just Say No." His head was down; presumably he hadn't seen them. Moulder waited until the man was under the El, then eased the Ford out, making a tight U-turn. Megan saw the video truck backing into the driveway and turning north. The man crossed to the far side of Shell, then started walking back the way Megan and Moulder had come from Manhattan, picking his way among the tow trucks and car wrecks. After a few blocks he turned left, walked half a block, then stopped under the entrance light of a wide squat commercial building. There was no question it was the same person whose photo appeared on the ID card of Ernesto Kim. He disappeared into the building. The sign over the entranceway read "Showtime Siding."

"The lighting isn't bad," said Moulder, looking about. "And I think we can get the truck reasonably out of sight but close enough in that lot by the church. You and I pull right up front and prepare for the confrontation."

"What confrontation?" asked Megan.

"We'll see if we can get an idea of what he's doing in there first," said Moulder. "Then one of us goes up to him when he comes out and asks him to explain what he's up to, about the Colombian rumors, his connections down there, the brother in jail, the cloud he left your station under, the works. The cameras"—Moulder made a cranking motion with his arm—"*roll*!"

"How do we decide who asks the questions?"

"Toss a coin?"

"And what is our justification for following an unindicted private citizen from his home in the wee hours to ask him impertinent questions he's not under the remotest obligation to answer?"

Moulder jerked his head in the direction of the video truck as it edged up behind them. "You think I'm going to charge

out that crew for a whole night at overtime and not come back
with some footage?"

It had become apparent during the stakeout that Showtime
Siding had something going on after-hours on the side. The
windows on the second floor had been blacked out, but the
sound of music and laughter and occasional orgasmic squeals
drifted down to the street. Moulder had struck a deal: The
"winner" would attempt to infiltrate the building, balancing
the risk of legal and personal damage against the possible
reward of an exclusive on-site story; the "loser" would stay
with the truck, directing the video maneuvers and picking up
the more likely prize of either footage of fleeing individuals
or any after-the-fact interviews. Megan had called "heads,"
and heads it was. So against whatever judgment she had left
she crossed the street, her sound equipment in a shoulder bag
and a cameraman in her wake.

The side door to Showtime Siding was not locked; it swung
open at her extremely tentative touch. Her nostrils were immediately assailed by the smell of tobacco and spicy food and
the sickly sweet odor of marijuana.

The noise was intense. She looked at her companion, a
good-humored and apparently fearless guy from Pelham Parkway named Gomez. He winked and nodded. Together they
crossed the threshold.

At just that moment, the lights went out.

CHAPTER 25

DESALES SAT ON THE overstuffed maroon sofa with the lace doilies on the arms. Teresa was bending over to peek through the Venetian blinds, having parted the heavy drapes; her ass, neatly outlined in her tights, was broader than Megan's but, he was willing to believe, no less miraculous. Miracles, after all, were everywhere. Miracles and martyrdom. Ever since he had walked through the door into the dim cramped space where Teresa's grandmother had raised her, he had felt as if he had walked back into his childhood. Blood gushed from the chests of tortured saints in the prints on the walls; roses bloomed from the stony hands of sepulchral-faced Madonnas on the Mass cards which littered the coffee table.

"The car isn't there yet," said Teresa—Terri—from the window. "You always know he's home when the car is in the driveway. Or when you hear the music. Of course the father plays loud music too, but he's usually passed out before I get home. The kid never sleeps. He's definitely on something." She sashayed over and sat next to DeSales on the couch.

"How long have they lived there?"

"Since I can remember. The parents—the generation older than us—were nice. The son was the neighborhood hippie. The parents died. Then the son got a wife and kid and took over the business. Same old Bensonhurst story. Only he decided to stay a hippie. His kid I don't know except by sight. Definitely an oddball. No mother, she split a long time ago. So these two creeps have been living over there, painting that shit on the house, for twenty years."

"Mob stuff?"

"Never."

"How about ethnic? Italian flags? Confederate flags? Nazi stuff? Anti-black? You know what I mean."

"Check it out. Looks like the opposite, and I've never heard anything except commie peacenik, that kind of garbage, about them."

"Violence?"

"Not until now."

"There hasn't been any for sure yet. Not here, anyway."

"*You're* here. Hey, I got the chief of the Violence Task Force. Right in my own living room. I'll have it announced at Mass on Sunday. Listen, you don't think I'm wasting your valuable time, do you, Frank? Just doing a favor for an old girlfriend?"

DeSales kept looking out the window, shaking his head. "It looks like what you think it is. A suspicious setup, especially with the car description fitting what we already had, and the decorations on the house are just what we were looking for. Worth a shot. Worth staying up for." He felt pulled two ways. Under any circumstance, the situation required close surveillance, but ordinarily the watching would be assigned to one of the Task Force's men on duty. Not the boss. But the boss found it hard to leave.

Terri had settled back against the cushions, crossing her

legs. The tights gripped her calves down to just above the ankles. A gold charm bracelet dangled there on the bone above shiny stiletto-heel pumps.

"Sure you don't want a drink?" she asked.

"I'm sure."

"Coffee?" She leaned farther back into the cushions, looking not at all about to bound into the kitchen, even just to boil water. She was wearing a cloth jacket with padded shoulders. The lapels fell back off her breasts, which were large and heavy, real women's breasts bursting against the constraints of the girlish top. Her eyebrows had been plucked and penciled, and her wide scarlet lips would certainly have been judged vulgar by certain people he knew. Her nose was probably too fleshy for the Ford Model Agency. This was no Serendipity—or Megan, for that matter. But the overall effect was like the sardine sauce and wine—what the doctor ordered.

"Thanks. No. Hey, how long have you been back here?"

She shrugged. "Three, four years. Nana dropped dead the day of my last divorce. So I figure, it's fate, just what I deserve for getting involved with so many losers. Why not move in? Rents are high when you got no alimony. This is still rent-controlled."

"Didn't you move up to Borough Park with your mother when she got married again? Around the time I was going away? What happened to that place?"

"Just up Eighteenth Avenue at Fiftieth Street. The Orthodox Jews started moving in."

"My aunt used to always say the Jews were good for the neighborhood. Raised the property values."

"These raised the property values. They also had about ten kids a family and no pets. Then they started bringing in the school buses to take them to the yeshivah. Suffocating. But the straw that broke the camel's back was the cement."

"Cement?"

"They cut down all the gardens, even the trees, and ce-

mented over everything. My stepfather had it then up to here.
He sold out and moved to Arizona. You should see it up at
Fiftieth Street now. It wasn't a rich street, but we had flowers
and trees and tomato plants and grapevines. Now it looks like
a parking lot. All cement."

"Why would they do that?"

"Somebody said it gives them more time to pray, read the
good book." She shrugged her shoulders and her bosom
heaved. "We always had Jews around before, but not the ones
with the black suits. The ones before didn't pray. They had
flowers too."

DeSales stretched against the wall and took in the room.
"Looks like you got religion too."

"What's that mean?"

"You kept all the saints on the walls, the missals and all."

Teresa started to laugh. "You investigating me now?" She
gave the interesting shrug again. "Sometimes I wonder myself.
Maybe it turns me on. Maybe I don't want to forget the old
lady. Maybe I'm lazy. Maybe I don't want to admit it's me
and not Nana living here now, back where I started. With
nothing."

"You look better than nothing."

"Romeo again. Here, I'll give you an eyeful. I could be
Miss America, this'll send you running like I was maybe like
the guy in *Psycho*."

She led DeSales toward the bedroom. From outside there
appeared to be an even dimmer light bulb burning in there.
But in the doorway, DeSales saw it was a votive candle in a
red glass jar at the foot of a five-foot-high statue of the Virgin.
A shrine, overlooking the narrow bed.

Teresa giggled. "Everything but the corpse or a bed of nails.
Like a wake, huh? Or a convent."

"How can you sleep at night?"

"How can I *not?* I gotta choose between sleep and the death
creeps." She paused, turning full front to DeSales. It was the

first time they had faced each other standing so close. DeSales remembered the first time they had danced. It was at the school, a Friday night hop. Ladies' choice. "Eddie My Love" by the Teen Queens. Had he been all of fourteen? Fifteen, tops. Now Teresa was running her hand over the teased hair; the spotty effect of the coloring was enhanced by the flickering candle. "Seriously, it's weird. I wouldn't live like this anywhere else, but I can't bring myself to throw any of this away. Sometimes I think the nuns are gonna come and get me for sacrilege. Sometimes it's like she's still around and I don't want to hurt her. Or *them*." She pointed to a grainy sepia photograph on the night table of an assemblage of unhealthy-looking short people in immigrant clothing: presumably Teresa's forebears. "Maybe I am like the guys with the watermelons. I don't want nothing to change."

"Maybe that's why I never took a chance on coming back to the neighborhood to buy my salami or cheese," DeSales said, looking at the Madonna's bare feet. "I'd never be able to leave once I got the smell back in my nostrils."

Teresa laughed heartily, so that her chest brushed his. She looked into his eyes; hers were a mixture of frivolity and deep sadness. "Frankie, you've always been a wiseass. But Frankie, speaking of the Lost Souls, whatever happened to your mother? After the fire?"

DeSales wished he could sit down. Or find an uncluttered wall to lean against. He tried to fold his arms, but doing so would mean brushing her breasts again. He said: "You don't fuck around, Terri. I've been in your place a half an hour and you're going for the jugular. You should be the D.A., not Guido Pasquale."

"I thought we were family, Frank. Kissing cousins. *Cugines. Paisans.* No secrets 'cause we all got the same secrets."

"After the fire she got better for a while. She had to move because the old place was ruined and because she thought the neighbors blamed her. I came home from school and got her moved. Then she tried it again; this was back in Red Hook, where she grew up. No serious damage, but I had to get her examined. They put her away and never let her out. That's when I quit school and joined the cops and moved in with the worldly Jews in the high rises on Ocean Parkway. No more *paisan* shit for Frankie. She's at a place on the Island. It's clean and they treat her nice and don't let her have matches or shoelaces or sharp objects. They have Mass very day. I went to see her every week for years. Every week she forgot me a little more until I became other people to her: my father, her father, the priest in Red Hook, Jack Kennedy, Frank Sinatra. Even Guido Pasquale. Now I call to check on her, and I go out during Christmas and Easter to take her something, but she doesn't know me from Sammy Davis, Jr."

"But you don't *look* Jewish!" Teresa had put her arms around him and he wasn't pulling back. He wasn't thinking of his mother now either but the school gym and "Eddie My Love" and the kind of hot dizzy feeling he'd got that first Ladies' Choice. Then they were on the bed kissing and slowly taking one another's clothes off in the light of the votive candle. DeSales had forgotten what women felt like before they started having personal trainers, going for Amazon status.

She seemed to read his thoughts. "I've gained weight and you haven't," she said. "You're probably used to young chicks with hard bodies. Like yours." She ran the sharp tips of her long nails across his stomach and down the inside of his thigh, then even more slowly stroked his erect penis from the root to the head, making it throb. A dewdrop appeared at the tip. Her tongue darted out and licked it off. "I was talking about hard bodies," Teresa murmured, pretending his sex was a microphone and she was crooning into it. Megan had become more reserved in such matters, especially after she had done a series of reports on AIDS. That was one of the problems with fancy career women. They liked to get ideas on their own, new ideas. It was interesting how these new ideas always seemed to involve finding more and better ways to say no. Teresa was now mounting him.

"I never grew up," he said. "That's how I stayed the same. You did, you grew into yourself."

"Like these?" she asked, holding her breasts, more than handfuls. She was laughing now. "You know what the *refined* people in the City would say about someone like me? 'Pizza-pasta-prayer' " She pronounced the phrase as one word, punctuating her move down onto him. "I see it in their eyes. So I know I need a sense of humor. You need a sense of humor to grow these." She had squeezed the bombshells together, the nipples cockeyed, almost touching. "And time, you need to take your time. Frankie, I don't think you been takin' your time." The left nipple grazed his lips. He opened his mouth. It was his turn to lick. "Frankie," she moaned. "Last time we had to hurry. Nana was coming home. Where she is now she can only watch. Let's take our time, okay?"

Francis DeSales was thinking of his first life-size Madonna. It had been at Our Lady of Peace Church down by the Gowanus Canal when he had been an altar-boy-in-training. One day he noticed that the nice lady in the blue gown was barefoot and had snakes under her long toes, and there was something about the conjunction of the bare toes and the snakes that made him not want to take his eyes off it. Yet at the same time he was afraid to be caught looking at it because he was sure it had something to do with what the nuns called sin.

Then Teresa was grunting unhappily. "Shit," she said. "I think I heard something across the street."

CHAPTER 26

BEN ASTERISKY CROSSED a bridge from West Seventeenth Street in Coney Island and found himself on Cropsey Avenue, Bath Beach. Bath Beach could have been anywhere, a distillation of the postwar pale scrubbed-brick conformity-on-a-freeway mentality. He checked his map and headed north, inland, in search of the fabled urban sprawl that was Brooklyn before the exodus, home of Dem Bums and "The Honeymooners."

And of Giovanni Bongiorno.

The old Bongiorno address was not far away. Asterisky passed the conjunction of a Bay street and the Eighty-sixth Street El and the Stillwell Avenue El. Then there was Avenue U and West Thirteenth Street and a series of squares with Italian names.

On virtually every street corner he found groups of idle young white males. Some ignored him, presumably in deference to his race, his age, and his harmless professorial bearing; others shouted, "What the fuck you lookin' at man?" when in fact he had been looking at nothing; others tussled with one another, punching and kicking and swearing. These young men were remarkably alike in appearance, wearing tank tops over tattooed bulging muscles, Jets and Mets and Islanders caps, earrings and shaved sideburns, hair in back flowing down over their collars, acid-washed jeans.

Most of the houses on the side streets were characterized by their sameness. They had been built between the wars, of weathered stone or stucco, semidetached with narrow driveways. Some of them had concrete arches over the front gates decorated with seraphim and cherubim and a crouching lion here and there. In enclosed front yards were stone displays of piety: a blue grotto, a shrouded Madonna, a Saint Francis with birds on his fingers and a birdbath nearby. Many of the denizens had jumped the gun on the Christmas season, already displaying on roofs and porches their crèches and Santa Claus sleds as holiday footnotes to the more permanent statuary. These blocks seemed self-contained, self-referential, institutional in their sameness, at once isolated from the pork butchers and bridal emporiums and churches that dotted the surrounding commercial avenues, and synonymous with them. This was neighborhood.

Johnny B. Goode's house stood out from the surrounding wasteland of sanctimony and sentiment. It was a kind of Pompeii of the sixties. The walls were covered with graffiti: "Make Love Not War," "Off the Pigs," "Up Against the Wall Motherfuckers," "Lucy in the Sky with Diamonds," with the *L, S,* and *D* embellished with psychedelic swirls and peace symbols. The largest statement seemed as much a response to the neighbors as an evocation of the good old days: "Hell No We Won't Go." In the driveway was a VW van, circa 1969, painted in Day-Glo flames. On a concrete archway over the entrance gate the bushy-haired black-faced head of Jimi Hendrix stuck out its tongue at its environment. A hanging sign underneath the archway said, "Bongiorno and Sons—Sewer Maintenance Since 1946."

Asterisky walked through the gate, head darting, taking it all in. Strobe lights flashed in the windows; rock-and-roll thumped dully through the walls. The rest of the block was silent, the houses darkened. He held his breath—this was what he had been searching for—and rang the doorbell.

Chapter 27

BONO GATHERED UP HIS TOOLS and weapons and explosives and crated them. Then he carried them down to the street. Neither Miz Raney nor her sons seemed to be taking any notice. Bono hoped they got a good night's sleep, considering it would probably be their last.

But he had forgotten about the limo. Not only might there be a bulletin out for it, but he had left the LTD back on the Lower East Side. He had wiped Remi's pad clean and then made doubly sure that the place wouldn't even *be* there in the morning, and now another piece of evidence had worked itself free. Evidence had a tendency to work itself free, he supposed. That was why he had to keep changing names, reversing the spin on the paperwork. The LTD had plates he'd lifted from the chop shop on McDonald. He'd bought the car under the name of John Baptist of Leonia, New Jersey, which was what his driver's license said. And he'd got his Social Security number from a dead illegal immigrant from Brazil who had bought it from a bartender on Staten Island who had the card because his brother had just jumped off the Verrazano Bridge and had left it behind in his pants. There were no flies on Bono. The real stuff—the name, the ID, the licenses—he kept at home, in the neighborhood. Where he couldn't ever be anyone else.

He loaded his stuff into the trunk of the limo. Nothing was permanent anyway—including the LTD—except the look in a creature's eyes: Anthony's dogs in the back of the Caddy after he had been screwed; the limo driver with the barrel of the Tec-9 down his throat in the basement of the abandoned tenement on Avenue C; Buzz and Reno keeping Remi company on the tape he had made before he left the Raneys' upper suite. If the car was still there in the morning, he would exchange it for the limo.

He drove back down Court Street onto the Gowanus and stayed on the expressway all the way to Caesar's and up Bay Parkway and home. It was a route he liked sometimes because there wasn't any more neighborhood in it than was strictly necessary. You sort of flew over and around it.

At the house, he carried his crates into the basement through the cellar door at the back. Then he drove the limo around the corner and parked it in front of Anthony Cardinale's mother's house. He cut across the back yards, knowing he could get shot. He felt like a kid, like he never had when he *was* a kid. He settled down to work in the studio. His father was having his usual party upstairs, so noise would not be an issue. Up to a point. There was some business with the tapes and then more wiring had to be done before dawn. On the big-screen TV with the Dolby stereo he ran the burning-house tape with the Hendrix "Star-Spangled Banner" overdub and was just beginning to relax, to concentrate, when he realized somebody was ringing the doorbell.

Maybe the shit was about to hit the fan in advance of all expectations.

CHAPTER 28

MEGAN GOT OUT of the darkness quickly. She led the cameraman around the back of the building and up a fire escape. As she climbed, she saw the lights in the windows go on again. A fuse must have blown, and no wonder—the music was deafening. Lots of drums. The sort of thing you would expect to hear from a live band in a topless bar. Her heart sank. One of the first pieces she had had to do as a radio reporter in the trashy old "Voice of the Big Apple" years was an afternoon of interviews with the patrons of a topless joint near Times Square. It had been skanky at first, then tedious. If good old Ernesto Kim was just getting his jollies in a tits-and-ass after-hours club, even selling or abusing illegal substances there, the end result was sure to be tedium.

And the footage worthless.

In a way, her apprehensions were overlaid with relief. Tedium and lousy footage translated into domestic bliss. DeSales would never even know she had *thought* about trying this end run around him or his precious Task Force.

She climbed into a window and found herself in a bare

hallway. She told the camera guy to wait outside the window. There was a metal door with a peephole. She thought about knocking and decided against it. She turned the knob and the door swung inward.

A hand grasped her arm and she felt faint. She turned. A short old Oriental man was looking at her impassively. "Ten dollar," he hissed. She found the money, paid him, and he was gone.

The room was dark and about as big as an airplane hangar. No sense calling for the camera yet. The music came from speakers hung from the walls. She was vaguely aware that there was a large crowd, mostly sitting, and that she had joined a knot of people standing at the back near the door. Nobody seemed to notice her. Far away, in the front of the room, was a giant TV screen, blank.

Megan edged against the back wall to get her bearings. She felt a curtain and backed into what appeared to be a coatroom. Her eyes began to adjust to the dark. She heard a kind of cheer, a low rumble of approval, sweep through the area like a wave. Keeping her body behind the curtain, she peered across the vast space, trying to make out what was going on.

The source of the crowd's pleasure was the appearance near the TV monitor of Ernesto Kim. He held up a small black rectangular object, bent over, and fiddled with some machinery. The TV came to life and the crowd cheered again. On the screen Megan saw the talking head of her network's nightly news anchorwoman, Charlene Chan, with her heart-shaped face, ivory complexion, ebony pageboy, and drop-dead earrings. Not only was she America's most highly paid female journalist but she was American TV's most highly paid Asian. Megan wondered why an audience—even, as it became apparent when her eyes adjusted to the dark, an Asian audience—would gather to see a show they could watch in the privacy of their own homes, free, five nights a week.

Soon she learned the answers to these questions. Charley

led off the show, as usual, with the headlines. Last month's headlines, Megan noted: Gorbachev's reaction to Armenian ethnic conflicts, a new AIDS drug, the John the Don hung jury. Then the famous anchorwoman introduced a commercial break. Charlene, wearing a red-and-black V-neck Armani number, sat silently poised to return to the air.

The tape jumped slightly and cut to a commercial—in Chinese—for a Chinatown fish emporium. At Showtime Siding, the aging Asians elbowed one another and guffawed. Apparently they had some idea what was coming.

It was time for Charlene to go back on the air. When she did, she was facing sideways, hair partially obscuring her features. "John?" she appeared to be speaking to one of the co-hosts, prompting him to take up the next news item. Instead of panning to John, however, the camera stayed with Charlene.

A Caucasian man in a business suit with a lot of pomade on his hair approached her. "Here it is, baby," he said.

Charlene's head was at the level of his waist. There was another cut and a close-up of Charlene, face front again, smiling in anticipation, then another cut to a close-up of the fly of the man's trousers. Fingers with long blood-red nails reached out, unzipped the fly, and reached in and extracted a long flaccid penis. In profile, the woman took it in her mouth. High-pitched hoots and cheers came from the crowd at Showtime Siding. The camera rolled back and showed more of the set, then closed in again on her oral ministrations. Pomadehead, no longer limp, grimaced in ecstasy. Charlene—or rather, as Megan now realized, a Charlene-lookalike porn actress—kept pulling her hair back over her shoulder so the audience didn't miss any climactic detail. Megan tried to focus on something else, noting that the actress's earrings were strictly dime-store stuff. Then three Asian men in Ninja garb arrived and ripped off Charlene's substitute's dress. She wore nothing underneath. The Ninjas took little time getting naked themselves. The porn actress was somehow turned over as two more Asian women appeared, wearing leather bras with holes cut out for the nipples. An orgy scene ensued, a jumble of martial-arts weapons and male and female genitals. The audience pounded on the tables, whistling madly. Then the tape cut back to the real Charlene at her desk, Armani and real jewelry intact. She wiped her mouth, looking anchorperson-serious, and breathed, "Thanks, I needed that."

Ernesto Kim was a real pro.

Megan slipped out the door among the whoops of laughter. She climbed out the window, took Gomez by the arm, and led him back down to the video van. Moulder was sitting at the controls, earphones on, intent on what he was hearing. Megan was breathless. As she began to speak, Moulder lifted one phone off his ear.

"It was incredible," she said. "Kim's got about a hundred Chinese waiters up there creaming themselves over outtakes of Charlene Chan's show spliced with porn footage that make it appear that Charley is actively involved in an orgy."

Moulder had a funny look on his face, distracted. "And she isn't?"

"Give me a break. She makes millions keeping her clothes *on*. You can write tonight off as a waste of time. Kim's just a very clever pornographer."

"Maybe that's what he was doing with the tape from your station and was why he got fired, but how do we know he didn't make the Dillard tape too?"

"This was a slick professional job, Glenn. The guy's a genius. Almost seamless cutting. If I weren't in the business, I couldn't tell the differences. All the spliced details—except her jewelry—are matched just right. Next to this the Dillard thing was a twelve-year-old's home movie. Write it off; the night's a loss."

Moulder had the earphones back on. He fiddled with some more dials. "I wouldn't be so hasty," he said.

"Why?"

"Because they think they've got Kaputz's killer cornered. There's at least two hostages and an arsenal of weapons and explosives."

"And we're out here sitting on our hands."

"Not exactly. First of all, I'm sorry to have to tell you that DeSales seems to be up to his neck in this, and the rumors I've got from the studio are that it's all happening right near here. We could even be the first crew on the story."

Megan sat down on the steps of the van and put her head in her hands. "And when do we find out exactly where. And if anybody's hurt."

"My producer's on to One Police Plaza now. DeSales is having trouble getting through to the perp. There's a woman with him . . . They're just pinpointing it . . . Ah, here we go."

Megan thought: a woman, deep shit, sitting on hands, the imitation Charlene Chan from the GYN perspective, Ninja swords. Blood spotted her consciousness, her conscience. She felt her teeth digging into her lower lip and wished she could go back to the topless bar, take back the years of striving for media success. If only she could change the history she had helped create.

CHAPTER 29

DeSALES FELT TERESA COME UNSTUCK from him as soon as she spoke, missed immediately the close synchronized breathing, the pounding echo, womblike, of his heart beneath hers in their postcoital embrace. The weight shifted on the lumpy old mattress and he was tilted toward the shrine side of the bed. He opened his eyes. In the candlelight, his original teen queen, all voluptuous shadow, was pulling on a short dressing gown and moving with stealth toward the window. She stood among the billowing curtains, a long fingernail depressing one slat of the blinds.

"He's home?" DeSales asked, trying to find his shorts in the tangled sheets.

"Somebody's at the door. Ringing the bell. A stranger."

DeSales stood behind Teresa and looked out the blinds. He pressed himself against her.

"Already? You one of these heat-seeking missiles?"

"You said you wanted it to last."

"Forget about it. Looks like you're back on cop duty. There's the father, Johnny," she said. "He used to be a tall skinny kid. Look at him now. It's like he's swollen from some disease. The Bensonhurst virus.''

DeSales saw the large man in work clothes usher the short fellow with the ponytail through the door. The two men embraced. The door swung shut.

Teresa must have felt something move in him. "You know them?"

"The visitor."

"Johnny Bongiorno doesn't have company. Not for years. Not since the kid was little. So who is this new guy?"

"He's a professor at the Institute for Urban Studies. Bongiorno was a student of his a long time ago. Name's Asterisky.''

"So why does he show up tonight?"

"They could be in something fishy together but I think it's because of the kid. Because the kid killed his old buddy, Kaputz. A warning was sent to Asterisky last week and he didn't get it. Now he figures it out and decides to play private eye. Or maybe he's got something to cover up.''

"You better get the guy out of there then, before the kid comes home.''

"Whatever I do, I think I ought to have my pants on.''

"The kid just came out of the basement. He must've left his car somewhere else.''

DeSales zipped up his fly, buckled his belt, and went down on his knees at the window, inching up the blinds from the sill. The block was the same. The monotonous line of stucco and brick mother-daughter combos. The religious statues. The half-constructed neon Christmas doodads. The crazy house in the middle that looked like an *Easy Rider* nightmare.

A short young man was standing on tiptoes at the ground-floor window between the section of the wall devoted to peace symbols and the section with the radical slogans. Apparently satisfied, he picked up a metal toolbox and headed past the flame-painted VW van to the porch across the driveway. Slinging the box around his neck by its strap, he shinnied up the porch pillar.

"That's the Gianellis' roof," Teresa said. "The Gianellis are always compaining about the noise from the Bongiornos. Of course, so do the Mazzolis on the other side, the ones with the blue shrine."

The young man on the roof opened the toolbox and inserted something into each section of the Santa's sleigh. Then he attached some wire from a spool and dropped the other end to the ground.

"Get me the phone," DeSales said to Teresa.

The boy let himself gently back down to the driveway. He carried the spool of wire with him as he went down on his knees in front of the blue Madonna next door.

"He's doing a penance," Teresa cracked. "Hail Mary, full of grace . . ."

DeSales was dialing the phone. The kid attached some more wire and trailed it back to his own house, where he picked up the toolbox and disappeared around the back.

"Who's on duty there?" DeSales barked into the mouthpiece. "Rinaldi? Okay. Tell him to prepare for a hostage situation. Probably explosives too. Get Kavanaugh and tell him to take charge. I've got a serious suspect in the Kaputz shooting under surveillance." He gave the address. "Now I want you to call me here when you get to Eighty-sixth and Bay Parkway. No sirens." He gave Teresa's number. "Call here. There's a woman named Terri might answer. She's working with me. Undercover." He winked at her. She looked frightened. "You can talk to her. But don't come any closer than Eighty-sixth. If we make this guy jumpy we could lose some innocent civilians."

DeSales hung up. He looked at Teresa. "You hear that?" She nodded, biting her lip. "So get *your* pants on too. I hate to be overdelicate, but I'm gonna have enough explaining to do when the media and the powers that be get here." He looked up and down the street again. Silent and empty. Young Bongiorno had disappeared. Then he noticed something he had missed before. "Hey," he called to Teresa in the bathroom, dressing. "What's the yellow ribbons on the lampposts?"

"For John Amalfi," she said, brushing her hair back. "A kind of welcome and congratulations when he beat that rap the other day. His brother lives on the street and some people figure he should get respect."

"I can't believe that shit is still going on."

"Listen," said Teresa. "Give me five John Amalfis, anytime, before one wacko like those two across the street. Maybe the goombahs who tried to get them out of here had a good reason."

Chapter 30

BEN ASTERISKY HAD TO BLINK as he crossed the
threshold into the Bongiorno house. A globe made out of
coin-sized mirrors hung from the ceiling. The strobe box in
the corner made it flash and illuminated in stops and starts
the snake-haired Bob Dylan poster that hung over the batik-
covered mattress which took up much of the floor of the front
room. Immense speakers stood on the sides of the bed like
monuments. Neil Young was singing in a whining voice. Down
by the river he shot his baby. Smoke curled from incense sticks
in clay holders on the odd pieces of low-slung furniture. A
brightly colored heart-shaped candle burned in one corner.
Giovanni Bongiorno, since his enthusiastic bear hug at the
door, had paced the room as if searching for something he
wanted to show off, looking coyly over his shoulder from time
to time. Finally he executed a half spin and lowered himself
onto the mattress, landing in a cross-legged sit. He beckoned
to Asterisky to join him.

"I was wondering when you were going to catch up with
me," he said.

"You mean it was you who sent that roster?"

Bongiorno had put on a lot of weight. He had been a tallish, slender boy with fine pale-brown hair that hung to his shoulders. Now his bulk seemed to have swallowed the old frame and he was skeletonless; his hair just managed to cover his ears, and his pate was almost bald. The folds of his jowls and neck had squeezed his features into a kind of V-pattern in the middle of the expanse of flesh. He raised an eyebrow—whether quizzical or ironic, Asterisky couldn't tell—and croaked: "I send my messages in lots of ways. I've been giving off *heavy* guilt vibes lately."

"So have I," said Asterisky. "That's one of the reasons I'm here."

"You?" What do *you* have to be guilty about? You didn't drop out without graduating. Without even saying good-bye."

"I thought we counseled you to drop out, to follow the muse."

"Did you? Maybe I forgot. Too much trouble in mind." Bongiorno looked away. He was wearing mechanic's coveralls, dark blue, with a "Bongiorno and Sons" patch and "Johnny B What U Wanna B" stitched in script under the left breast pocket. He reached for a wooden cigar humidor, opened the top, and extracted a joint. Furrowing his brow, exaggerating the downward V-patterns of his features, he wetted the end of the cigarette with his tongue, extracted a book of matches from his pocket, and lighted up. He took a toke and proffered the joint to Asterisky.

Asterisky hadn't turned on in a decade. He accepted the burning stick, put it to his lips, and sucked the smoke into his lungs, holding on tight, recalling the lingo of history. "Go with the flow," he exhaled, passing the joint back to Johnny. "Good shit."

Bongiorno nodded. "It is. Sensimilla. Improved agricultural techniques. Domestic, too. No imports from the banana dictators. My kid gets it for me."

"You've got a family?"

"It's a long story."

"That's why I'm here. I want to hear the long stories now, the ones I've been afraid to hear for all this time."

Johnny smoked, looked toward the ceiling, then sucked in his cheeks, keeping his eyes as wide open as possible, a look of slapstick surprise. Then the expression vanished and he was solemn, concentrated. "Remember that year I was at the Institute? You took us to that revival movie house in the Village. James Dean. *Rebel Without a Cause*. Marlon Brando in *One-Eyed Jacks*. Brando was a cowboy that offs the dude in the saloon and goes, 'He didn't give me no selection, man.'" Bongiorno held an imaginary pistol and blew on the muzzle. "Well, my story is sorta like that. No cause and no selection. I saw you last, like, in the early summer of '69, and then I went up to Woodstock. Righteous. I got high with Hendrix behind the stage just before he did "The Star-Spangled Banner." I had this sweet little hippie chick from Toronto with me. And we went out in the mud and balled our brains out during the set. Time passes."

He did three quick hyperventilated tokes. "I'm back in Brooklyn, getting my shit together. Garage band. Gigs on the Island. 'Play "California Girls"' they used to scream. And I was thinking I might go West. Who turns up at the door with a big belly but my hippie chick from Toronto. Oh, don't ask me why I bought into it, man. My old man had just died and I was about to sell this sewer business, but here was this chick, and there was also maybe the Selective Service System to deal with. So I took the easy way out and stayed, settled into Guinea heaven here. *Bambino*. Business with my own truck with the name on the side. No armed service because of my paternity. Then the kid is only a few months old and his mother splits, just like that. I become the Man." He pointed his thumbs backward at his chest, joint burning down to nothing between the index and middle fingers of his right hand. He felt the burn and stubbed it out in an ashtray on the floor by the bed. "Anyway, like that's how I got from backstage stud at Woodstock to Sewer Rooter in one short year."

"Your son must be grown."

"If you call it that."

"Is he in your business?"

"Shit, no. He's a free-lance entrepreneur. A little dope, hot car accessories, arcade games, computer black market, video and audio equipment. He plays with the moving pictures too. I guess you could say he's a criminal who wants to make movies. A perfectly logical product of our times: a child of the Reagan-Bush administrations, a product of the triumph of the military-industrial complex."

Asterisky laughed weakly. He was feeling a short wavy rush, seeing again the celluloid nightmare at DeSales's office. Groping for words, he finally managed to say to Bongiorno: "And you've held on to the sixties, the idealism . . ."

"It's the only way I keep my fucking sanity, man. On the one hand I got a pure capitalist in my house and all around me . . . Hey, you see this neighborhood, the saints and Santas? All around me I'm living in the middle of the fucking Middle Ages. Everybody's got a hard-on about them killing this black kid, but what else is new? The black kid had an idea. He wanted to buy a car. He wanted to go to a strange place in the middle of the night. He had fucking *adventure* in his bones, man. Wasn't that what we were supposed to be all about?"

Bongiorno stood and began to bounce on the mattress, more slowly and softly, with greater delicacy, than his immense girth would seem to allow. "You wouldn't believe these people I have to live with. I don't know if it's because they're Italian or they become Italian or it's Brooklyn and it doesn't matter. You get burrowed into the deep parts of Brooklyn—they don't only got *cugines*, you know? They got *kosher* cugines. They got *mick* cugines. Anyway, they all got one purpose in life: stifle adventure, sit on the face of creativity. The black kid makes newspaper headlines because he's black, but they killed me too. Here, in my motherhumping dago heart. And they killed my kid's heart when I tried to raise him on progressive principles. Fucking pea brains. You'd think they fell asleep on V-J Day and woke up when Reagan got elected. A lot of them, though they don't even know it, they're still in some hillbilly town in Calabria or Sicily in the fucking thirteenth century, man. There's gonna be another Holy War. A Crusade. Only instead of us going to clean out the Moslems, they're gonna go through here like shit through a Christmas goose."

"Everybody Knows This Is Nowhere" was playing. Bongiorno stepped off the mattress and turned up the sound, fiddled with the bass until it was impossible to hear anything else. He suddenly whirled and pointed a grimy thick index finger at Asterisky. "You got family?"

Asterisky coughed. The grass had been hot on his throat. And stronger than he remembered. He tried to imagine the face of Betty Robinson's daughter and came up with his grandmother's. "I don't know," he said.

Bongiorno sucked in his cheeks again.

"That's the point," Asterisky went on. "I guess. Like I never found out what happened to you, I never found out whether I had a kid of my own. I mean I never tried to find out until today. See, Artie Kaputz got shot and . . ."

"I heard it on the radio. In my truck." He turned and addressed himself to the audio controls again. "Now there was a slimeball if there ever was one. When you talked to him, he looked right through you, at like something else in the next room. What was it? Money? Power? Universal fucking brotherhood? Heaven?" He giggled, selecting another record. "Well, I guess he's seen it by now. We were talking about your family."

"Remember Betty Robinson?" Asterisky felt a kind of a surge in his chest. He was finally going to get it out. It was why he'd had to walk down the street of Mermaids, listening to the siren song again.

"No," said Giovanni Bongiorno.

"The one in your class who did the Aretha Franklin imitation. 'R-E-S-P-E-C-T'?"

"Maybe I do. I was a majority of one in a minority class. Remember?"

"One afternoon I went home with her to help her with a paper. She had a kid, remember? The kid was asleep in a crib in this one room she lived in. We ended up balling . . . I mean making love. On the roll-out bed."

Johnny was lip-synching with Otis Redding. He paused to say: "The chick from Toronto was named Doris, Doris Dunstable, but she called herself Beaver, as in Eager. We fucked in the mud, underwater, in a wigwam. We made it once on a bum trip cot in the Diggers' Medical Emergency tent."

"I assumed Betty was on the pill. Everybody was back then, especially somebody who already had had one mistake. When we finished I asked her and she looked at me like I was crazy. She had this big round Afro and a gap in her teeth. And I thought to myself, here I am trying to stop this cycle of illegitimacy and poverty and oppression. Through education. Awareness. Raised consciousness. And here I was just like the rest of them. I got horny and careless too."

"Come where you can," said Bongiorno.

"The baby in the crib started to cry. She had to go get his bottle. I saw myself as just another one of *them*. Adding to the welfare rolls."

Bongiorno had brought out a bottle of sambuca. He poured the clear syrupy liquid into a cracked cup and drained it.

Asterisky continued: "Don't you see? It wasn't that I had made it with a student, none of that old bourgeois ethical stuff. It was that I had declared myself the solution to social evil and here I had become part of the problem. I *was* the problem. That's why I never moved the EOA program to the next stage, to tracking down effectiveness, to finding what happened to you all. I wasn't only afraid that maybe we didn't succeed in making you into members of the college-grad elite. I was afraid that I would find my own issue littering a slum, in jail, dead of poverty and oppression."

For a moment Bongiorno seemed tuned-in, sympathetic. "You could have taken the kid on, if there was one, like I did. Shit, mine's a half-breed. Half spaghetti-bender and half Presbyterian.

Asterisky croaked: "I couldn't face it. A *black* kid, mine? What would anybody think. How could I handle it? It was like an invisible shield and I couldn't break through it. It would have been admitting to myself, to the world, that I was part of the problem." He sank to the floor, muttering. The dope had gone to his stomach, the roller-coaster feeling.

Bongiorno was now navigating the perimeter of the room, snapping at the walls with his fingers. The joking mood had evaporated. "You asshole," he shouted. "You think my kid was like *me?* That he looked right or acted right to fit into the world I brought him into? Ha! You're part of the problem, I *am* the fucking problem, my kid is beyond that. He is the *son* of the problem." He poured himself another drink and took it down in a swallow. He strode to the window and threw up the sash, pointing into the silent street. "There's a world you oughta try to straighten out. Check it out. They wash their cars, water the lawn, grease their hair, shine up the shrine, put the sauce on the stove, and pull out the lawn chairs every weekend. They sit there with their thumbs up their asses waiting for the Mets to win another pennant or maybe for World War III so they can march their kids down to the draft board behind the priest to sign up to kill or be killed. And I have to clean up their shit. The Sewer Rooter Man. So I give it back a little. They could do without us here, but hell, no, we won't go!" He began jumping up and down again. "Kill or be killed!" he screamed into the Bensonhurst night.

Asterisky heard the door fly open behind him. Out of the side of his eye he saw a short heavily muscled young man draw a bead with his rifle on the hanging globe, which highlighted his father's contorted features in stuttering frames of progression. Then he fired, the globe shattered, and the room was briefly ablaze with glitter. Darkness fell on the household, except for the flickering heart-shaped candle. The boy pointed the gun at Bongiorno, motioning him back to his cross-legged position on the mattress. Then he held the barrel against Asterisky's ear.

"He didn't give me no selection, man," he said.

CHAPTER 31

DE SALES STATIONED HIMSELF at the window, dividing his time between the crack in the blinds and the telephone. He had been successful in establishing troops of police in the area surrounding the block, but he had not yet managed to get through to the number listed in the phone book for the Bongiorno homestead. Without some kind of direct communication with the inhabitants of the house, terrorist or victim, there was little he could do but wait. Terri, clad now in tight designer jeans and an oversized nubbly wool sweater, rubbed the back of his neck and paced the room on the heels of her sling-back pumps.

She was fretting. "I'm having second thoughts on this, Frank. What if somebody gets hurt unnecessarily? What if they're just doing drugs or making book over there, and we bring in an army of cops? Then I got the neighbors, not to mention the Amalfis, all over me like a hot shower."

"The *omertà* code's getting under your skin: silence, never turn anybody, tie a yellow ribbon . . ."

She pinched his neck hard. "You know I'm bigger than that,

Frank. I still got a right to my feelings. Who's not gonna feel
scared now?"

DeSales squeezed the pinching fingers, gently. "No sweat.
I'll get you in the Witness Protection Program. And I'll be
the guard. How about me and you in a motel in Arizona with
a pool and air conditioning and free tennis for the rest of our
lives?"

"I don't play tennis, Frank. And I sunburn easy. You want
some coffee? You wanna just get under the covers with me
until the shit hits the fan?"

"Hail Mary Full of Grace would be watching."

"She didn't seem to hold you back any before."

"Don't you remember your catechism? It's only a sin if you
do it more than once a night."

"That wasn't the catechism: That was the sign in Louie
Gaja's rec room: 'Once a King, Always a King. Once a Night
Is Enough.' "

"You've got a good memory for a Bensonhurst broad."

"The New Year's Eve party was there. Our first official date,
after all the dry-hump slow-dancin' Friday nights at the gym.
'Moonglow,' remember. I liked dancing to that with you that
year. Gaja wasn't hip to the new music. The latest records he
had were his oldest sister's. So all New Year's we only had
'Moonglow' and 'The Isle of Capri' by the Gaylords and 'Memories Are Made of This.' Was that Dean Martin or Vaughn
Monroe?"

"It wasn't the Teen Queens or Little Richard, I can tell you
that. Couldn't do the fish to the Gaylords. Hey, Bensonhurst
culture owes a lot to the blacks after all, right?"

"In those days you'd see mixed doo-wop groups singing on
the corners around here."

"You think these Guidos today, the ones that shoot blacks
and beat up strangers, they're something new?"

"They were always here. But the rest of the world changed,
passed them by. They got scared, defensive, more closed-in

if that's possible. They watch TV, go to Manhattan, they see the black guys with the white girls, a black running for mayor. They get scared they don't got the biggest balls anymore. And the rich Europeans and Japanese are pushing the yuppies out of Manhattan into downtown Brooklyn and the yuppies push the blacks into Flatbush and the blacks push the Jews out of Flatbush into Borough Park and the Jews push you and the rest of the Italians down here. Gravesend and Bath Beach are the last stops. "Our backs are to the water. The Guidos are the last line of defense."

"Where's the draft board? I wanna sign up." DeSales's eyes were slit in mock solemnity. Teresa threw her arms around him and squeezed. "Remember, my grandmother called you the Little Pistol? The Pistol *paisan,* she would say. She was a good woman, even with all the crucifixions on the walls."

DeSales took a deep breath, squinted through the blinds, laid his head on Teresa's breast. "She was good to me. That *paisan* business, it made me feel good. I was always half-and-half, right—mixed marriage, my Canuck father was away, then gone, there was the trouble at home with Mom. So I never felt like I fit in. Your grandmother made me feel at home."

Teresa nodded toward the window. "Somebody should've done that for that kid over there. A loony father, always taking on the neighborhood, no mother. All he needed was some-body to put her arms around him, call him *paisan* or *bambino.* Show him he belongs. Then he wouldn't be where he is now."

The phone rang. DeSales picked it up, listened intently, and said, "Give me that number again." He scribbled something on a pad. Terri raised an eyebrow as he laid the receiver in the cradle.

"You wanna hear the good news or the bad news first?" he asked.

"Good."

"Good news is we've got another number at that address. It's listed under the name "Woodstock Nation.""

206 • THOMAS BOYLE

"So now maybe you can call the kid up and start a dialogue, cool him down. What's the bad news?"

"Not only have His Honor the Mayor and an army of press people joined the police units at Eighty-sixth Street, but we are also honored by the presence of our leading candidate for next mayor, Harry Bosch's personal choice, Harrison Dillard."

"I don't think it's safe for him down here, especially after dark. He didn't have enough shit for one day?"

"He's supposed to be not only well educated but a very tough guy."

The scream broke the still surface of the night: "Kill or be killed!"

Then they heard the shot ring out and watched through the blinds as the lights in the Bongiorno ground-floor front room blazed and died.

DeSales stood up, gently moving Teresa aside, stretching, reaching for the phone. "I don't think it's going to be safe for anybody now," he said.

CHAPTER 32

ASTERISKY AND HIS FORMER STUDENT, Johnny
B., sat bound in chairs in the darkened anteroom next to the
kitchen on the ground floor. A TV, playing a tape of burning
buildings, glowed in the corner.

"I saw part of that tape this afternoon, at police headquarters," said Asterisky. "Why does he have it on now?"

"He's a good-hearted kid," said the father. "Just not too
smart. He used to do his homework in here. He always said
the tape kept him warm, like one of those fireplace tapes they
sell. Makes things cozy?"

"Like of buildings with hostages that were fire-bombed by
cops?" Asterisky's palms were very damp.

But Johnny wasn't following Asterisky's train of thought:
"Believe me, it was no picnic being a single parent. Finally I
had to renovate the basement so he could have his own pad.
The tape and the music and the mechanical toys were all over
the place. Thank God I got him contained down there."

Asterisky watched the flames licking the walls of the California house, trying to formulate a thesis statement for a lec-

ture about the secularization of Mission-style architecture in the City of Angels, but it was no good. He could only see Johnny B.'s son setting up his stage, breathing heavily into the phone, arranging weapons, dancing frenetically. The kid was out of control and it didn't seem to have yet occurred to his father that they were in his control. In deep shit. Asterisky had never been a prisoner before, at least in this sense, and it took a while for him to initiate some form of practical discourse with Johnny in regard to some goals, like getting free. And it wasn't all Johnny's fault. The high from the short toke of sensimilla he had taken kept coming back and wrapping around his brain. After thinking about it for a long time he asked: "What was that orange goopy stuff he was bringing out to show off before he brought us upstairs from the basement pad?"

Johnny shrugged his shoulders. "Dunno. Look at that. I got a water stain on the ceiling. Must be a leaky pipe in the bathroom. Never saw it before. Never sat in this position, I guess. Wouldn't you know it'd be the plumber who don't know his pipe is leaking."

Asterisky realized his wrists were rubbed raw from the ropes. He pleaded: "Johnny, you and I don't seem to be on the same wavelength. Your son is dangerous. He's going to hurt somebody. He's armed and . . ."

"Nah." Johnny shook his head. "I'll take care of him. I'll beat the shit out of him as soon as he comes back up here. He knows I can do it. Even with those store-bought muscles of his, he can't lick his old man."

"But you're tied up!"

Bongiorno's wink was just discernible in the glow from the screen. He held out a hand, almost loose of the ropes. "See, I'm working these off. He can't tie for shit. Couldn't even tie his own shoelaces until eighth grade. Man, those kids in front of the candy store down the street used to get on him for that.

But they wouldn't fuck with me when I went down to clear up any misunderstandings."

"If you can get free, why don't you untie me so I can get out of here? I think I'd like to leave, John. This is strictly family business—yours, not mine."

"Hey! I said I was *getting* loose. Gimme time. We gotta wait until he leaves his toys downstairs anyhow. In that place of his, he can be a bitch to deal with."

Asterisky tried to stretch, wiggle his hands and ankles, but he found no imperfections in young Bongiorno's knots. "What about Ray Martinez?" he asked. "Your son was talking about him to the camera. What does he have to do with this?"

"Hey, Ray—he called himself Remi after he left the Institute—is the kid's fucking godfather, right? We baptized him down here in the birdbath outside St. Francis of Assisi. A couple of hippie parents with a fairy spade for a godfather. You think *that* didn't blow the collective mentality around here! Father Cabrini's eyes were fucking popping out."

"But your son was talking about Ray being a victim, about him being *dead*."

"Junior talks a lot of stuff." Johnny Bongiorno closed his pig's eyes and put his head against the back of the chair. He spoke in the direction of the spreading stain on the ceiling. "I tried to raise him right. Remi was like an uncle to him, man. And after a while Remi started making a lot of bread in the rag business. Went from window dresser to theater-costume design, a big success. We bought the kid what he wanted, took him to the aquarium to see the sharks and shit. Privileged. Not like these little white-trash Brooklyn rats around here. I even tried tutoring him at home. Maybe that's where I fucked up. He missed the point."

"What point?

"Like, remember that poem you had us do the free writing about? William Blake—that guy who inspired the Doors? It was a poem about London at the beginning of the Industrial Revolution, and everybody and everything was down and out. You could recite it by heart. That impressed the hell out of us."

"Still can." Asterisky cleared his throat.

> I wander thro' each charter'd street,
> Near where the charter'd Thames does flow.
> And mark in every face I meet
> Marks of weakness, marks of woe.
>
> In every cry of every Man,
> In every Infants cry of fear,
> In every voice: in every ban,
> The mind-forg'd manacles I hear
>
> How the Chimney-sweepers cry
> Every blackning Church appalls,
> And the hapless Soldiers sigh,
> Runs in blood down Palace walls
>
> But most thro' midnight streets I hear
> How the youthful Harlots curse
> Blasts the new-born Infants tear
> And blights with plagues the Marriage hearse.

"Right on!" Bongiornio cheered. "That's *it*. Far fucking *out!* There was a war like Nam and the ruling-class oppression and the military-industrial complex and all that shit. Even in the seventeen hundreds. You said that it wasn't just the material slavery of capitalism that was the problem, but the idea of things being even named, chartered, like the streets and the rivers, and that giving names to things that should run free and loose was the same as making rules, and it was the rules, any kind of law, that were the problem. Especially marriage, where the church and state ganged up to control your freedom by making the ecstasies of sex into a set of conventions. It was why John Lennon sang 'Why don't we do it in the road.' A road without a name, you said, just a road to keep moving on. It sounded good at the time. And shit, the Doors must have known something. They named the band after something this dude was into, right? Hey Prof, you could get *behind* some poetry! Remember how you could do Poe's "Raven" and say he was the first acid-head? You'd hold your arms out like broken wings and say 'Nevermore' like a real freak."

Asterisky's head was drooping. Some youthful extravagances were perhaps best forgotten. Into his chest, he asked: "What was the point Junior missed?"

"That this 'London' number was just a poem and we weren't talking about how fucked up his parents' marriage was or what kind of a baby he was or how fucked up the social conventions of Bensonhurst were. Not *literally*. Put it this way—he didn't miss the point, he just didn't *get* one."

"It was only a *metaphor*," Asterisky caught himself protesting.

"Of course."

Asterisky felt a desperate need to change the subject. What had they been talking about? He remembered. "Ray's dead?"

"Could be. He got sick and lost his job. I always suspected it might be AIDS."

"You went to see him?"

"Hardly, man. I was too busy cleaning the sewers around here. But the kid went, took him things. Like I said, the kid's got a good heart. You just got to get to know him."

"He was your old buddy, your kid's godfather, and you didn't even bother to find out if he was dying?"

"Shit, man, we all gotta die sometime. A long time coming and a long time gone, remember? And anyways, the longer I live the more it seems like we die from doing the things the Establishment was always telling us *not* to do. Like maybe they were right all along. We die from what was fun and freaky. It's a real bummer, like original sin and penance, just from doing it in the road . . ."

"And mud," Asterisky supplied.

Suddenly Johnny was leaning forward, nasty. "Or to Betty Robinson."

Nevermore, thought Asterisky.

But of course it was too late.

CHAPTER 33

OUT IN THE STREET, DeSales said to Teresa: "Get back in your apartment now. And stay there."

She put her hands on his shoulders and he put his arms around her. They held each other close. Slow dancing without moving your feet. Then Teresa was gone, back to her house, and he stood alone on the streets of Bensonhurst. The citizenry, honest and dishonest, had been shut up in their homes on his orders. Visitors were kept off the block by blue sawhorses. The world had been reconstituted as a field of endeavor—a stage, in fact—on which the only players were the media, the agents of law enforcement, and the inhabitants of the house with the VW van out front.

DeSales turned toward the ramp leading up to the large trailer they had established as crime lab and video headquarters. Then he saw her. Megan—looking remarkably fresh and fashionable considering the hours which had passed since she had climaxed beneath him while at the same time bathing in the warmth of her own video presence—was standing at the side of one of the media mobile units that were double-parked at the avenue. The look she gave him was one of bitter longing. It said that she had seen him and Teresa in their parting clinch. It was not the kind of look one would want to engage over any significant period of time. He nodded brusquely and trotted up the ramp.

He had not seen the mayor in person since his last operation. Harry Bosch without TV makeup looked remarkably puffy and pasty sitting in the van. By contrast, Harrison Dillard, standing against a wall to the rear, looked quite robust considering the draining events of his day. He wore khaki trousers and an open-necked brown shirt that suggested something between a back-yard barbecue and a paramilitary operation.

Kavanaugh was sitting at a table sorting files, a computer terminal and telephone at the ready. Behind him the lab technicians lounged in their folding funeral chairs, patiently awaiting the opportunity to analyze any available mortified flesh or bodily fluids. Behind them a bank of flickering video monitors were all showing the same still life of the darkened Bongiorno house. Other cameramen-officers and selected media techs were stationed on the perimeter of the operations area, plugged into monitors of their own, but under orders not to activate their equipment until they got the word from DeSales in the war room.

Charley Garvin, the plainclothes cop in charge of the videotaping, was standing at the instrument panel. Charley, who called himself the Director, often told his colleagues that at retirement he had standing offers from both NBC and CBS to spend his Sunday afternoons in a similar mobile unit outside Giants Stadium pushing buttons to select the best angles, not for crime scenes but for instant replays of football action, at twice the salary.

Dillard had his arms folded across his chest, grim. "And what is the situation, Inspector?"

DeSales looked squarely at Dillard. "The kid is holding his father and this teacher from the Institute for Urban Studies in there somewhere. He's got at least a rifle; we heard him fire it."

"Is anybody hurt?"

"The kid says no. Rather, he grunts. I've had him on the phone twice. Like he's an ape-man or something. He climbs like an ape-man. Anyway, he managed to get across that no one's hurt, but that somebody may be. Soon."

"You're sure he shot Kaputz?"

"As sure as I can be with what we've got. Even if he didn't, it's all the same. He's armed and dangerous and we have to get these people out."

"What does he want?"

DeSales shrugged. "He wants to send us a videotape to make his demands perfectly clear. The phone won't do."

"And how do we acquire this tape?" asked Dillard, sitting down next to Kavanaugh and looking strategic.

"Simple procedure. He wants someone to approach the house, no closer than the curb. Arms in air. No weapons. He'll throw the tape out the upstairs window."

"Who's going out?"

"I am," said DeSales.

DeSales had removed his shirt to demonstrate the unlikelihood of his carrying a concealed weapon. Now, wearing the same snug corduroys he had put on that morning outside Megan's steamy bathroom, he walked slowly down the ramp of the truck with his hands up. All of his senses seemed preternaturally tuned in to the environment. He felt Megan's eyes from inside the TV van, where he was sure she was now standing watching a monitor with Glenn Moulder. He imagined he heard Moulder chuckle with glee at the indignity of his favorite debonair but surly Italian sauntering around deep Brooklyn in the wee hours with his shirt off. He could see the empty beatitudes in the blank eyes of each statue on the silent stretch of workingman's sanctuary. Keeping his head rigid, he allowed his own eyes to elevate slightly and was sure he saw the protruding tongue in the Jimi Hendrix mouth over the Bongiorno gateway waggle with insolence.

He looked up at the second story and saw the barrel of the rifle gleaming in the streetlight, tracking him. Now he heard chanting coming from the end of the block and saw the waving banners and thought, oh shit, I'm dead; the kid is going to see the Reverend Luke's hired hands coming and blow me off the face of the earth. But the curtains parted slightly on the second story, and fingers could be seen releasing a small black box, which landed softly behind and to the right of DeSales, rolling over a couple of times. The detective managed to force himself to turn his back on the gaudily decorated house. He made his way to the box, a soft vinyl container bound with rubber bands. Bomb or videocassette? He picked it up and strode back to the truck and up the ramp without looking back.

His hand was not blown off. No shots were fired. There was a ringing in his ears, however, which gradually subsided. Then he heard behind him the rhythmic slogans of the black protesters wafting across the pavements to which he had come to feel so anchored. He had roots among the patron saints of that cracked concrete and muddied asphalt, and this made him mightily resent the cries of "No justice, no mercy!"

CHAPTER 34

BERNIE KAVANAUGH WAS WAITING anxiously at the door of the truck to see if DeSales was okay. The mayor was on one of the phones. He looked up. "It's Reverend Luke and the Bed-Stuy contingent. They're at the corner. We've got to head them off."

"They're already headed off," said DeSales, pulling his shirt back on and handing the tape to Garvin. "No way they go through the barriers. Luke and I go way back and he gave up on that tactic, over or around any obstacle, when he passed two-fifty on the bathroom scale."

"But the media will find them. One of the news programs is already running a story on Luke recruiting an army to invade the area. It'll be another circus." Bosch turned to Dillard. "Harrison, can you go over and calm them down? They're your constituency."

Dillard waved him off. "Tokenism, Harry. Sheer tokenism. All blacks aren't the same constituency, even if we have common cause. We're citizens of the same city, don't need a passport, don't need Harrison Dillard to pat them on the head or stamp their visas. My job is here. Somehow this violence was predicated on my candidacy, and I want to stay with the action."

"Let Crowd Control do it," DeSales snapped at the mayor. "If we send Dillard over there, we turn a one-ring media circus into a three-ringer."

Everyone in the van was watching Garvin as he inserted the tape in the replay monitor. On the screen, a hand-held camera panned around a disheveled room with a bomb-shelter air about it. Rock posters covered the walls. There were bookcases lined with videocassettes. Rifles and other military paraphernalia were stacked in each corner. There was video and audio equipment all about. An anomalous jumble of assorted cellular phones lay on top of some Indian blankets.

The camera settled on a slightly raised platform against one wall. On it was an electronic keyboard, at which was seated a fairly authentic-looking skeleton. Also on the platform were a white wicker wing chair of the sort one might find on a porch in Key West and two bound and trussed figures. Close-up: Ben Asterisky, squirming, looking pained but keeping silent. Close-up: a heavyset, fortyish man in work coveralls, face bloated, eyes squeezed and indifferent. The insignias on his coveralls read "Sewer Rooter" and "Johnny B What U Wanna B."

"That's the father," said DeSales. "The big one. I saw him greeting the little guy, Asterisky, at the front door."

The screen went blank for a moment, then the picture became more stable. The hostages had disappeared from the platform. The long instrumental opening to the Doors' "Light My Fire" was heard on the soundtrack. A figure emerged from behind the camera and started walking toward the platform, his back to the lens. Afro hair cinched with a headband made of knotted tie-dyed cloth. Thick neck, broad shoulders, heavily muscled arms tattooed with death's heads. Stepping up on the platform, the figure suddenly whirled to face the camera. He was wearing extra-large reflector shades which covered not only his eyes but most of his forehead. Above his jeans he wore only an open leather vest, some African beads, and an earring. He held a microphone to his lips.

"Looks Latino," said Dillard, breathless.

"It's a wig," DeSales responded. "He's Italian. Grew up here. Been here all his life."

On the tape, the boy made some clumsy passes at playing air guitar, then leaped from the platform to the floor, landing flatfooted and attempting a kind of shimmy. All the while he lip-synched the tremulous Morrison vocal.

"He *is* like an ape," said Dillard.

The boy with the Afro and the shades danced around the room, occasionally glancing back to make sure he was in camera range. From each corner he collected various weapons— an Uzi, an ammo belt, a couple of grenades, which he fixed to the belt. He remounted the platform just as the song was ending and sat in the thronelike chair, draping himself with the belt and balancing the automatic rifle on his knees.

"Remember that Black Panther poster? Huey Newton? He's imitating it," said Bosch.

The boy pulled a sheet of paper from his jeans pocket, spread it out in front of him, and began, haltingly, to read, from time to time looking tentatively at the camera from behind the impenetrable spectacles.

" 'I am a guide to the labyrinth,' " he read. "Jim Morrison said that, and this moment is dedicated in part to his memory. When our cause is achieved, our first act will be to follow his wishes and declare a national Week of Hilarity."

" 'Hilarity,' " Kavanaugh sneered. "The kid looks like one of the Munsters. An undertaker for the Grateful Dead."

Dillard smiled for the first time. "It's what the shrinks call 'misplaced affect.' "

"I wish he'd misplace it in another jurisdiction."

The boy squinted at the paper and went on: "I also hereby

dedicate this occasion to Mr. Jimi Hendrix. I would like to read the unsolicited testimony of one of America's leading pig weeklies, their unbiased assessment of his enduring contribution to American culture." The young Bongiorno cleared his throat and intoned the words from the magazine as a minister might the Thirty-third Psalm. " 'Jimi Hendrix was to the electric guitar what Horowitz is to the piano—and more. Left-handed, he played right-handed guitars upside-down and behind his back. He broke new ground in electronic innovation, pioneering experiments with the wah-wah pedal, fuzz box, and Univibe. His tape-delay mechanisms and sound distortion created the explosive, extraterrestrial swirls of his music. He could make "The Star-Spangled Banner" sound like a B-52 bombing raid.' " The boy took a deep breath. " 'Hendrix died in London in 1970 from the aftereffects of a B-52 bombing raid.' " He looked confused, held the paper up to his face. "I mean, 'from the aftereffects of barbiturate intoxication.' " The overdubbed soundtrack kicked in again: "The Star-Spangled Banner" as air raid, a flaming building on the screen instead of the boy.

Mayor Bosch let out a squawk that was barely distinguishable from the guitar solo and put his fingers in his ears.

"The same fire footage your son brought home this afternoon," DeSales said to Dillard, who looked shaken for the first time.

"I am a guide to the labyrinth," the kid was repeating, no longer reading. The camera had zoomed in and now the screen was full of the masquerade outline of the Afro and oversized shades against the blank wall. "My name is unimportant. I am the son of one of these men I have taken into custody, who cursed me with his slave name and then threw in a 'Junior' just to make it stick. The other man enslaved my father before I came along with his bullshit teachings, his false prophecies of equality and mind-expansion. The labyrinth is paved with false teachings and ethnic-name labels and diminutives like 'Junior.' Hell is the culture-label closet.

"The bullshit-teaching man also enslaved Raymond Martinez, who did not deserve the suffering they laid on him. This event is also dedicated to Raymond Martinez, who had to change his name to Remi Martin to escape the culture label, to get work in a business where you cocksuck your way to fame and fortune and top prize is disease and death. One culture closet to the next. In Brooklyn he was the nigger sissy. In the City he was just another pretty black asshole to the disco darlings, the same people who look at me and see a Guinea with the wrong shoes on, the guy you don't want to let past the velvet rope. It's the Chuck E. Cheese factor again. And when you get to the bottom of it, none of them know shit.

"I look at the Doors, I look at Remi, I figure you can only take so much so long. Wait'll you see the surprise I got in store for you in Miz Raney's upper suite. How many know that Jim Morrison was really a Native American. He had to change his name from Chief Ironcloud. Watch your TV listings for the story that tells the truth about Jim Morrison the Indian chief."

DeSales said: "Martinez was a name on that roster they sent Asterisky."

The boy was now standing, pointing his weapon left and right, then training it on the camera lens. "There's a chain of oppression that goes back through history. A chain of culture closets. Skin closets, name closets, Junior closets. The celebrity closet killed Ray Martinez in the end. But you'll be happy to see that he's going out in celebrity style."

Footage of Remi, his swollen tongue hanging out, next to Reno and Buzz, bug-eyed and naked, took over the screen for a full minute.

"Oh my God," said the mayor.

Dillard said: "It's that jerk from the Olympics with the movie-star girlfriend. They're in the papers all the time."

DeSales nodded.

Junior Bongiorno was back at center stage. "See how they cornered Remi. But you're not gonna get me anymore. I'm gonna get you. You heard what the pig newsweekly said about Hendrix, whose African name was taken away. How the fuck you think I feel over here in this place, man? Fucking Bensonhurst. You know what growing up here was like for me? It was like being left-handed and somebody decided there should only be right-hand guitars. I had to play my music behind my back, upside-down, when nobody was looking, when I was down here in my shelter, man. It was like a bombing raid, and unless you give it up, right now, you're getting blown away. One big extraterrestrial swirl is gonna take this shithole block and put it back in the motherfucking *original* labyrinth it all came from. Asses to asses, mud to mud. You get my meaning, Mr. Cop?"

"He's a lunatic," said Bosch, somewhat recovered.

"We didn't think he would be Mr. Rationality, Your Honor," said DeSales.

"But what's he talking about? What does he want? If anybody can cut a deal, I can."

"I'll tell you what I got here," said the boy. He pulled off a gob of orange clay and smeared it around each grenade. "This is Semtex. It blew up the Lockerbie plane. I got it spread around the neighborhood. I got detonators. I got us all wired, man. Now lookie here. I got my war paint on." He was smearing his face with the plastic. "I'm a human bomb. A *time* bomb, man."

"What does he want?" cried Bosch.

"That's what I got, what I am," the boy continued. "Now I tell you what I want. I want the works. A fresh start for everyone. No names. Everybody gives up names, dago names, nigger names, spic names, Polack names, the works. Then repatriation. I mean resettlement. We get a lottery. A computer can do it. Everybody gets thrown into the database and gets randomly assigned to live somewhere. So the meatballs can't gang up on me on the corner. So the fucking Koreans can't gang up on the vegetable business. You get my meaning? Maybe I go to South Dakota, Anthony Cardinale goes to Outer Mongolia, Jimi Hendrix is reincarnated in a cave in South America. But of course none of these people have names, so nobody knows who they are. *Everybody* is a stranger."

The boy paused for breath, looking confused. He pulled some cash from one pocket, wrinkled papers from another. "Oh, yeh," he breathed. "How many people on this block? Two hundred? Five hundred? I can take them all out by pushing a button. Anybody touches me, I get to the button first. Anybody gets me before the button, *I* go up on my own and take everybody with me. So"—he perused one of the papers—"here's step one. I need TV. I wanna be on the news, conduct my own press conference, spread the word about my plan to save the planet, explain why I had to waste that mushroom Kaputz to show running as a black isn't better than running as a white. You start out square, you don't gotta run as *nobody special,* dig?

"The press conference. I want the right people there to ask the questions. Charlene Chan, Mike Wallace, Ed Bradley, Glenn Moulder, Mary Gay Taylor, Gabe Pressman, John Miller, David Diaz, Megan Moore, Al Roker. Bring back Tex Antoine! I got the answers. I want to dance on MTV with Downtown Julie Brown. I just learned the Lambada!" He pumped his fists with the grenades in them and executed a couple of ungainly steps.

"Now it's time for a little entertainment." He dropped the rifle and put the grenades down softly. He adjusted the camera so that the entire stage was in view. His father and Asterisky were still out of sight. Satisfied, he rubbed his hands together, then pushed a button on the keyboard. The volume was turned up full blast. He sat down and began to sway to an instrumental of "I'm In with the In Crowd." He smiled at the camera, pretending to tickle the ivories, head flopping loosely on his shoulders, just another blind superstar at the keyboard.

The mayor had his head in his hands. "We can't take this seriously, DeSales, can we?"

The boy at the keyboard looked up, took off the dark glasses and the Afro wig, and ran a finger along his upper lip. He blinked, then consulted a watch he picked up from the floor. He raised his prominent eyebrows melodramatically. Beneath them, the eyes were strangely without affect, but his cheeks were wreathed in smiles. "And if you don't take me seriously, check this out." He pointed at the camera. "By the time you get to watch this tape, a little accident will be taking place. A house on Bond Street, near the Boerum Hill projects, containing the remains of Ray Martinez, a.k.a. Remi Martin, and his celebrity guests, is blowing up just about right now. You check it out. You'll see that if you fuck with me here"—he held his hands out—"poof, there goes the neighborhood."

The tape went blank.

CHAPTER 35

THERE WAS SILENCE in the video truck as the various city employees appeared to be scanning the walls and ceiling for answers.

Finally Dillard spoke. "Did he actually say he shot Kaputz?"

"He implied it." DeSales lighted his first cigarette in what seemed like hours. Teresa's encouraging him to light up in the restaurant had made him feel self-conscious about his smoking, when a hundred screaming yuppie abolitionists wouldn't have made the slightest impression. If he had another life, he thought, maybe he'd go to a shrink and figure out why he always found himself straddling fences, heading in opposite directions. But there was only one life for the moment, and in it he had committed himself to enforcing the law and not fucking around with too many complicated ideas. "Whatever. Bernie, get on the phone and do what Junior says—check him out. Any houses blowing up on Bond Street these days?"

"I think he's bluffing," said Bosch, his Adam's apple bobbing, looking around for reassurance. "He's one of these copycat people. It's the media blowing everything up out of proportion."

"Bond Street houses and your press releases," DeSales muttered under his breath. Out loud, he announced: "Look sharp, you guys. Prepare for the worst. Medics at the ready. We got the bomb squads outside? The fire engines? Okay. They got the sniffing dogs? Good. It doesn't look like this guy is going to walk into our hands. We've got to assess his capability and then move fast. Placate him until we get him isolated. He wants press, we can offer him press coverage in exchange for Asterisky and his father. We'll need a negotiator. If he won't talk on the phone, someone's going to have to approach in person."

"Bluff or not," Dillard interjected, "I think we should just charge the house, take him by surprise. I was an Airborne Ranger in the early days in Vietnam, when we were winning. Look what we did in Suez. Direct attack. Hit the beaches."

"I thought you were a liberal," said Kavanaugh, waiting for someone to pick up the phone on the other end.

"I've been trying to get across throughout my entire campaign that African-American men have been fighting wars for this country since its inception. I'm a domestic liberal with a tough stand on crime at home and on defense abroad. And the best defense is a good offense. Whites always look at my skin color and not my record . . ."

"I got Fire. Healy. You know Healy, Frank? He thought he was dreaming when he first got the report: an explosion on Bond Street; a tall naked blond woman runs out of a flaming brownstone trailing a ball of fire on a string between her legs. With two heavyset black men wearing only pajama tops in hot pursuit. Get it: *hot*."

"It sounds," said Bosch, "like that kid called this in out of his fevered imagination. To fake us out."

Kavanaugh shook his head. "Nothing doing, Mayor. Healy's men are over there with hoses now. The second and third floors are on fire. Containable, they think, but a three-alarmer. The blond woman's okay, but she's worried she got separated from her boyfriend inside. The two black guys are the land-lady's sons. They thought the blonde was the arsonist. Now they're each in a state of shock. The kid's bluff has been called and he's holding cards."

DeSales took his shirt off. Then he raised his pant leg and checked the tiny pistol in the ankle holster. He picked up the phone and dialed the Woodstock Nation number. The person who answered said nothing, just breathed heavily. DeSales used his loving-uncle voice. "Listen, we've confirmed the Bond Street event, and anyway we think you've got a legiti-mate gripe there. About people being cursed with names and neighborhoods. We *all* want to be free of that shit. They named me after a saint and I got beat up every day after school. In Bensonhurst. In Red Hook. But I got another problem. I'm a cop. My family needs to be fed. I gotta keep my job. And to keep my job I have to make sure the people in the house with you and the neighbors don't get hurt. So why don't I come in and visit? And in exchange you send out the other people in the house. My name's DeSales. You threw the tape to me. I'll take off my shirt again so you'll see I'm not packing. And my arms in the air, so I don't do any funny reaching. I'll be carrying a sheet of paper with a list of TV news people you can talk to. You got it? I come in unarmed with the TV deals on paper and you let your father and Asterisky go. I'll ring the doorbell once. You open it. I'm standing there as your shield, you know they won't take a chance on shooting me. You push the hostages out on the street, you take me in. That simple."

The voice on the other end of the line was faint, almost childish. "You can't have my father. The other guy okay." The line went dead.

"I'm going in," said DeSales, standing up. "He'll give us Asterisky, but not his old man. The thin edge of the wedge.

I think I can soften him up. Type up the names of some of the news people you've seen around, Bernie. I'm going to offer him the moon, but he's got to give up the old man and his weapons and detonators before he gets to smell the roses."

"Look at Garvin!" cried one of the techs.

Charley Garvin, ashen, had slumped to the floor. Two medics were over him immediately. "It looks like a heart attack," said one.

"We can't have ambulances leaving, sirens. The kid would blow up the block. You've got life-support systems here and there's a doc outside, right? Just take care of him until I get inside the house."

"He should be in a hospital, Inspector."

"Right, and he's an old friend of mine. I'm a godfather to one of his kids. But we got more than one life at stake and Charley's the cop. He signed on for dangerous duty." DeSales laughed bitterly. "Except he figured cutting tape on a machine in an armored truck wasn't going to be particularly dangerous. Get the doc."

Bosch protested. "We need a video editor. There could be a billion dollars in lawsuits before this is over. The whole procedure has to be on tape, on the record, to show we followed standard operating procedure. There are five cameras covering every angle to keep us posted in here when you go in, so we can protect you. And to show the public there was no reckless endangerment, no disregard for life. That's why we spent all that money on this goddam studio-on-wheels."

DeSales headed for the ramp. "Get one of the news people, Bernie. The first one you see who can edit. I'll wait until he gets in here before I approach the house. But hurry the fuck up."

Suddenly Dillard was standing between DeSales and the ramp: "*I'm* going in, Inspector."

"This is none of your business." DeSales watched Kavanaugh slip down the ramp and around the corner of the truck.

"Until you're elected and sworn in, you don't even have any official capacity. You're here as a guest of the mayor. And at my sufferance."

Dillard looked like he wanted to grab some lapels, but DeSales was bare-chested, so he stuck a finger into the detective's sternum. "Look at it this way. This is *my* problem first. You heard the boy. My candidacy is what set him off. It was my assistant who is the only murder victim we know of so far. It was my son who was assaulted and given the tape. The threat is clearly to me and my people. It's my responsibility to persuade this boy that my election is a blow against stereotyping and oppression, not an intensification of the problem. Back to the future, like Artie Kaputz said." He took his finger out of DeSales's chest and pointed at the phone. "Call him again. Tell him I'll come in. Harrison Dillard is a juicier catch than some anonymous cop. For the media coverage alone, if you want to be cold-blooded."

At that moment Kavanaugh led Megan Moore up the ramp into the truck. She touched DeSales's arm. "Frank?"

DeSales brushed her off, looking only at Kavanaugh. "You couldn't do better than a lady talking head, Bernie? I asked for a fucking *director,* not a *socialite.*"

"The media's pooling its resources out there, Frank. Apparently she's as qualified as anybody who isn't already occupied. She and Moulder and all the rest who qualified drew straws. Here she is."

"Besides," Megan intervened, "Moulder's got his own van and crew to run. I don't. I was only along for the ride tonight. I'm expendable as no one else is. I'm a pro. My skills are valuable, too."

DeSales was now glaring at Dillard. "I don't want her."

The mayor came forward and took Megan's arm. She had done a number of favorable pieces on him. "Here, sweetheart. We're all a little uptight. I'll show you where Garvin was working and make sure you get audio contact with the camerapersons." He turned to DeSales. "She's doing it, Inspector. That's an order."

Megan headed for the bank of screens, then turned her head. "You don't have to be defensive, Frank. I don't care what you did tonight, personally or professionally. It's been a bad day for remembering where our commitments are. I've had my problems, too. Look"—she tapped the Police Special earrings—"a sign."

DeSales did not look. He turned to face Dillard. "See, the media knows *me*. I'm not just some anonymous cop. And anonymous or not, this is *my* job. These are *my* people, the people I come from. You didn't listen close enough to that kid. He needs a sense of belonging; he's an outcast. He needs a real father—God help me—and he's even willing to keep the crazy one he has around so he's not totally alone. He looks at *your* skin, he sees another alien."

DeSales realized he had made the sign of the cross when he said "God help me." He hadn't made the sign of the cross since his mother went batty and he joined the force. Now here he was heading out into no-man's-land, blessing himself like a twelve-year-old shooting a foul shot in a CYO game. Why not call in the priest? *Confiteor Deo.* Bless me, Father, for I have sinned. I banged two women I wasn't married to today. I didn't obey my parents and it's been thirty years since my last confession. "Fuck you, Mr. Candidate. This isn't the sands of Iwo Jima. This is my world—South Brooklyn. Like I said, these are my people, the people I come from. That John Wayne shit doesn't work around here. Neither does John Lindsay or Jesse Jackson. And you don't got the rhythm. I do. It's all tribal signs, smoke signals, war drums. I speak the language. So you either go home or sit here in the corner like a nice boy and wait and see whether you still got as much city left to run when this is over as you thought you would when you decided you wanted to be mayor."

Dillard raised his fist. DeSales waited, the bare sinew of his shoulders and chest twitching under the streetlights. Then Dillard dropped his arm, hung his head, and retreated to a seat next to the mayor, behind Megan at the control panel.

They could all settle in now and watch the concluding episode on TV.

DeSales put his bare arms in the air, like a long-distance runner crossing the finish line, and paced deliberately across the street. He gave no indication if he was aware that he was being filmed from five different angles, and that the woman who had been his only lover for well over a year—until tonight—was manipulating the controls that would determine the image he projected on the central monitor, which was in turn being fed to the TV studios of the city, and presumably all of that portion of the world which was dying to know what was happening in Bensonhurst. He took note of the yellow ribbons on the telephone poles. Welcome Home, Francis Carmine DeSales. John the Don got welcomed home. When DeSales's father came home from the war they had a welcome-home celebration, even if he was just Merchant Marine. Now little Frankie had grown up and come home in triumph, a big shot, a detective inspector, and he had a right to imagine the yellow ribbons were out there just for him.

He stepped up onto the curb and approached the house, passing beneath the Hendrix gateway and by the psychedelic bus, and standing still on the little stoop in front of the door emblazoned in red with "Hell No We Won't Go." He remembered other doors in Bensonhurst before which he had stood trembling: the first time at Teresa's grandmother's; once when the nuns had summoned him to the convent after school; on his twelfth birthday, when a small-time *capo* in one of the mob families had invited him over. Each time the door had opened and the feared grown-up on the other side had greeted him with open arms and gifts. Teresa's grandmother wanted him to have Teresa; the nuns had a citizenship award for him; the *capo* was practicing a certain *noblesse oblige* and was giving poor boys from the neighborhood ten dollars when they turned twelve. This was his chance to give something back for the embraces, the protection. This kid needed to be taken in, but to be cared for, not punished.

He slowly lowered one arm and put a finger on the doorbell, then raised it again.

He stood there feeling helpless, knowing he had no way of reaching the revolver in the ankle holster in time should he need it. The door opened an inch and one of Junior's eyes scrutinized him. Then the door quickly opened wide and the unsteady figure of Benjamin Asterisky was propelled, face first, to the pavement. He landed hard and lay still. Before DeSales could act on his instinct to help the fallen man, however, his own outstretched arms were bunched at the wrists by a powerful grip and he was pulled into the house. The door slammed behind him.

Step one accomplished. He could have allowed the force of being dragged into the house to propel him to the floor and, while gathering himself up, found his own gun and shot first, taking the kid down. But the kid was a walking bomb, and if he went down, the house and all that was in it went up. Besides, that would preclude salvation. For anybody.

DeSales faced his host, arms still aloft. The boy had put back on the Afro wig and shades and gun belt. He had the orange plastic smeared all over his face. He was training a World War II Luger at DeSales's head. The desperate plea for recognition which this pathetic costume constituted was infinitely more pathetic in person than it had been on the small screen of the video monitor. It wrenched something in DeSales's gut, some unresolved and inarticulate echo of childhood helplessness. His father coming home from the war a hero, then going away on the same ship and never returning.

DeSales felt his heart melting all over again. He reached toward the boy with open arms. "*Paisan,*" he called, his voice cracking.

Junior Bongiorno fired twice. First he hit DeSales's right knee and then his left. The detective went down like crumpled toilet tissue. A burning sensation raced briefly through each leg and then they ached dully.

"Dad," the kid yelled out. "I kneecapped the motherfucker. Twice. Just like the IRA on the Education channel."

CHAPTER 36

MEGAN MOORE STOOD AT THE KEYBOARD of the Betacam Edit Control Unit trying to sort out the various mechanisms which she had been trained to use in case of a technicians' strike. She checked over the insert and assemble editing, video and audio tracks, the CD player and the sound-mix system, the source deck and recording deck, and the various receivers. At the same time she kept an eye on the progress of DeSales across the street as it appeared on the monitors. She saw him hesitate, hold still, then ring the bell. The door opened a crack and then the chubby fellow came tumbling out as DeSales was pulled in and the door closed behind him. The guy on the pavement took a long time getting up. When he finally staggered to his feet, he seemed disoriented. Camera three zoomed in nicely. The event became more intimate. His nose was spurting blood. His hands were tied but his feet were free, and after gazing at the rooftops up and down the street for a while and scuffing his feet, he stumbled toward the police lines.

Megan typed a command, changing angles, and now her

main monitor was showing the view from behind Asterisky as he collapsed into the arms of the uniformed cops, who untied him and carried him toward the truck she was standing in. Good dramatic touch. She felt omniscient, removed, as she assessed her work. She pressed the freeze-frame command and held the moment of Asterisky's ascent up the ramp, contemplating the pathos of the moment, imagining millions of viewers contemplating the pathos of the moment. On another monitor, the house was still and dark. Then they were carrying Asterisky to the medical area in the van. She had not yet released the freeze-frame, so she pushed some more buttons and the professor was no longer caught in his ignominious progress up the ramp. She felt more and more disoriented. Since DeSales had made his speech and almost come to blows with Dillard, she had felt that something was adrift. In all their time together she had never seen Frank so passionate. These are *my* people, he had said. Without irony. What could he mean? Of all the men she had known, or women, Francis DeSales was the most cut off from any sense of community. Perhaps she had misapprehended that which was too physically and emotionally close to her.

Then she heard the shots, at once distant and deafening, from the other side of the door that said "Hell No We Won't Go." The door DeSales had just been dragged through. The mayor was breaking up, hoarse and faint. "I told you we should have charged. I've lost my best man!" On the screen, the house hadn't changed—it was still and dark, as if *it* were in freeze-frame—but cops could be seen scurrying from neighboring back yards and running low in front of the cameras.

The video truck had come to desperate chaotic life. The mayor and Dillard were shouting, urging anyone within earshot to action; Kavanaugh was working three phones, deploying squads of attack forces; the medics got Asterisky propped up against a wall, where he sat goofily, apparently healthy but unraveled. Then Garvin rose partway up from the

pallet where he had lain, like something out of a Dracula
movie, and mumbled directions. Incomprehensible. One cop
was back from the dead. Another, her own personal cop, was
on his way out.

New York's Finest were going in, the real battle, and Megan
Moore had become merely the projectionist of a movie about
the war, not a soldier in the war itself. She was rapidly losing
focus. Madly she pressed the buttons, searching for the present
tense.

Inside the house, DeSales was alert. He kept his eyes at half-
mast. It was possible he was paralyzed from the waist down,
possible he was only suffering a mild case of trauma. He
watched Junior's back as the boy dragged him, sliding in his
own blood, to the doorway leading to the kitchen and an
anteroom. In the darkened room, the only light came from a
TV with a raging fire on the screen, and that light illuminated
Junior's father, sitting bound in a straight-backed chair.

"Who the fuck's that?" the father asked.

"A cop. Exchange for your old teacher. Came to negotiate
but he's just another name-game artist. Gave me the *paisan*
routine. Maybe he shoulda tried 'wop-a-lop-and-boom.' "

" 'A-wop-bop-alu-bop-a-wop-bam-*boom*,' " the father corrected.

"You always gotta be fucking right, don't you?"

"With a loser like you around, somebody's gotta know
something. What's your strategy now, Einstein?"

"I don't need no strategy." Junior reached into the old-
fashioned refrigerator, bumping one of DeSales's legs. The
pain brought tears to the detective's eyes but he managed to
hold still. The kid pulled out a liter of Diet Pepsi and swallowed some pills, washing them down with the soda. "I can
go head-to-head with anything they send in." His eyes were
yellow at the edges.

"And take us all out with you."

Junior shrugged. "Why not, you been taking me along on your dead-end escapades all my life."

"Maybe this guy's got somebody out there needs him. Give him a chance. Give *me* a chance. Maybe I can turn things around. You want the cops to help you commit suicide, you don't need to take anybody else along. I shoulda let you die when you were sixteen and got into the sleeping pills. Shouldn't of let the stomach pump in the house. Untie me and I'll take him outta here. Drive your own hearse. You customized it!"

"That the same marriage hearse you read about in college and been running your mouth about ever since?"

Junior pulled the piece of paper from DeSales's hand. He read it slowly. "I don't need help. You see who's waiting to put me on the air?" He gestured at the paper with the backs of his fingers. "All the big shots from network news. And local. And print!"

DeSales's pants were soaking. He wondered how much blood he had lost. He thought about going for the pistol, but it was impossible to bend his legs or waist to reach it. He needed arms like Plastic Man.

"Is that why you got that orange shit on your face?" asked the father. "To go on TV as the lone surviving member of the lost hippie tribe? Well, let me tell you, as someone who was actually *at* Woodstock, you look like an asshole, not a hippie. Muscles and guns are not the symbols of the love generation."

"Don't tell me what I look like. You fat Guinea bastard. The Roto-Sewer man. You got all the rhythm of a sump pump."

"Look at yourself in the mirror, Junior. Don't call names."

Obediently, Junior went to the mirror in the front hall and turned on the lamp, laying his guns on the table. Next to them he put the remote control he had had dangling from his belt. He contemplated his features, smoothing the gobs of Semtex here and there. He removed the Afro wig and began to apply himself seriously to his makeup, raising and lowering the Ray-Bans.

DeSales saw the father—Johnny B. Goode, Asterisky had called him—out of the corner of his eye as the man began to move. Somehow he had slipped his knots and the kid didn't know it. The elder Bongiorno lowered himself silently to the floor. He made eye contact with DeSales, forming with his lips the one-word question: "Packing?"

DeSales nodded, indicating his ankle with his eyes. Bongiorno seemed to understand. Without taking his eyes off his son's back now, he raised the detective's pant leg and took the pistol in his palm. Then he crawled back into the chair.

"You never answered me," he said to his son. "What's the orange shit? You smell like a two-bit whore. Or is that the oil you put on to make the store-bought muscles shine? I never thought I'd raise a faggot around here . . ."

The kid picked up his Luger with one hand and the remote control with the other. A gunfighter's knowing grin twisted the corners of his mouth. He was about to whirl, but his father was already pulling the trigger. DeSales saw the concussion of the bullets in a neat vertical trail of splats where the leather vest hung open, more or less splitting Junior's magnificent physique into two separate entities. DeSales heard the boy's gun clatter from his hand. But the kid tumbled after it, still gripping the remote control. The last sequence of events the detective remembered was the kid's lower half exploding like a human land mine, the Afro wig catching fire, and the flames licking the walls. He remembered the day he found his mother's mother-of-pearl-handled combs that she had inherited from her mother blackened after the fire at the apartment in Red Hook. He remembered the exposed springs in the charred cushions of the cheap sofa under the burnt plastic covers and the smell of candle wax and smoldering rubber from the kitchen. He remembered that he had been unable to get that smell out of his nostrils for years. It had killed his appetite for the *salumeria* and here it was again.

Now the stains in the Bongiorno ceiling seemed to be separating from the rest of the plaster. There were exposed pipes and a smoking mattress on the floor and flames shooting out of Bob Dylan's nostrils in the alcove. The TV with the taped fire popped and fizzled its way to extinction. The father stood over his son, pumping more bullets into the lifeless torso, swearing unintelligibly, and then there was another explosion and Johnny B What U Wanna B was history.

The walls came tumbling down.

On the screen, Megan watched the windows blow out on the ground floor, then the second, then she saw Santa and sleigh and eight tiny reindeer evaporate into puffs of smoke and residual pockets of brush fire. Mechanically, unfeeling, she cut to camera four or three or held a shot for the duration of one concussion or another. Then she saw the top of the Bongiorno house erupt in towers of red and blue flames, the stuff of gothic fairy tales, an incendiary nightmare cathedral. She shielded her eyes from the sight of the cops and firemen who had been approaching the house dropping back as if in awe. It was time to bring it all to an end, avert the screams and sights of carnage which were already crowding in on her fevered imaginings. She hit the freeze button, stopping Time. "Fuck the present tense," she thought. She fell back against Garvin on the makeshift hospital bed, muttering, "Freeze Frank, Freeze Frame." She remained curled there beside him, dead weight. She whispered: "There's nothing to do about it. He's caught a bad case of Brooklyn Three."

Teresa Colavito was sitting by the window doing her nails when the house blew. For a moment, she continued to file the cracked tip. She was feeling the way she always did after finding a new lover—even if he was an old one. It was a sense of anticipation, as if it were the morning of a holiday and she was a little girl; there would be festivities and she would be allowed to stay up late. It was the Fourth of July and the

Amalfis had paid for the block party's annual fireworks display. Then she looked up and realized what had happened. She got up suddenly, spilling the polish on the floor, then sank to her knees, elbows on the windowsill, and began to pray. She started to say a Hail Mary but couldn't get beyond the line, "Blessed is the fruit of thy womb Jesus," which she kept repeating until she summoned the strength to run down to the street to see if she could help.

Ben Asterisky was convinced he was having an acid flash, a retribution wreaked on his brain cells for having abused them so many years before. What, after all, could this scene be but a hallucination, treading the dangerous line between bum trip and hobo voyage? The mayor of the Big Apple and his anticipated successor, who happened to be black, were climbing the walls like competing Spidermen. There was a skull-faced man lying on a cot next to a woman curled up in a fetal position. The woman he had seen on TV. She kept breathing the word *three* into one of the man's bony eye sockets. Behind the couple was an edit control panel and a bank of screens. On the principal monitor a still-life house of ill fame kept re-creating itself, an architectural phoenix out of the valley of ashes that he dimly remembered as Bongiorno's Bensonhurst. Then he recognized in the screen's rendering a rough draft of the Disneyland logo: Cinderellaland towering above the drive-in culture, a blackning church appalled. Wasteland as kiln. Mind-forg'd manacles. Benjamin Asterisky, the new paladin of the West, riding his white hearse across the desert, a casket full of ex-wives: wombless, cursing. He was tuned in to the airwaves on the wraparound speakers. Light My Fire. Checking into the air-conditioned motel, turning on the TV, selecting a tape, keeping a cool eye on the holocaust, beating the heat.

Quoth the Raven: Nevermore.